BEAUTIFUL DREAMER

It would be simple—almost too simple—to scare Miss Mary Goodwin out of Jason's life. But thus far she hadn't reacted to Vincent's ghostly presence.

He frowned. She must be a heavy sleeper. Perhaps this would be more difficult than he'd thought. He concentrated once more, allowing the energy in him to build and expand and intensify. When it reached a critical level, he released it.

"OOOOOOOOooooooooooooHHHHHHH."

It was a sound to make hair stand on end and flesh creep and crawl. It was a lament to make one's blood run cold and petrify one's bones. It was a wail of sorrow, the cry of a tormented soul, an unearthly requiem for the dead. The eerie sound echoed around the room. It rose and fell and then rose again to a shrieking sob before dying away to a sighing moan.

Truly, he had outdone himself. Proudly, expectantly, he looked at Mary.

She emitted a small snore and slept on peacefully, her hands folded under her cheek.

Books by Angie Ray

Ghostly Enchantment
Sweet Deceiver
A Delicate Condition
Ghost of My Dreams

Published by HarperPaperbacks

Ghost of My Dreams

ANGIE RAY

HarperPaperbacks
A Division of HarperCollinsPublishers

HarperPaperbacks
A Division of HarperCollins*Publishers*
10 East 53rd Street, New York, N.Y. 10022-5299

ISBN 0-06-108380-1

HarperCollins®, 📖®, HarperPaperbacks,™
and HarperMonogram® are trademarks of
HarperCollins*Publishers* Inc.

Cover illustration by Jim Griffin

First printing: December 1996

Printed in the United States of America

Visit HarperPaperbacks on the World Wide Web at
http://www.harpercollins.com/paperbacks

❖ 10 9 8 7 6 5 4 3 2 1

For my mother, Betty Scharf.

Heartfelt thanks to Sandra (Paul) Chvostal, Colleen Adams, Barbara Benedict, and Victoria (Bruce) Bashor.

And, special thanks to Gus Chew of the Orange County Badminton Club for his expert opinion on badminton injuries.

Prologue

Vincent Parsell, sixth earl of Helsbury, sat alone at the scarred trestle table that could comfortably seat twenty, sipping a snifter of brandy. Rain lashed at the windows, and the dining room was chilly with only a few candles to disperse the shadows, but he didn't summon a servant to tend the fire or light the candelabra. He didn't notice the cold darkness creeping along the walls and sending curling tendrils out across the floor. His entire attention was focused on the portrait that hung on the far wall.

The portrait, with its gilded frame and luminous colors, contrasted sharply with the gloom-filled room. The artist, in some magical mixture of hues, had managed to capture the woman's image perfectly—the ebony curls swept up into a high chignon to reveal the delicate line of her jaw; the gold locket in the hollow of her throat nestling against her creamy skin; the high-waisted gold silk dress that shimmered and hinted at the sweet curves beneath; the full, ruby red lips that smiled seductively; and the brilliant midnight blue eyes that danced with teasing laughter.

Vincent averted his gaze. That laughter had been absent the last time he'd seen her—the night of the Helsbury masquerade. The night she'd broken off their engagement.

He lifted the snifter to his lips and drank deeply. The brandy burned its way down his throat and settled in his stomach. He waited.

Nothing.

He swore. He'd been drinking for the last two hours now, and still he felt none of the numbing warmth he was seeking. Setting down the snifter, he picked up the bottle. As he poured, brown droplets splashed onto the dull oak, and the clinking of glass echoed in the cavernous room. He became aware of the silence, the emptiness of the entire house.

He set down the bottle with a loud thump. He wasn't accustomed to being here alone. Usually, one or another of his brothers was in residence. But they were all in London, enjoying the entertainments. All except Gilbert, of course, who was living in bucolic splendor with his wife, Jane, and their little boy, Jason.

Vincent shaded his eyes with his hand. Gil had always been a trifle different from the rest of the Parsell men—less distrustful and more stubborn—but they'd all been surprised when the boy had proclaimed his love for Jane. He, himself, had laughed at little Gil's avowal of love. But now the memory of their earnest, glowing faces made him feel even more empty, more alone.

Perhaps he should go to Elizabeth. Talk to her. Apologize. . . .

No.

Everything inside him recoiled at the thought. The earls of Helsbury did not apologize, and they certainly did not go crawling after women. She would have to come to him, and she'd better do it soon, or he might decide not to take her back—

"My lord?" a hesitant voice said from behind him.

Vincent turned and focused with difficulty on the short, brown-haired man standing in the doorway. He frowned. "What is it, Wilmott?"

"I beg your pardon, my lord. But this just arrived." Wilmott advanced and handed him a letter, then stepped back a respectful distance. "The messenger is waiting for a reply."

Vincent turned his back on Wilmott, barely hearing the

servant's last sentence. He stared down at the familiar, feminine scrawl on the missive. For a moment, he felt light-headed. Then he smiled.

So she'd come to her senses at last. He had known she would. He had known she would beg for forgiveness sooner or later. The letter would no doubt be smudged with tears and full of pretty apologies. He turned the folded paper over. He didn't know if he should accept them—she truly had behaved quite abominably.

A faint perfume, like roses in spring, wafted upward from the letter. Growing still, he inhaled. His loins tightened, and suddenly, his hands were shaking. The missive slipped through his fingers and fell onto the dark wood of the table, soaking up the drops of brandy he had spilled. No longer smiling, he scooped the paper up and broke the seal.

Dear Vincent—
I hope this letter finds you well. Although we did not part on the best of terms, I wish to assure you that I bear you no ill will. I hope that you, too, are willing to put the past behind us. I would like for us to be friends, Vincent.

Vincent closed his eyes for a second. Yes, he was willing to put the past behind them. And yes, he wanted them to be "friends." God, how he wanted it. Perhaps he would forgive her after all. He could exact his revenge for her stubbornness *after* they were married—he would keep her in his bed for a week. . . .

A faint smile curling his lips, he opened his eyes and continued reading. His smile disappeared.

In the spirit of friendship, I would like to ask that you return the portrait I gave you as a betrothal gift. I am sure you will agree that it is not quite the thing for you to keep it. Especially now, since I have fallen in love with another man and am shortly to be married. . . .

The words blurred. The blood grew still in his veins and the room darkened. A heavy pounding beat against his temples, and a loud ringing filled his ears.

"What reply, my lord?" Wilmott asked.

Vincent stared at him uncomprehendingly.

"My lord?" Wilmott's dark, bushy brows lowered in an anxious frown. "What reply?"

Vincent looked down at the letter, crumpled in his tightly closed fist. He inhaled, his nostrils flaring. Abruptly, he stood up, the legs of his chair screeching on the floor.

Without answering the startled butler, he strode out of the room and into the marble hall where a rain-drenched servant stood, twisting a sodden hat between his hands.

Vincent thrust out the crumpled paper. "Did you bring this missive?"

The stocky messenger gripped his hat. A steady stream of water dripped from the cap and his rain slicker onto the floor. "Y-y-yes, my lord. Miss Vale said that I was to return this painting"—he nodded to a canvas-covered frame resting against the wall—"and receive one from you in return. I have a carriage outside."

She had returned the portrait of him? With an effort, Vincent tamped down his rage. "Miss Vale must want this painting very much," he drawled.

"That is true, my lord." The man began to twist his hat again. "She wishes to give it to Lord Haversham."

The muscles in Vincent's neck and shoulders tensed. "Haversham?" he repeated, his lips barely moving. "She is marrying Haversham?"

"Yes, my lord. Tomorrow."

A reddish haze rose before Vincent's eyes. Haversham. She was marrying the marquess of Haversham tomorrow. The wealthiest man in the country—and the biggest fop.

The jade. The greedy, faithless jade.

Clenching his teeth, he turned to Wilmott. "Summon three footmen to help you take down the portrait," he ordered.

The messenger stepped forward. "I'll be pleased to help, my lord."

"That won't be necessary." Vincent barely spared him a glance. "You will not be taking the portrait to your mistress."

The messenger's mouth fell open. "But . . . but, my lord, what shall I say to Miss Vale?"

Vincent narrowed his eyes. "You may tell Miss Vale that I intend to build the largest bonfire this shire has ever seen and burn the portrait. If it were only a few hundred years earlier, I am certain she would burn along with it. Now," he said in a dangerously soft voice, "I suggest you leave before I decide to gut you and throw your carcass out for the crows."

The messenger's hands froze on his hat. Then he slapped it back on his head and turned, almost slipping in the puddle he had created. He scuttled out the door.

Smiling unpleasantly, Vincent turned, only to see Wilmott standing frozen in the middle of the hall. "Well?" he asked, still in that soft voice.

Wilmott opened his mouth as if to say something, but apparently thought better of it. He hurried toward the servants' stair.

Vincent returned to the dining room. He picked up the glass of brandy and drained it in one gulp. As he lowered the glass, his gaze fell once more upon the portrait.

Her brilliant blue eyes seemed to glow in the dim room. They laughed down at him, mocking and beguiling at the same time. He could almost hear her laughter. Low, enticing laughter that made a man insane with longing and desire.

His hand tightened on his empty glass.

Now, Haversham would be the one to hear that laughter. Haversham would have Elizabeth's sweet smiles and honeyed kisses. Haversham would have Elizabeth in his arms and in his bed—

No!

He hurled the glass away with all the force he could

summon. It crashed against the wall, splintering into a thousand glittering, tinkling shards. Brandy dripped down the wall. He stared at the stain, then turned on his heel and strode to the door, almost bumping into the footmen who were about to enter.

They took one look at his face and fell back, their expressions fearful, but he ignored their fright. "One of you see that Zeus is saddled and at the door," he ordered harshly. "The other fetch my hat and cloak."

They goggled at him, and he snapped, "At once!" They scurried off to obey.

In no time at all, he was mounting his powerful black stallion and spurring the animal forward into the storm. Swathed in his greatcoat, his hat low over his forehead, he rode down Helsbury House's long drive toward the main road. The wind and rain beat against his face and crept under his collar, but he didn't notice the cold. Rage generated a scorching heat.

Haversham! He should have thrown his glass of wine in the fop's face three months ago at the Helsbury musicale when he had the chance. He should have challenged the milksop to a duel and sliced him to ribbons. He should have carved out the miserable cur's liver with his sword and fed it to his dogs.

And Elizabeth! He should not have been so lenient with her, either. He should have locked her in the ancient dungeons below Helsbury House and kept her there until she agreed to marry him without delay. She didn't love Haversham—she couldn't! The man was a mincing, prancing fop. He wore a corset and padded his calves, for God's sake. He wrote the worst poetry imaginable. And if his voice was any higher, he'd sound like a choirboy.

Vincent reined in Zeus as they rounded a sharp turn in the drive, then urged the animal forward again. Specks of mud and gravel stung his face as he rode, but he didn't slow his wild pace.

No, Elizabeth wasn't in love with Haversham. She was only marrying the fop to punish him, Vincent. To punish him for wanting too much, for asking too much, for demanding too much. He should never have given up so easily—

Lightning flashed and thunder boomed. The stallion shied, and in the blaze of light, Vincent glimpsed a swollen, frothing torrent blocking the path. The rickety bridge that had spanned the usually gentle brook was gone.

Cursing, he drew back hard on the reins. Zeus whinnied in protest. Vincent pulled the nervous stallion in a circle, a small voice of common sense telling him to return to the house. The night was too dark, the rain too heavy, the road too treacherous.

As treacherous as Elizabeth Vale.

Hot blood surged through his veins again, wiping away all reason. He spurred Zeus forward, into the rushing river.

The chill water lapped at his legs and splashed onto his arms. He could feel the current tugging at him, but he paid no attention. He had to keep going. He had to prevent Elizabeth from marrying Haversham.

He clenched his jaw. How could she stand for that worm to touch her? After everything they had been to each other, how dare she let another man touch her?

How could she have betrayed him so?

For a moment, Vincent's grip on the reins slackened. He slid sideways. Gritting his teeth, he wound his fingers in the stallion's dank black mane, ignoring the numbness creeping through his flesh, and urged the horse forward.

Torrents of water swirled around them, tugging at him and the horse. Vincent dashed the water out of his eyes and peered through the gloom. He could barely make out the opposite bank. Between his knees, he could feel Zeus's powerful muscles struggling against the current. The water soaked Vincent, pulling and dragging at him. Tightening his grip on the mane, he leaned forward. "You can do it, boy," he murmured.

Zeus's ears flickered, then pointed forward again. With

a sudden burst of strength, the stallion surged against the current, battling the water with its strong legs. A moment later, the horse's hooves scrabbled on the rocky bank.

Vincent rested his head on Zeus's neck for a moment, his breath coming in harsh gasps. Damn, he was a fool to be out on a night like this. It was all Elizabeth's fault. As soon as he could lay his hands on her, he was going to punish her for putting him through this. He was going to kiss her until she begged for mercy, until she begged for forgiveness. And then he was going to kiss her again. Kiss her until she admitted that she didn't love Haversham, that she could never love anyone else except—

Lightning flashed again.

Zeus reared. The reins slipped through Vincent's numb grasp. He fell onto the rocky bank, his head striking a sharp stone.

Pain exploded through him. All vestiges of warmth disappeared, and suddenly he was cold—chilled to the very marrow of his bones. He couldn't move. His eyes drifted half-closed.

Water rushed by inches from his face. A twig churned out of the water, scratching his cheek. The fresh pain prodded him from his daze. He sat up and rested his aching head on his knees. He wanted to sit there on the wet bank and allow the pain to subside, but he couldn't. He didn't have time.

Sluggishly, awkwardly, he rose to his feet. Black shadows whirled in front of him, making him dizzy. Stumbling, he reached out blindly for the stallion.

His hand encountered wet, sleek hide. Zeus sidled nervously, knocking against him.

He fell back, splaying his arms outward, trying to regain his balance. The spinning shadows whirled faster. He fell back, back, back. . . .

The impact of the icy water hit him with the force of a bludgeon. Oxygen whooshed out of his lungs. He sank below the water, the sounds of the storm becoming muted.

Then he was swept upward. His head broke the surface, and the howling wind and raging river pounded at his eardrums. He gasped for air, barely filling his lungs before the current jerked him under again.

He kicked and clawed at the water, but it filled his boots and weighed down his clothes, dragging him deeper and deeper toward the bottom. He strained to kick off his boots, but they were too tight. He fought to untangle himself from the stranglehold of his heavy cape, but it only twisted more tightly around him.

He thrashed in the water, the sound drowned out by the blood pounding in his head. His arms and legs grew leaden. Water pressed against his eyeballs and his eardrums. His lungs were bursting from lack of oxygen. He realized he was going to die.

Rage boiled through him.

Elizabeth . . . you jade . . . damn you . . .

The world grew quiet. Dark and quiet and freezing cold. His anger faded. The pain in his head and lungs was excruciating, but the ache in his heart was greater.

Elizabeth . . . you can't marry him . . . you can't . . .

Water, tasting of dirt and mud, poured into his mouth and down into his lungs. Numbness crept through him, sweeping away the pain.

Beth . . .

1

25 years later

Mary Goodwin stared out the dirt-streaked window as the train rattled along the tracks. With the windows closed, the compartment smelled of coal and smoke and unwashed bodies, but Mary barely noticed. She was in her own little world, dreaming about Jason . . . dear Jason.

Almost a year had passed since she last saw him, but she could still picture him as clearly as if she had seen him yesterday—the gentle blue-gray of his eyes, his thick, dark brown hair with the stubborn curl, and the white flash of his sudden smile. He was tall and strong, but very kind—he had often fetched her shawl or sewing basket for her—and extraordinarily gentle. When he had proposed, he had held her hand as if it were made from the most fragile glass, and when he had kissed her, his mouth had been so warm, so sweet, so reverent—

The train rattled, and an exclamation of "Oh, bother!" distracted Mary from her thoughts.

She glanced around to see the elderly woman seated across from her frowning down at the knitting in her hands. Mary, who had exchanged introductions with her earlier, smiled. "Did you drop another stitch, Mrs. Tern?"

Mrs. Tern nodded. With a sigh, she folded the mittens she was making and tucked them and her needles into her traveling bag. She looked around the crowded compartment, her brow furrowing. "It is very warm in here. I do hope the engine isn't overheating. Did you hear about the train that exploded last week? Twenty people were killed! I would have preferred to travel by carriage. It is so much more comfortable. One doesn't need to worry about being blown up."

Smiling, Mary shook her head. "The train can't blow up. It is impossible for something so dreadful to happen on such a wonderful day."

"Anything is possible," the older woman said gloomily.

Still smiling, Mary patted Mrs. Tern's hand. "Train explosions are very rare," she assured the woman. Hoping to divert Mrs. Tern from her fears, Mary asked, "Would you like a peppermint?"

The older woman's face brightened. "Yes, thank you."

Mary rooted around in her bag and pulled out two small pieces of the candy. She gave one to Mrs. Tern and put the other in her mouth. The strong, minty flavor burned against her tongue, vivid as her memories of Jason.

She could still barely believe that she was going to marry him. As a twenty-four-year-old paid companion to the invalid wife of Mr. Cooper, a not-too-prosperous merchant, she had been aware of the stark reality of her lack of prospects. She had always prided herself on being sensible, however, and had accepted her lot in life with determined cheerfulness.

Jason's arrival on Mr. Cooper's doorstep in Liverpool had changed all that.

He had been a law clerk from the firm Mr. Cooper did business with, and he'd accompanied the senior partner to discuss some lawsuit Mr. Cooper was embroiled in. Immediately struck by Jason Parsell, she'd watched him from the corner of her eye all through dinner. Later that night, when she'd sneaked from the stuffy house to sit in the jasmine-scented garden, she'd even allowed herself to dream about him a little.

But in spite of her wistful dreams, she'd had no real illusions. She'd known she was unlikely to attract him. With her straight brown hair and unremarkable face and figure, she'd known it was doubtful he would even notice her.

So she'd been surprised when he'd struck up a conversation with her at breakfast the next day. And again at luncheon and dinner. That night, when she sat quietly sewing in her corner in the parlor, she noticed him watching her, a warm smile in his eyes. The next evening, he sat next to her and talked to her while she sewed.

In the days that followed, she had often run into him in the corridor, on the stairway, or in the garden. She found herself talking to him, confiding in him, laughing with him. In a short time, he became a friend, one that she'd felt she'd known all her life.

Then one afternoon, she'd been cutting roses in the garden. Hearing a noise, she turned around, her arms full of flowers, and bumped into him. His hands came up to her shoulders to steady her. Laughing, she looked up to see him staring down at her, a serious, intent expression on his face. The warm sunshine, the buzzing of insects, the heady scent of the flowers pressed between them, all seemed to melt into the background. For a moment, a delicious, impossible, giddy hope had unfurled inside her.

But he had stepped back and turned away. In a rather stifled voice, he told her that he'd just received word that his uncle had died and he had inherited not only a tidy fortune, but an earldom as well. Her foolish hope had shriveled and died.

Shifting on her seat, Mary sucked on the shrinking peppermint and stared out the window.

She had been glad for him, of course, but she had known he would have to leave the Coopers' house and go to London to find himself a wealthy, titled bride. Blinking back tears, she had smiled up at him and congratulated him on his good fortune.

But instead of thanking her, and taking his leave, he

had gathered her in his arms, roses and all, and kissed her gently on her lips. Then he had asked her to be his wife.

Mary gazed dreamily at the countryside speeding past. She'd said yes, of course. He'd had to leave her to straighten out the details of his inheritance, but when she'd accompanied him to the train station to say good-bye, he had promised to send for her as soon as everything was settled. And he had promised to write.

"Even though," he'd said in a sheepish voice, "I'm not much of a letter writer."

Which had certainly proved true, she thought with a wry smile. He'd written her a total of exactly three letters. The first hadn't arrived for almost three months, but she had read and reread it until she could recite it from memory:

> *Dear Mary—I apologize for not writing sooner, but I have been very busy in London dealing with the legalities of my inheritance. I only arrived here at Helsbury House a week ago, and I must tell you, it's a very odd feeling to know that I am now the owner of this huge old barn of a place. My aunt Weldon (a distant relation—her sister married one of my father's cousins) has offered to make the wedding arrangements. I told her we wish to be married as soon as possible, but she has informed me of several Helsbury House traditions that we must follow, including being married in the village church. I agreed, since it seemed very important to her. Is this acceptable to you? If you are not happy with these arrangements, tell me so, and I will speak to Aunt Weldon. Although I warn you, she is quite formidable, and my knees quake at the thought of naysaying her. But I will do anything for you, Mary.*

Mary smiled, remembering this piece of silliness. Of course she had written him that she was happy for his aunt to make the arrangements. It was incredibly kind of the woman to do so. Mary was looking forward to meeting his aunt and thanking her in person—in spite of Jason's joking comments about her. At times he had a very reprehensible sense of humor, which he had displayed quite outrageously in the rest of his letter.

There is one more thing I must tell you—now, promise you won't laugh—I think this house is haunted. Will it bother you to live in a haunted house, Mary? I will protect you from the ghost, I promise. I will never leave your side. Especially at night when ghosts are known to roam.
Yours, Jason

Mary blushed, remembering that last sentence. But she had read the words over and over again, her heart pounding at the images they conjured up. It was wicked of him to tease her like that. She would definitely have to scold him when she saw him.

The second letter had come a few months later.

Dear Mary—
I apologize again for not writing sooner. I am involved in a border dispute with a neighbor (the man is trying to claim over an acre of the South Woods and I am having difficulty finding the deed to the property), and it is taking up all of my time.
I miss you terribly, and I wish we could be married right away, but it is impossible. Being an earl is more difficult than I thought it would be, Mary. I must decide on everything, including when to plant the crops, how much rent to charge the tenants, what school to send some young relatives to, which families to call on, and even how to carve the roast! But I don't mean to burden you with my troubles. I hope everything is well with you, and I will write again once this suit is settled.
Jason

Although she sympathized with his problems, she'd been disappointed by the delay of their wedding—especially since he hadn't written again for almost six months. She'd been growing worried when his third letter—a note, really—had arrived.

> Mary—
> *I apologize for neglecting to write. I am very busy with estate matters and my new duties, but now would be a good time for you to visit and meet my family. The wedding will take place one week after you arrive. A ticket is enclosed.*
> *Yours, etc., Helsbury*

Mary smiled, remembering how excited she'd been. Finally, after a year of waiting, they were to be married! She'd barely paid any attention at all to the way he'd signed the letter—she was certain he must have written the signature without thinking. And although the note was perhaps a bit curt, the intent was clear—he wanted to marry her right away. At last!

The squeal of metal brought Mary back to the present. The engineer applied the brake again, and more squealing ensued. The train slowed and the conductor called out, "Manchester! Manchester!"

Mary looked up. This was her stop. Hastily, she chewed the tiny sliver of candy still in her mouth and swallowed. She checked her hat to make sure it was straight and glanced down at her dress. The brown merino was a bit worn, but she had sewn new cuffs and a collar on it, and she thought she looked quite respectable, in spite of her sister-in-law's opinion that she should have bought a new dress.

"You're going to be a countess!" Kathryn had scolded when Mary visited her a few weeks ago. "Buy a new wardrobe and send the bills to your fiancé. He will expect you to dress well."

Mary had disagreed. Jason didn't care about clothes.

Besides, the idea of his buying her clothes had seemed inappropriate. Instead, Mary had hoarded every penny she earned from Mr. Cooper to buy the silk for her wedding gown, and sat up late at night, embroidering the bodice with silk floss and seed pearls. Every stitch had carried a hope and a dream for the future—her bright and rosy future with Jason.

Mary smiled, thinking of the dress in her satchel. It was very nearly done. She only needed to embroider the hem.

The train chugged to a stop, and Mary peered out the window. But the platform was crowded and she could see no sign of Jason. Bidding farewell to Mrs. Tern, she rose, clutching her satchel as a great deal of polite shoving and pushing ensued. The conductor handed her down the steps onto the platform.

The train huffed and puffed and squealed even though it was standing still, and the humid air made Mary's skin feel clammy. Wiping her brow with her handkerchief, she looked around again and caught sight of a familiar tall silhouette, half-turned away from her.

A smile burst from inside her and impetuously she stepped toward the man. "Jason!" she called, waving her handkerchief in the air.

The train belched and hissed, nearly drowning her out, but the man must have heard her, because he turned.

For a moment, looking at the elegant figure before her, she thought she had hailed the wrong person. But no, it was Jason. Her smile faded. Slowly, she lowered her handkerchief and pressed it against her breast.

He had changed.

2

Instead of the rusty black coat that she remembered, with frayed cuffs and a patch on the sleeve, he wore a dark green frock coat and a waistcoat embroidered with an intricate pattern of leaves. The crumpled, slightly askew neckcloth of thin black muslin he'd once worn was gone—now, he sported a striped silk cravat tied *à la Byron*. He carried a black silk top hat and fine leather gloves in one hand.

Mary slipped her handkerchief into her pocket, her fingers brushing against the fabric of her skirt. Suddenly, her worn brown traveling dress seemed old and ugly. She wished she had listened to her sister-in-law and purchased a new one.

He had been twenty-nine when she first met him, and she'd always thought he looked younger. Now he must be thirty, but he looked older—his face thinner, more stark, with new lines on his forehead. At least his dark brown hair was the same, and he was still tall and broad. But his eyes seemed cooler, more gray than blue, as his gaze wandered over her.

He looked aloof, imposing . . . aristocratic.

Instinctively, without thinking, she curtsied. "Good afternoon, my lord."

As soon as she had done it, she felt foolish. This was *Jason*, for heaven's sake. Her fiancé.

She half expected him to laugh at her, but he only said, "Good afternoon," and held out his hand.

She stared at it, uncertain what he wanted. His hand looked hard and smooth, no telltale splatters of ink marring the skin, the calluses from holding a pen gone. His nails were evenly cut and well-cared for.

"May I take your satchel?"

She looked up and saw his brows were raised. Blushing, she gave him the bag. He handed it to a servant standing discreetly behind him, then offered her his arm. Conscious of the immaculate fabric of his coat and of her fingers, sticky from the peppermint, Mary gingerly placed her hand on his sleeve.

He even smelled different, she thought dazedly. He smelled of expensive soap and clean linen, of fine wool and exotic tobacco.

He led her across the platform, a path through the crowd somehow magically appearing before him, to a shiny black carriage with an elaborate crest painted in gold on the door.

Inside, Mary sank down onto the plush red velvet seat. Jason sat across from her and rapped on the ceiling. The well-sprung carriage set off with barely a jolt.

For several minutes, while the carriage maneuvered through the busy streets, Mary could think of nothing to say. All the small things she'd been storing up to tell him fled from her brain. She felt extraordinarily awkward—and strangely hollow inside.

It wasn't until the carriage had left the smoke and crowds of the city behind and was tooling down a wide road that she recovered her wits enough to give herself a mental shake.

It wasn't so strange she should feel a trifle awkward—they had been apart for almost a year. It would pass, she was certain, once she became accustomed to Jason's new persona. She just wasn't used to him looking—and smelling—so grand. But surely he was still the same person inside. Becoming an earl didn't change a person that much.

Did it?

Absently, she stroked the fine, soft velvet seat.

"How was your journey?"

His voice was cool and impersonal. She glanced at him from beneath her lashes, wondering what he was thinking. His gaze was fixed on her hands. Flushing, she lifted her fingers from the velvet cushion and clasped them in her lap.

"It was very pleasant, but I am happy to be here."

"That is very apparent."

Hearing the sardonic edge to his voice, Mary's flush deepened. Was her discomfort so obvious? She licked her lips, tasting a lingering vestige of peppermint, and fell silent.

After traveling several more miles, the carriage turned onto another road, and she gathered up her nerve again.

She forced herself to smile. "I am looking forward to spending the week becoming reacquainted with you."

"And I with you," he said, still sounding sardonic. "In between the numerous entertainments we have scheduled for this week and the business I must finish before our wedding—including finalizing the arrangements for our honeymoon."

Entertainments? Business? *Honeymoon?* Mary swallowed. They had barely discussed a honeymoon. Oh, she had mentioned she loved the seashore, but that was all. The carriage turned sharply into a narrow lane. "Honeymoon?" she echoed.

"I wanted to surprise you." He looked out the window. "We are going to Paris."

"Paris!" Mary gasped, her discomfort forgotten. She had never dreamed that she would ever have a chance to see the foreign city. She smiled radiantly. "Oh, thank you!"

He glanced at her, his expression unreadable. "No need to thank me. Paris is the fashionable place to go for one's honeymoon." He looked out the window again. "We are almost at the house. You will be able to see it when we come around this bend."

Mary stared at his averted profile for a moment, then obediently turned to look out the window.

They were traveling through a thick forest of oak and yew trees, alongside a winding brook. She could hear robins and sparrows chirping in the trees, and she caught a glimpse of a hare dashing through the thick underbrush, before the carriage rounded the bend and Helsbury House burst into view.

She gasped again.

The house was not a house at all—it was a mansion, with a white marble facade, ornamented with columns and pediments and statues, and chimneys too numerous to count. Against a backdrop of dark green pines, it stood on a broad, flat expanse of lawn. Several fluffy white sheep clustered beneath a huge elm there, chewing on the grass, while a few others drank from the sparkling brook that wound its way across the lawn and in and out of the woods.

This was the "old barn of a place" he'd mentioned in his letter? "It's beautiful!" she exclaimed.

"It's very cold," he said, tapping his fingers on the window ledge.

She looked at him quizzically. "Surely there are fireplaces?"

He shrugged.

Mary was struck again by how different he seemed. Although he had always been fairly quiet and serious, she didn't remember him being so unforthcoming. "Do you and your aunt Weldon live here alone?" she asked.

"Several other of my relatives reside here also," he said as the carriage bumped and the wheels clattered on the wooden slats of a bridge. "Lady Weldon, who acts as my hostess, has a daughter named Beatrice. Two of my father's cousins live here—Horace Quimby, who serves as vicar for the village, and Miss Sarah Parsell. But I doubt you will meet her."

"Why not?"

"She is very reclusive. She takes all her meals in her rooms and never comes out."

Mary was confused. "Is she ill?"

"No, she just likes to stay to herself."

"But isn't she lonely?"

Jason shrugged again. "Perhaps. However, it is her choice to remain there."

Mary stared at him. His response seemed a trifle unfeeling. But she didn't know the whole story, she told herself hastily. Perhaps Miss Parsell truly preferred her own company.

"I have another relative who lives here, but she is temporarily residing in Bath to take treatment for her arthritis," Jason continued. "In addition, I have two distant cousins who are currently making mischief in London, and one who is at Eton. One or all of them may return at any time. My cousin Cecil Parsell is here also, but he is only visiting. He is one of my few relatives who has his own household."

"I will enjoy meeting him," Mary said as the carriage pulled up to the front of the house. "And the others, too. Especially Lady Weldon. I want to thank her for her kindness in handling the wedding arrangements."

Jason, looking sardonic again, did not reply. He climbed out and held out his hand to help her down, then escorted her up a flight of marble stairs to where a regal butler stood by the imposing front doors. The butler bowed and ushered them inside to a beautiful but very chilly hall, with floors, pillars, and staircase all made from white marble.

A tall, gray-haired woman in a black silk dress and a young, very beautiful girl wearing a fashionable yellow gown that set off her long red hair were just coming down the stairs. They stopped at the bottom and stared at Mary. Seeing the resemblance in their brown eyes and aquiline noses, Mary realized they must be Lady Weldon and her daughter, Beatrice.

Jason performed the introductions. "Aunt Weldon, Beatrice, may I present Miss Mary Goodwin," he murmured. "My fiancée."

Her guess confirmed, Mary smiled and stepped forward. "Lady Weldon, how pleasant to meet you! I want to thank you for your help with the wedding plans."

Lady Weldon's expression did not change, and Mary's smile faltered. She had never seen brown eyes that could look as cold as Lady Weldon's. The woman looked down her nose as she spoke. "Miss Goodwin, I am sure you will want to freshen up and change into something more suitable"—her gaze wandered over Mary's brown dress—"for dinner."

Mary flushed and stepped back. "Yes, I would. Thank you, Lady Weldon."

"Is your maid following with your luggage?"

"I don't have a maid. Nor any luggage except for my satchel. Although," she added hastily, seeing the older woman's shocked expression, "it's a very large satchel."

The news of the satchel's size did not dispel Lady Weldon's air of disapproval. "Miss Goodwin, are you saying you traveled on the train *alone?*"

"Now, Mother," Beatrice said, moving forward to Mary's side. "You mustn't lecture Jason's fiancée on her first day here. Come, Mary, I'll show you to your room. Mother has had the Yellow Bedchamber prepared."

Thankful for the girl's intervention, Mary followed Beatrice toward the stairs.

"Wait."

Jason's command halted Beatrice in her tracks. Mary looked at him, thinking perhaps he was going to offer to escort her. But instead, to her surprise, he said to his aunt, "I prefer that Mary stay in another room."

Lady Weldon's brows rose nearly to her hairline. "The Helsbury fiancées always sleep in the Yellow Bedchamber."

"Nonetheless, I prefer a different room for Mary," Jason said.

"It seems ridiculous to change rooms when one is already prepared." The lines bracketing Lady Weldon's mouth deepened. "You cannot intend for her to stay on the same floor of the house as you? That would be most improper."

"No, of course not." Jason brushed a fleck of dust from his sleeve. "I wish her to stay in the Blue Room."

Lady Weldon's eyes widened and her neck grew stiff. Beatrice, too, became very still. Mary glanced around at the silent figures, wondering why they seemed so tense—

With a crash, the front door slammed closed.

Mary jumped and turned to look at the butler.

He was standing next to the coachman who had just entered with Mary's satchel.

The butler's gaunt cheeks were almost as snow-white as his few remaining strands of hair. "I . . . I beg your pardon, my lord. The door somehow pulled out of my hands."

"Probably the wind," Jason said. "Have one of the servants take Miss Goodwin's bag to the Blue Room."

"Yes, my lord," the butler muttered.

"But Jason," Lady Weldon protested, "it's not ready."

"I ordered the room cleaned and aired yesterday," Jason said.

"I see. It would appear that everything is taken care of, then." Her lips stretched in a thin smile, but her eyes looked positively glacial. "Please excuse me, Jason, I must speak to the cook about dinner." With a bare inclination of her head in Mary's direction, Lady Weldon swept from the room.

Jason, appearing astonishingly unmoved by his aunt's displeasure, turned to Mary. "I'll escort you to the Blue Room."

Beatrice seemed to recover from her stupor. With a playful smile, she said, "No, no, Jason. You must allow me a chance to further my acquaintance with your fiancée. I will show her to the Blue Room."

Jason studied Mary a moment, his expression unfathomable. She hoped he would insist upon accompanying her, but he merely bowed and strode off in the opposite direction. She watched him go, the hollow feeling returning to her stomach.

"I hope you don't mind," Beatrice said. "But I wanted to give Jason a chance to apologize to Mother for usurping her duties."

Mary stared at her. "Did he do that?"

"Yes, indeed. Although I'm certain he didn't intend to. He would not wish to undermine Mama's authority with the servants." Beatrice turned and hurried up the stairs.

Mary blinked, then gathered her skirts in one hand and hastened after the other girl. She thought Beatrice's comment rather odd. Didn't Jason have the ultimate authority here? But she didn't press Beatrice on the issue. She was more curious about everyone's strong reaction to the Blue Room. "Is there something wrong with the Blue Room?"

Beatrice laughed lightly, her heels clicking on the marble stairs. "No, of course not. It's just that no one has slept there in twenty-five years."

"Whyever not?" Mary asked as they reached the top of the staircase.

Beatrice turned down a long corridor, its walls covered with portraits of old, grim-faced people and dark, gloomy landscapes. "Because of the ghost," she said in a low voice.

Mary's mouth fell open in surprise. Then, remembering Jason's joking comments about a ghost in his letter, laughter bubbled up in her throat. "The room is haunted? How charming!"

A tiny frown knitted Beatrice's brow. It smoothed out, though, when she saw Mary looking at her. "I'm so glad you're not superstitious. Most people would be afraid to sleep in the Blue Room." Quickening her steps, she turned a corner that led to another corridor.

"Oh, is it an unfriendly ghost?" Still smiling, Mary increased her pace to keep up.

Beatrice hesitated. "I'm certain you have nothing to worry about," she finally said. "There's no point in telling you stories that would only serve to make you uneasy."

"No point at all," Mary echoed. It was a good thing

she didn't believe in ghosts, or Beatrice's statement would have made her very nervous indeed.

Beatrice stopped in front of a paneled ebony door in the middle of the corridor. "Ah, here we are." She pushed open the door.

The room was furnished in ebony, white silk, and blue satin. There were two large windows on the south wall. The room was warmer than the rest of the house, perhaps because of the fireplace tucked into the corner and the pink and blue carpet on the floor. "Why, it's beautiful!" Mary said, walking over to the bed. A large conch shell lay on the small ebony bedside table. She picked up the seashell and stroked the hard, slightly bumpy surface.

"I'm glad you approve." Beatrice smiled. "I'm so delighted you've come. I've always longed for a companion close to my own age. I hope we will become good friends, Mary."

Smiling, Mary glanced up from the shell. "I hope so too, Beatrice."

The other girl plucked at the huge sleeve of her yellow dress to puff it out. "It's Lady Beatrice."

Mary's brow wrinkled. "I beg your pardon?"

"My father was an earl." Beatrice lifted her lashes, a pleasant smile on her face. "I am called 'Lady Beatrice.'"

A blush warmed Mary's cheeks. "Oh. I beg your pardon, Lady Beatrice."

"Never mind. I know you aren't familiar with all the ways of fashionable society." Beatrice's warm smile took some of the sting from her words. "I am sure you will learn. If you need any help, please don't hesitate to ask my mother or me."

"That's very kind of you, Lady Beatrice," Mary murmured.

With another pleasant smile, Beatrice left.

Mary stared after her, then looked down at the seashell in her hands.

She could almost hear Jason's voice saying, *Paris is the fashionable place to go for one's honeymoon.* She traced the seashell's protruding points. For some reason, her enthusiasm for Paris had dwindled.

She held the seashell up to her ear. She could hear a faint roar. A picture flashed through her brain of Jason and her strolling up a pebble-strewn beach to a cozy, intimate cottage. She put the shell down. Paris would be much more exciting, she told herself sternly.

But as she changed for dinner, the image of the tiny cottage at the seashore lingered.

3

Jason carefully folded the starched cravat, inserted a ruby stickpin, and studied the result in the mirror. The left side of the bow drooped limply. Frowning, he pulled out the stickpin and yanked the muslin from around his neck. His valet, prudently silent, handed him another length of muslin. Jason started again, but he found it difficult to concentrate on his task. He couldn't stop thinking about Mary.

About how she had changed.

So much time had passed since he'd last seen her, it had been difficult to remember the exact details of her appearance and demeanor. Perhaps that was why he had been so shocked when he first saw her shabby gown. The threadbare brown dress was more suitable for a scullery maid than his future bride. Why hadn't she asked him for money so she could purchase a new one?

He did not like her severe hairstyle, either. It made her look like a governess. Had she always worn it that way? He couldn't remember. But he knew for a certainty that she had never curtsied to him or called him "my lord" before. There had not been a hint of a smile on her face as she did so. She had seemed cool and remote. Somber.

He didn't know what he had seen in her a year ago. He couldn't remember. He vaguely recalled thinking that she had a sweet smile—a smile like an angel. He remembered thinking that heaven must have sent her down especially for him. . . .

He winced. Had he truly been so foolish?

"I think you almost have it, my lord."

Jason glanced at his valet's narrow, sallow face. The man was watching him tie the cravat with intense concentration. To Everitt, the matter was one of great importance. The servant had been near tears over some of Jason's earliest efforts. It had taken weeks of practice for Jason to improve enough to meet the valet's strict standards.

Being an earl, Jason thought wryly, was very different from being a law clerk. A year ago, no one had cared how he dressed. He had simply been Jason Parsell, a man in love with a pretty girl. Now, in this new world, he was the earl of Helsbury, he wore only the finest clothes, and love seemed like a strange, almost alien emotion. The earls of Helsbury, as he was frequently reminded, did not fall in love.

"Perfect, my lord."

Jason glanced at his valet, who was nodding in approval. He looked back at the mirror and saw that the cravat was indeed a perfectly arranged masterpiece.

"Thank you, Everitt." Jason allowed the valet to help him into his dark blue coat, then went downstairs to the drawing room, his thoughts returning to Mary.

He supposed that whatever his reason for proposing to her, it didn't make much difference now, not at this late date. He wouldn't be such a cad as to jilt her, even if he wanted to. Which he didn't. It was his duty to marry, and considering the history of the Helsbury earls, it behooved him to marry as quickly as possible. Mary would suit him well enough. He wasn't foolish enough to yearn for some puerile emotion brought on by a sweet smile—

He heard laughter as the servant opened the door to the drawing room. He went inside, then stopped, staring at the cozy couple sitting on the sofa.

His cousin Cecil's silver-blond head was bent close to Mary's golden brown one. Cecil laughed at something Mary said, and she laughed too, her eyes smiling up at the other man.

Jason tensed. He stood there, watching them, until Mary turned and noticed him.

Her smile disappeared. "Good evening, my lord," she said, looking at him warily.

"Good evening, Mary." His voice was level, polite. So why was she looking at him like that? He had an odd urge to stalk over and pull her away from Cecil, but he restrained himself. He was being ridiculous. It was a good thing that Mary was becoming acquainted with his relatives. There was no reason to feel annoyed.

"There you are, Jason!" Cecil exclaimed. "I must say, your fiancée is most charming. I'm quite envious of your good fortune."

"Thank you," Jason said coldly. He felt someone take his arm, and turned to find Beatrice, who had been talking to her mother by the fireplace, linking her arm with his.

She smiled up at him. "Good evening, Jason."

He smiled back absently before glancing over at Mary again. She looked prettier this evening. She wore a blue dress, which although plain was more becoming than the brown one she'd had on earlier. Her hair was arranged differently too, pulled up high on her head. The style emphasized the delicate line of her cheek and jaw.

"Mary and Cecil seem to be quite taken with each other," Beatrice said softly. "Mary has drawn him out quite amazingly."

"So she has." Jason's voice sounded stiff, even to his own ears. He supposed he shouldn't be surprised that Mary had drawn Cecil out of his shell—he *did* remember her as being very pleasant and friendly. But he was still surprised that she'd managed so quickly. Beatrice, who was beautiful and charming, hadn't been able to elicit more than a word or two from Cecil. Clearing his throat, Jason said more evenly, "I'm glad she's found a friend."

"She's found two friends," Beatrice said. "I like her very much also. She's so . . . unassuming."

Jason frowned a little, his gaze straying to Mary again. He noticed that the arrangement of her hair left the nape of her neck bare. A loose strand of rich golden brown hair curled against the vulnerable skin.

"Jason?"

He tore his gaze away from Mary and looked down at the girl at his side. "I beg your pardon, Beatrice. You are right, Mary is very unassuming. I hope you will help her if she needs it."

Beatrice's lashes fluttered downward. "Of course I will, Jason."

The door opened again and Horace Quimby entered, his tufts of white hair sticking straight up, a Bible tucked under his arm.

With a vague nod to the other occupants, Quimby rushed to Jason's side. "Cousin, you were right about Blevins!" he announced, clutching his Bible. "I checked with his previous employer and discovered that he had a history of drinking quite heavily!"

"That's unfortunate." Jason frowned, remembering the desperation he'd seen in the man's eyes. For a moment, the weight of responsibility pressed down upon him. "I will have to speak to him tomorrow."

Quimby nodded. "I shudder to think how close I came to recommending that you hire him for the mill position. To have a devotee of Bacchus in our community is wholly repulsive—ah, thank you," he said, taking a glass of wine from a passing servant. He sampled it and smiled in approval before glancing around the room. His gaze lingered on Beatrice with almost palpable longing before moving on to Mary. Something sparkled in his rheumy blue eyes. He swallowed the rest of his wine and stepped forward. Taking her hands, he clasped them between his. "Ah, I see we have a guest. Cousin, you must introduce me to this beautiful lady."

Annoyed, Jason complied. In spite of his age and religious training—or perhaps because of them—Quimby had something of a roving eye. Jason had not thought Mary was the type of female that would appeal to the vicar. He should have known that Quimby would make up to anyone in skirts—even skirts as shabby as Mary's. Their shabbiness was even more apparent as Mary stepped past Beatrice. The younger girl was garbed in emerald silk and Valenciennes lace with a matching feathered hat adorning her brilliant red locks. Mary wore the simple blue gown and an unembellished cap.

He frowned.

Lady Weldon stepped forward. "Shall we go in to dinner?"

Jason held out his arm to Mary, his gaze meeting hers. He searched her eyes, looking for . . . what? He wasn't sure exactly. For whatever it was he had seen there a year ago.

But it wasn't there. Her clear blue eyes were polite, but cool.

Strangely, that made him angry. But he did not show it as he escorted her into the dining room.

If he'd learned anything in this last year, it was how to conceal his emotions.

4

Mary sat at Jason's right at the dinner table, watching him from the corner of her eye. She wanted to stare at him, to try to define the changes in him. She could identify some of them—the vertical line between his brows that gave him a permanent frowning expression; the thinner, straighter line of his lips that made him look harsher; and the tense set of his jaw and shoulders—but there was something else, something that eluded her. In his immaculate dark blue coat and white trousers, he looked every inch the earl, haughty and arrogant. But he also had an air of self-confidence, an aura of power and complete control that was strangely attractive.

If only he didn't seem so . . . intimidating.

She wanted to say something to him, but her earlier awkwardness seemed to have increased rather than diminished. He seemed so cool, so distant. She didn't even know how to address him. She thought of him as Jason, but perhaps he expected to be addressed by his title now, like Beatrice. At the train station, he hadn't objected when she'd called him "my lord."

She watched him lean toward Beatrice, seated to his left, listening to something she was whispering. Mary felt a twinge of envy. She wished she possessed the poise the younger girl did. Beatrice looked completely at ease with Jason, laughing at his response to whatever she'd said, her hand resting casually on his arm.

The two of them were so elegant, so handsome, so refined. They looked so *right*. As if they belonged together.

Mary shook away the disturbing thought. Jason loved her, she assured herself, sipping her turtle soup. Perhaps he was a little stiffer, a bit more formal, but she was certain she would discover that underneath he hadn't changed.

Her discomfort must be because of the house, not Jason. She wasn't accustomed to so much grandeur. Such as this dinner, with its acres of linen and crystal and silver, and servants almost bumping into each other in their efforts to offer traysful of exquisite food. And this dining room, with its mile-high ceilings, white marble floors, and woefully inadequate fireplaces.

Mary shivered, wishing she had a shawl. In spite of its magnificence, the house lacked warmth. At her brother's home, the rooms were warm and bright, and there had been lots of laughter and noisy conversation. Even the Coopers' drafty house had seemed warmer and the meals livelier.

Here, the fire did not give off any appreciable heat, and the candles in the chandelier were curiously dim. No one talked above a whisper or laughed or even seemed to enjoy their meal—except perhaps Mr. Quimby, who sat on the other side of Beatrice. He ate with a dedication that precluded him from conversing. Mary was glad someone appeared to appreciate the food—the soup was excellent. If she weren't so nervous, she would be reveling in it.

Forcing herself to concentrate on the soup, she took a sip. Some of her tension eased as she held the creamy liquid in her mouth for a moment to savor the taste.

Swallowing, she glanced up to find Jason staring at her. Did she have soup on her chin? She put her spoon down and wiped her mouth with her napkin.

Without comment, he turned back to Beatrice.

Still unnerved, Mary turned to Cecil on her right. She was glad he was there. So far, he was the only person in the house she did feel comfortable with. When she'd first met him in the drawing room, something about him had reminded her of the way Jason used to be, even though Cecil was blond and more slender, less muscled than his cousin. The resemblance had more to do with his slightly reticent air—as if he were not quite at ease in the company. Her heart had gone out to him, and she had set herself to making him comfortable. She rather thought she had succeeded quite nicely.

"Do you always dine so formally?" she whispered to him now.

Cecil grinned. "Isn't it awful? I say, do you know which fork I should use for this fish?"

Mary inspected the three forks lined up by her plate and shook her head ruefully. "I have no idea."

Cecil picked up the one closest to his plate. Immediately, Lady Weldon cleared her throat. Frowning at Cecil, she pointedly picked up the fork on the outside and took a bite of fish with it.

Cecil's ears turned bright red as he changed forks. "I hate all this nonsense," he muttered.

Mary felt sorry for him. "My first act when I am countess will be to prohibit having more than one fork at any meal," she said jokingly.

Just as she spoke, a sudden lull fell in the dinner conversation, and her words boomed around the table. Seeing Jason's raised brows, Mary blushed.

Lady Weldon's cold brown eyes raked over her. "I do hope you're not serious, Miss Goodwin. As the wife of an earl, you will be expected to maintain certain standards, standards that I have taken great pride in perfecting."

The heat in Mary's cheeks increased. "I'm sorry. I didn't mean to imply—" She glanced at Jason and saw he was frowning now.

"Of course you didn't," Beatrice said, smiling. "Mother, you mustn't be too hard on Mary. Remember, her background is very different from ours."

A small silence fell around the table. Nervously, Mary

picked up her glass of wine and drank, hoping the liquid would help cool her hot face.

Cecil cleared his throat. "Personally, I think Miss Goodwin will be an asset to our family. I only hope she lasts longer than the earls' other fiancées."

Mary choked on her wine. Gasping for breath, she turned to Jason. "You've been engaged before?" she croaked.

"No." He glanced at a servant standing by the sideboard. The servant hurried over and poured Mary some more wine.

"Forgive me, Miss Goodwin," Cecil said. "I was referring to the previous earls' fiancées. No earl of Helsbury since the fifth earl has ever married—although all of them were engaged at least once."

Mary's eyes widened. "None of them married? But why not?"

Mr. Quimby stopped eating for the first time since dinner had started, his eyes darting around the room. Leaning forward, he whispered, "Because of the ghost."

"The ghost?" Mary laughed, the discomfort she'd been feeling all evening waning. "Don't tell me you believe in that silly ghost story, too."

A loud clinking noise made Mary look at Jason. She saw his hand grip the fork on his plate. He was not smiling.

"You mustn't laugh," the vicar said anxiously.

"I beg your pardon." Mary tried to assume a more serious expression. "Who is this ghost?"

The vicar nodded toward the wall behind Lady Weldon. Mary turned and stared.

On the wall above two crossed swords was a portrait in a heavy gilded frame. The man depicted was very handsome—and looked as though he knew it. Dressed in the style fashionable some twenty-five years earlier, he had golden, windblown hair and held a jeweled snuffbox in one hand. Below straight black brows and surrounded by thick dark lashes, his cool green eyes were painted in such a fashion that he seemed to be staring directly at her.

"He looks harmless enough," she observed.

A loud clatter drew her gaze to Jason. A servant rushed to his side and picked up a knife that Jason had knocked to the floor. Oddly tense, Jason seemed to be glaring at the portrait of the sixth earl.

Another servant placed a succulent slice of pheasant on Mary's plate. She took a bite, reveling in the taste and texture, before turning her attention back to Quimby. "Even if there was a ghost, why would that fact prevent the previous earls from marrying?"

The vicar had just taken a large bite of pheasant. Cecil, seeing Quimby's difficulty, took up the story.

"Vincent was one of a long line of Helsbury earls who suffered betrayal by a woman. The story is that Vincent swore at his death that no future earl would again endure this indignity. 'Tis said that his ghost now judges all the fiancées to see if they're worthy."

"Worthy? How does he determine that?" Mary speared a piece of the pheasant with her fork.

Cecil shrugged. "Who knows? But however he makes his decision, the results have been discouraging."

"What do you mean?" Mary placed the bite of meat in her mouth.

"Aaron, Vincent's brother and the seventh earl, had been engaged for several years, but had never set a date for the wedding. He finally did so and brought his fiancée to Helsbury House a month before their wedding. That night, she heard footsteps pacing all around her room. She was so frightened that she broke off the engagement, packed her bags, and left."

"How foolish of her." Mary nodded to the servant offering her some salad. "A few creaking floorboards are not proof of a ghost."

Cecil shook his head solemnly. "Perhaps not. Aaron rejoined his regiment and was killed several years later at the battle of Talavera. Roger, the next brother, became the eighth earl. He was quite a ladies' man and had no desire to settle down, but he dutifully engaged himself to a Miss

Dalrymple. But she saw strange lights in her room. She also broke off the engagement, packed her bags, and left."

"Dear me," Mary murmured.

"A month later, Roger engaged himself to another lady and brought her to Helsbury House to be married, but he suddenly became the clumsiest fellow imaginable. Although an excellent athlete and sportsman, he tripped and fell everywhere he went. Lady Diana broke off the engagement."

Mary looked up from her salad, frowning. "How shallow of her."

"Yes, exactly." Cecil nodded to the servant offering him some peas. "I think Roger had a lucky escape from that one. But he was still determined to marry, and after that he realized what was happening—that the ghost was frightening away the unworthy brides. So he chose the next one with care. He selected Miss Hortense Grimshaw, a devout Christian, who said prayers every morning and every evening. But as soon as he brought her to Helsbury House, a strange thing happened—every time he opened his mouth, an oath came out. He swore—in between profanities—that the ghost was making him do it, but Miss Grimshaw was so offended, she left the next day. Roger gave up and led the rest of his life in, er, sinful pleasures. His dissipations caused him to die early, and thus Timothy, Vincent's third brother, became earl."

Beatrice set down her fork. "Cecil, perhaps it would be best not to repeat this story. It can only serve to make Mary nervous."

"Ghost stories don't make me nervous," Mary said. "Please continue, Mr. Parsell."

Cecil swallowed some peas. "Timothy was nearly sixty and still a bachelor, but he promptly engaged himself to a young heiress. He brought her to Helsbury House." He paused as the servant reached in front of him to take his plate.

Another servant took Mary's plate, but she barely noticed. "What happened?"

"No one knows." Cecil looked at her solemnly, but with a slight twinkle in his hazel eyes. "She ran screaming from the house in the middle of the night."

"Good heavens!" Mary leaned back in her chair as the servants rolled up the tablecloth and removed it. "The poor thing!"

"Poor thing, indeed," Lady Weldon said disdainfully. "She was definitely unworthy to be a Helsbury bride."

Quimby put his Bible back on the table and rested his hand on it. "Let us hope Vincent finds Mary worthy."

Mary would have commented, but she was distracted by a servant offering her a slice of cake. She nodded. Taking a bite of the rich chocolate, she sighed with pleasure.

Beatrice declined the cake. "Really, these tales have no bearing on Mary's situation. I'm sure she is worthy of our dear Jason. He would not have chosen her otherwise." She turned to Mary and smiled. "I am sure you needn't worry that the ghost will appear in your bedroom and try to frighten you away."

Mary looked at the painting and laughter bubbled up inside her once more. "It will take more than the ghost of a puffed-up coxcomb to frighten me away."

A dull thud made her look toward Jason. He had spilled his wine. "I beg your pardon," he muttered. "I am unaccountably awkward tonight. Aunt Weldon, isn't it time for the ladies to withdraw?"

Lady Weldon rose majestically to her feet. "It most certainly is. I do not approve of this talk of ghosts."

The gentlemen and Beatrice stood also. Mary, her laughter evaporating, followed suit. She had been enjoying the fanciful stories and the delicious food. For the first time since she'd arrived a few hours ago, she'd felt at ease. But now Jason seemed almost eager to have the ladies withdraw.

At the Coopers', Jason had always been reluctant to divide the company. He'd often forgone his port so that he could join Mrs. Cooper and her in the parlor. Mary glanced at him now. Perhaps he was planning to come with the ladies?

As if sensing her stare, he turned and met her gaze. He gave a slight bow, his face remote and withdrawn.

No, apparently not.

Suddenly feeling cold again, Mary followed Lady Weldon, passing by the fireplace as she did so. The flames burned high, but even standing right next to the fire, Mary could feel no warmth.

Shivering, she left the room.

"I say, Jason, your fiancée seems a good sort," Cecil said as soon as the door had closed behind the ladies. "I like her."

"I'm glad to hear that," Jason said, accepting the bottle of port from Quimby and pouring himself a glass. "I thought perhaps you were trying to frighten her away with those stories about a ghost."

Laughing, Cecil reached for a bowl of walnuts. He cracked one open and dug out the contents. "She was bound to hear about it sooner or later. And I must say, she didn't seem at all frightened."

No, she hadn't. Jason sipped his port thoughtfully. Her reaction had surprised him. Most women would have been at least a little uneasy, but Mary had only laughed. She had the most extraordinarily attractive laugh—

"She's not at all like the usual society lady," Cecil said.

"A charming, unaffected flower of womanhood," Quimby agreed. He tilted his glass up, swallowing the entire contents. "Ahhh. And quite beautiful in her own way. Hair like burnished golden oak, eyes the clear blue of a hedge sparrow's egg, and a figure as delicate as a wood nymph's—"

"Horace . . ." Jason said, his fingers tightening on his glass.

"What? Oh, forgive me." Quimby picked up the bottle and poured himself some more wine. "It's just that I find

Miss Goodwin extremely appealing. I look forward to becoming better acquainted with her. In fact"—he drained his second glass and smacked his lips—"if you gentlemen will excuse me, I think I will join the ladies right now."

"Horace," Jason said again, fixing him with a steely eye. "Don't you have to prepare your sermon for Sunday?"

"No, I don't." Quimby picked up his Bible and rose to his feet. "I've already finished it."

"Then perhaps you need to check it over."

"No, I—" Meeting Jason's gaze, Quimby paused. "I, ah, now that you mention it, that would be a good idea. Please excuse me." Clutching the Bible to his chest, he left the room, his step a little quicker than usual.

Cecil raised his brows at Jason. "Practicing autocratic stares, cousin?"

Jason frowned forbiddingly, but Cecil only laughed. "Quite effective. Very well, I can take a hint. If you wish to be alone, I will leave." He grabbed a handful of nuts and strolled out the door.

Jason made no effort to stop him. Cecil was a good friend, but there were times when Jason wished him to the devil. At dinner, for instance—it was just like Cecil to fill Mary's head with stories about the ghost. Fortunately, Mary hadn't seemed frightened.

But she had seemed quite taken with Cecil.

Moodily, Jason poured himself another glass of port.

Cecil appeared somewhat enamored of Mary, also. Which did not seem quite as strange as it had a few hours ago. There was something about her that drew one's gaze—his own included. At dinner, he'd had a hard time listening to a word Beatrice had said, he was so intent on watching Mary.

She ate with quite obvious enjoyment. He'd heard her sigh with pleasure after she took a bite of the dessert. While she'd been eating her pheasant, her eyelids had drooped heavily. And while partaking of her soup, she'd rolled the liquid around on her tongue before swallowing.

Watching her, a memory had come to him, of the first day he had met her. He hadn't noticed her overmuch at first. But after dinner, when he went outside for some fresh air, he'd seen her walking alone in the Coopers' garden, moonlight gilding her hair, her face pale and serene. He'd stayed out of sight, behind a tree, feeling foolish and guilty for spying, but there was something about her, something about the way she'd moved around the garden, cupping a bud here, stroking a delicate petal there, that had rooted him in his place, unable to move, unable to tear his gaze away from her.

Jason shook his head to dispel the image. He was behaving like some moonstruck youth. If he weren't careful, he would start bleating like a calf. He poured himself a glass of port and lifted it to his lips. He had other things to think about—

The fire sparked, a bright flame flaring high, before dwindling down lower than before. The candles flickered, and the room grew cooler. A smell like autumn leaves wafted through the air.

Lowering his glass, Jason looked across the room.

A glowing, slightly transparent figure stepped down from the portrait. As Jason watched, the figure grew more solid and Vincent Parsell, sixth earl of Helsbury, stood before him, a cynical smile on his face.

Jason's fingers tightened on his glass. "Why the devil don't you go to Hades where you belong and stay there?"

5

Vincent laughed. "Mayhap I will—once I've saved you from the clutches of this female."

"As I've been telling you for the last six months, uncle, I don't need your help."

"Oh?" Vincent strolled forward, his aura making his golden hair glow like a halo—an angelic image that contrasted sharply with the cynical glint in his green eyes. "You seemed glad enough for my advice when you were in such a quandary over how to deal with your bailiff and tenants."

Jason lowered his gaze to the pile of walnut shells Cecil had left on the table. "Yes, I was very grateful—"

Vincent stopped at the opposite end of the table and took a jeweled silver snuffbox from his pocket. "You did not object when I told you where the deeds were that proved that the property in the South Woods was Helsbury property."

"Your knowledge of Helsbury affairs has been most useful—"

"And who taught you how to tie your cravat?" Vincent tapped the lid of the snuffbox with one long, elegant finger. The lid sprang open, and he took a pinch of snuff. "You would undoubtedly still be sporting that limp, crumpled bow if I hadn't been here to instruct you."

An unwilling laugh escaped Jason. "True, you saved me from becoming the sartorial laughingstock of the shire.

However . . ." Jason's smile faded, and he lifted his gaze to Vincent's. "However, I prefer to deal with Mary myself."

"Bah!" Vincent closed the snuffbox with a snap, his mask of lazy good humor slipping a little. "You need help more than you realize. This one's worse than any of the others. Did you hear her laugh when Quimby told her about me?"

"I heard."

"What kind of woman makes a mock of the dead?" Vincent paced around the corner of the table. "She has no proper respect at all."

"She is very sensible."

"Sensible!" Vincent strode past Jason, a chill breeze following in his wake. "Did you hear what she called me? A puffed-up coxcomb. Me! The earl of Helsbury! I've never been so insulted in my life—or in my death! Why didn't you defend me?"

Jason rolled his eyes in disgust.

The heavy drapes swayed as Vincent stalked past the spot where Cecil had sat. The walnut shells slid to the edge of the table and fell to the floor. "It's obvious that you can't marry this woman. She will make you miserable."

Jason watched the shells' descent. "You know nothing about her."

"I know that she was flirting like a spinster at her last prayers with your own cousin at dinner. She must have heard that he's as rich as Croesus."

Jason's gaze snapped back to Vincent. "She was being polite."

At the end of the table again, Vincent paused and glanced over his shoulder. "You sound jealous."

Jason kept his face impassive. "I am not jealous."

Vincent smiled mockingly. "Of course not." Lowering his eyelids, he watched Jason from beneath them. "I was rather surprised you put your little fiancée in the Blue Room," he said casually.

"Were you?" Jason's bland expression did not change.

"Yes, I was. The Helsbury fiancées have always slept in the Yellow Bedchamber."

"So Aunt Weldon informed me," Jason said calmly. "However, Mary hates yellow. I know that the Blue Room once held some unpleasant memories for you, but I am sure that after all this time it can no longer hold any significance."

Vincent's eyes narrowed. "It doesn't."

"I'm glad to hear that, uncle."

Vincent's brows drew together. Then, he shrugged. "I suppose it doesn't matter. She will be gone by tomorrow. I suspect it will be quite easy to frighten her off. She's a mousy-looking little thing. She will no doubt run screaming from the house the first time I whisper 'Boo' in her ear."

Jason drank the rest of his port. "I don't want you saying boo in her ear. In fact, I would prefer it if you would refrain from playing your usual tricks."

"Tricks? You make me sound like some cheap sideshow magician."

Jason ignored this remark. "I think you should consider what will happen if none of the Helsbury earls marry—eventually the title will die out."

Vincent glanced away. "I assure you, I only wish to make certain that the woman is worthy of the family name."

Jason set his glass down and rose to his feet. "I will decide that for myself."

A frown creasing his forehead, Vincent stared at him. Jason met his gaze steadily.

The clock on the mantle ticked loudly in the silence.

Vincent's eyelids drooped, and his forehead smoothed. "If that is what you wish, then of course I will not interfere," he murmured.

"Thank you, uncle. I'm glad we agree on something for once."

Vincent arched his brows. "We agree often enough.

Tell me, what do you plan to do about the Blevins situation?"

"I am going to the village tomorrow to discuss it with him."

"To discuss it? What is there to discuss? You must take action—"

"Thank you, uncle," Jason interrupted. "I am sure I will be able to handle it. Now, if you will excuse me, I would like to join the ladies."

"Certainly." Vincent kept his expression blank until the door closed behind Jason, but once the boy was gone, his brows drew together again.

This was the third time in the last week that Jason had refused to discuss an estate matter. The boy was acting strangely—he had been ever since his announcement a fortnight ago that Miss Mary Goodwin would be coming to Helsbury House and that the two of them would be married forthwith. The household had been thrown into a turmoil, Lady Weldon complaining bitterly of the short notice and having to scramble to organize the traditional parties. Beatrice, stepping up her campaign to steal Jason from his fiancée, had sought him out and brushed up against him whenever possible. Quimby and Cecil had peppered him with questions about the girl—but Jason had said very little.

His frown deepening, Vincent began to pace restlessly around the room. He was fond of Jason—Jason was very like Gilbert. Gilbert, the baby of the family, had always been Vincent's favorite brother. Gil had been good-natured, but intense—always determined to keep up with his four older brothers—and impossibly stubborn. Jason had clearly inherited that trait.

Vincent stopped by the fire and stared down at the glowing logs. He knew that six months ago Jason had fancied himself in love with this Mary. Although the boy had never actually said so, the look in his eyes when he mentioned her name had made his feelings plain.

Fortunately, the long separation and the stresses of his

new position—not to mention Vincent's frequent homilies on the perfidy of the weaker sex—had extinguished Jason's ridiculous emotions.

Or so Vincent had thought.

Now he wondered if perhaps a tiny spark of affection had survived. If so, it was up to him to prevent that spark from reigniting. Or at least, it would have been, if Jason hadn't refused his help.

Vincent shook his head. He was only trying to spare Jason pain. The boy had no idea what it was like to be betrayed by a woman. . . .

Vincent's hand tightened on the snuffbox. A jewel pressed against his fingers, causing a faint sensation that was almost like pain.

Vincent stared down at his hand. If Jason refused to listen to reason, there was nothing he could do. He must respect the boy's wishes.

Which he would, of course.

That settled, he inhaled deeply, drawing energy from the heat of the fire and the flickering candles. The flames dimmed and his aura grew brighter, strength flowing through him.

Now all he had to do was think of a way to welcome Mary to the family.

A visit to her room might be just the thing . . . say in an hour or two.

A smile curved his lips. Returning the snuffbox to his pocket, he stepped back up into his portrait.

Midnight couldn't come too soon.

6

In the parlor, Mary bent her head over her sewing and wished with all her heart that she could excuse herself and go up to her room.

It wasn't because she was tired—she wasn't. And it wasn't because of the cold—she'd retrieved her shawl along with her sewing things, and in truth, the room with its soft candlelight was quite pleasant. It wasn't even that Lady Weldon was ignoring her—Mary didn't mind at all that the older woman had chosen to sit in a thronelike chair next to the fire and engross herself in a book of sermons.

No, it wasn't any of those things. It was Beatrice. She was being so . . . kind.

Holding a quill, Beatrice sat at a small writing desk, a sheet of paper before her, but so far she hadn't written anything. She was chatting with Mary in the nicest way possible, telling her numerous anecdotes, and Mary appreciated her kindness—she truly did—but as she listened, her spirits were sinking lower and lower.

"And the duke of Stafford's ball was the social event of the year," Beatrice was saying, her rosebud lips smiling. "Everyone was scrambling for invitations. People came all the way from London to attend. My poor friend Clarice had influenza and couldn't come. I wrote her all about it, but of course it wasn't the same. I haven't felt so sorry for her since the headmistress caught her cheating on an examination. That was when we were attending Miss Finch's Seminary for Young Ladies," she explained to Mary. "We were bosom bows."

"How nice," Mary murmured.

"Yes, one can form quite excellent friendships at school. Clarice is related to a bishop and a viscount. Tell me, where did you go to school, Mary?"

"I didn't go to school," Mary said quietly. "My mother taught me at home."

"Oh. How . . . unusual. And how unfortunate. It's important to have connections, you know."

"No, I didn't."

Beatrice traced a finger down the sheet of paper. "Don't worry, I'll tell all my friends about you. After you and Jason are married, you will have to give a ball so that I may introduce you to them. You will, won't you? As a countess you will be expected to entertain frequently."

"Will I?" Mary asked, carefully embroidering the hem of the blue silk dress in her lap.

"Of course." Beatrice brushed the quill along a red curl on her shoulder. "You simply must. You enjoy balls, don't you?"

"I've never attended one," Mary replied.

Beatrice's brown eyes widened. "Never attended a ball?"

"My brother and his wife often hosted parties, though," Mary said.

"Oh." Beatrice looked away, as if Mary had said something embarrassing. "Well, I am certain you will enjoy giving a ball, then. Of course, you will be expected to act as hostess. But it is not at all difficult. I am sure I can advise you, if you need help."

Restraining a rude impulse to tell the girl she didn't need any help, Mary nodded and propelled her needle into the blue silk as Beatrice rattled on. What could be taking the gentlemen so long? Surely they would not spend the entire evening in the dining room, drinking and conversing amongst themselves? Surely Jason would come in, at least to say good night?

"There are many things that will be expected of you as countess, Mary," Beatrice's voice interrupted her musings again. "For example, you must remember to patronize the village shops on occasion. Of course, you would go to London if you needed something nice, but for odds and ends, the village is fine. Jason bought a fan from the haberdasher's there just last week. He gave it to his aunt Sarah, since it was too ugly for anyone else."

Mary looked up from her sewing at the mention of Jason's other aunt. Sarah Parsell, she remembered. "Did Miss Parsell like the fan?"

"I don't know. Jason is the only one who ever speaks to her. He insists on visiting her every afternoon, even though Mama recommended against it."

Lady Weldon laid down her book, deep lines forming above her upper lip. "I have informed Sarah many times that her fear is irrational and foolish, but she refuses to listen to me. I finally washed my hands of her."

Mary frowned. "What is she afraid of?"

"She committed the ultimate betrayal of Vincent," Beatrice said. "She was a friend of his erstwhile fiancée. Now Vincent waits outside Sarah's door, ready to wreak horrible revenge on her." She smiled. "Or so Sarah says."

Mary was shocked. "The poor woman!"

"She does not need sympathy," Lady Weldon said. "She needs to face reality. I am sure the quickest way to bring her to her senses would be to completely isolate her."

"Oh, but surely that would be needlessly cruel," Mary protested without thinking.

Lady Weldon stiffened. "Sometimes one must be cruel to be kind, Miss Goodwin. It is best you learn that as soon as possible." She resumed reading her book.

Beatrice glanced from her mother to Mary, then dipped the quill in the inkstand and wrote something on the sheet of paper. The scratching of her pen could be heard in the silence.

Biting her lip, Mary lowered her gaze and continued

sewing. She couldn't agree with Lady Weldon, but she didn't want to start an argument. Besides, Jason would never consent to such inhumane treatment, she was sure.

The scratching of the pen stopped.

"Mary, what is that you're sewing?" Beatrice asked, dipping the quill into the inkstand again.

"My wedding dress," Mary said quietly, pushing the needle through the fabric.

"Your wedding dress!" Beatrice exclaimed. The hand holding the quill froze in midair.

Lady Weldon laid down her book again. "Surely you must be joking."

Mary's fingers tightened on her needle. "Why do you say that?"

"You are marrying an earl." Lady Weldon stared down the length of her aquiline nose. "People will expect you to be suitably dressed."

"Now, Mother. With her background, I'm sure Mary is an excellent seamstress." Beatrice smiled at Mary. "I think what Mother is trying to say is that the fashion now is for white wedding dresses. I know a dressmaker in the village. If I speak to her, I am sure she can come up with something more modish."

Mary shook her head. "I prefer my own dress, thank you." This was one thing she *was* sure about. Jason had always liked her in blue. Besides, she didn't really like white. It was such a cold, emotionless color.

Lady Weldon closed her book with a snap. "I do not think—"

The door opened. The three ladies' heads swung in unison. Jason stood in the doorway, his broad shoulders nearly touching the frame.

Instantly Lady Weldon was all smiles. "Ah, there you are, my dear boy. I was just wondering if you'd decided not to join us."

"Not at all," Jason said politely, glancing at Mary. He crossed the room and sat on the sofa next to her chair. He was close enough that she could see the crisp hair curling in the nape of his neck and smell the scent of his soap. Her heart beat a little faster.

Lady Weldon looked back and forth between the two of them. Her smile grew less warm. "It's fortunate you didn't come any later. I will have to retire shortly. There is much to do on the morrow, what with the entertainments we have planned for introducing Mary to everyone."

"Entertainments?" Mary repeated, her heart sinking. She glanced at Jason, remembering that he had spoken of some such thing in the carriage on the way here, but she had been distracted by his mention of their honeymoon.

"Yes, indeed," Beatrice said, putting the sheet of paper in the desk drawer. "Traditionally, there is always a musicale, a breakfast, and a masquerade ball before the wedding to introduce the Helsbury fiancée to the community."

Mary struggled to hide her dismay. She had not brought any clothes suitable for such grand parties. "Surely there isn't time for these events."

"Aunt Weldon has managed to arrange all of them for this week," Jason said. "The musicale will be the next night after tomorrow and the breakfast the following day. The masquerade will take place two days after that."

Mary's heart sank farther. She glanced at Beatrice, wondering if she could ask the other girl to lend her a dress. But somehow, in spite of Beatrice's offers of help, she couldn't bring herself to do so. She would have to wear her wedding dress, she decided reluctantly. It was the only thing she had.

"The entertainments aren't usually all crammed into one week," Lady Weldon said, glaring at Mary as if this was somehow her fault. "I only hope you're still here. I've arranged similar events for the previous earls' fiancées, and they all left before the musicale. I trust you won't be so inconsiderate."

"I have no intention of leaving." Mary inspected the hem of the silk dress. Thank heavens it was almost finished. She shouldn't have any problem completing it in time.

"Don't worry, Mother," Beatrice said. "I am sure Mary is not one to be frightened off by a few odd noises. Are you, Mary?"

"No, not at all." Mary glanced up at Lady Weldon. "It was very kind of you to make all the arrangements."

Lady Weldon inclined her head in an infinitesimal nod.

"You'll enjoy the musicale, Mary," Beatrice said, curling a red ringlet around her finger. "We play a game—it's a tradition. All the ladies put one glove on a tray and the gentlemen select one. The lady may then demand a favor from her sweetheart."

"What if the gentleman doesn't choose his sweetheart?" Mary asked.

"The servant who carries the tray gives little hints so that won't happen—unless the gentleman *wants* it to happen." Beatrice smiled. "You needn't worry, Mary. A Helsbury earl has never failed to pick out his fiancée's glove. It would be a terrible insult if he did."

"Then let's hope I won't be the first Helsbury fiancée in history to suffer such a terrible insult," Mary said, half joking, half nervous.

"You needn't worry," Jason murmured.

"Oh, dear, I'm afraid I'm giving you an exaggerated idea of the glove game," Beatrice said. "It really is not very important. The highlight of the evening is actually the Helsbury fiancée's performance—traditionally, she always sings or plays."

Mary tied a knot slowly and cut the thread. "I'm afraid I can't do either."

"Oh dear, that is a problem."

Mary glanced up from rethreading her needle to see a worried frown on Beatrice's face.

"You shall have to sing in her place, Beatrice," Lady Weldon said.

Beatrice lowered her lashes modestly. "Oh, no, I couldn't."

"Nonsense. You sing beautifully. Tell Beatrice she must sing, Jason," Lady Weldon commanded.

"Please do," Jason murmured.

Beatrice fluttered her lashes. "If you insist."

Mary looked at Jason. He appeared not to have noticed Beatrice's alluring lashes. Instead, he seemed to be staring at Mary's hands. Surprised, she pushed the needle unwarily and pricked her thumb. With a small exclamation, she lifted it to her mouth and sucked. As she did so, she noticed Jason's gaze was now on her mouth.

Flushing, she lowered her hand. Undoubtedly it was improper to suck on pinpricks. Hoping to distract him from her gaffe, she asked, "Will there be dancing at the musicale?"

"No," Jason said, his gaze returning to her hands.

"But there is dancing at the masquerade," Beatrice reminded him. She turned to Mary. "And there's battledore and shuttlecock and a fencing match at the breakfast."

"A fencing match?" Mary remembered Jason telling her he'd taken lessons at school, but she could not like the sport—it seemed extremely dangerous.

"It will be quite exciting." Beatrice rose to her feet and strolled over to sit by Jason on the sofa. She touched his arm. "I am sure you will win."

For a moment, Mary could not tear her gaze away from the sight of Beatrice smiling up at Jason. The twinge of envy she'd felt at dinner grew. Everything about the girl seemed perfect. She was kind and beautiful. She was accomplished and had wealthy, important friends. And, no doubt, she had scores of beautiful dresses in her wardrobe.

A sudden urge to be away from the parlor seized Mary. She folded the blue silk quickly, picked up her sewing kit, and stood. "I hope you will excuse me, but I am very tired from my journey. Good night, everyone."

Jason rose to his feet. "I will escort you to your room, Mary."

Beatrice's fingers tightened on his sleeve. "Jason, I have a small matter I would like to discuss with you, if you don't mind."

Jason hesitated.

"You don't need to escort me," Mary said hastily. "I remember the way." She left the room quickly and grabbed a candle from a table in the hall. She hurried up the stairs and down the art-lined corridor, unable to restrain her eagerness to be as far away as possible from the parlor.

Turning into the corridor where the Blue Room was, Mary slowed her pace. She should be ashamed of herself for being so envious of Beatrice. The girl was doing her best to make her feel welcome—it certainly wasn't Beatrice's fault that Mary didn't have any proper clothes or important friends, and couldn't sing or play the piano. She must be tired from her journey after all. That must be the reason why she was feeling so low—

The door to the room beside her opened, and Mary almost bumped into the servant girl coming out, a potted plant clasped to her chest. The girl bobbed a curtsy and hurried on her way.

Mary gazed after her for a moment, then looked at the door. It must be Sarah Parsell's room, she realized. She hesitated a moment. If Lady Weldon did not want Miss Parsell to have company, then it really wasn't Mary's place to intrude.

But wasn't the poor woman terribly lonely?

Straightening her shoulders, Mary stepped up to the door. There could be no harm in just meeting her. It was the polite thing to do, after all. She would introduce herself and say good evening. If the woman was upset, she would leave immediately.

She knocked, and a voice called out, "Come in." Mary opened the door.

A slender woman with graying blond hair, dressed in a frilly pink bedgown covered by a smock, was watering a row of plants by the high arched window in the corner of the room. She turned, eyeing Mary in surprise. "Who are you?" she asked, her watering can half-tilted.

Mary curtsied. "I am Miss Mary Goodwin, Lord Helsbury's fiancée. We are to be married in a week."

"Oh, are you?" Sarah Parsell watered the plant and moved on to the next pot. "I suppose Vincent will frighten you off like all the others."

Mary laughed. "No, he won't. I don't believe in ghosts."

"You don't?" The woman straightened the can and turned to stare at her with wide brown eyes. "Hmm."

Seeing the fine lines around her eyes, Mary realized the woman was older than she'd first thought—perhaps close to fifty. Her wrists looked very frail. Mary glanced at the large tin watering can. "May I help you water your plants, Miss Parsell?"

The older woman hesitated, then nodded. "If you like."

Mary crossed the room and took the heavy watering can. The sweet scent of lavender, sage, and thyme wafted up from the pots.

"So," Miss Parsell said, settling herself in a spindly chair next to a shelf full of small bottles and jars. "Tell me what you think of Helsbury House."

Mary carefully watered the plants. "It's very beautiful."

"You don't find it cold?"

"Perhaps a little." Mary moved to the next row of plants. "I think a carpet in the hall would help."

Miss Parsell gave a rusty-sounding crack of laughter. "It will take more than a carpet to warm this house. It's been cold for the last twenty-five years and more."

Mary glanced up. "You've lived here that long? Did you know Jason before he became earl, then?"

"I met him once or twice. I believe he visited here a few times. For the funerals of the various earls."

Mary blinked. "Oh."

Miss Parsell pointed to some pots on a table in the opposite corner of the room between the bed and a small bookcase. "Don't forget those."

Mary moved over to the table and watered the plants, taking care not to drip on the pink ostrich-feather fan lying next to the pots.

When Mary finished watering, Miss Parsell beamed. "Thank you, Miss Goodwin. That was very kind of you."

"I don't mind. I used to be a companion, and I often did odd jobs for Mrs. Cooper."

"A companion!" Miss Parsell's arched brows rose nearly to her hairline. "Does Eugenia know that?"

"If you mean Lady Weldon, then yes, I believe so. She does not appear to approve of me."

"No, she wouldn't," Miss Parsell said, a sly smile curving her lips. She looked at Mary. "I like you, Miss Goodwin."

"Why, thank you," Mary said, surprised.

"No need to thank me," the older woman said. "I can tell you will be perfect for Jason. The only problem is—what about Vincent?"

"I told you, I don't believe—"

"Yes, yes," Miss Parsell interrupted. "You don't believe in ghosts. But I don't doubt you will be gone by tomorrow. Unless . . ." Her voice trailed off and she stared into the distance.

"Unless what, Miss Parsell?" Mary asked.

Miss Parsell's gaze swung back to Mary. "Oh, never mind," she said. "But please, you must call me Aunt Sally. And I will call you Mary, if that is acceptable to you. We are to be related soon, after all."

Mary smiled. After her uneasiness with Beatrice and Lady Weldon, she was delighted to find a female member of the Parsell family whom she liked unreservedly. "Of course, Aunt Sally."

There was a tap at the door and a maid came in with a tea tray. She stared at Mary with wide eyes, then curtsied and left.

Aunt Sally looked at Mary. "Will you take a cup of tea with me?"

Mary nodded.

Sally rose to her feet and inspected the bottles on the shelf next to her. "I always brew my own tea. I have a special camomile blend I think you will enjoy." She sprinkled a few dry leaves into a teacup. "I am something of a naturalist."

"And this is your garden?" Mary asked, looking around at the various pots.

Sally nodded. "I grow many medicinal plants, including toothwort, poppies, and valerian." She took a bottle from the shelf and added a generous amount of liquid to Mary's teacup.

"What is that?" Mary asked.

"My own secret ingredient." Sally poured hot water over the mixture and handed the cup and saucer to Mary. "Sit down, my dear. Drink it, and tell me what you think."

Mary sat on the spindly chair and sipped the tea. She almost choked. The brew was the worst-tasting concoction she'd ever tasted. It burned down her throat and had a sickly sweet flavor. The camomile was so strong it tasted bitter.

"Do you like it?"

Mary wanted to say no. But she didn't want to offend the kind woman, so she smiled. "It's very unusual." She forced herself to swallow the rest. Afraid that the older woman would pour her a second cup, Mary hastily rose to her feet. "Now I must say good night. It's been a pleasure meeting you."

"Visit me anytime," Aunt Sally said. "Good night, Mary. Sleep well. Don't let Vincent frighten you."

Mary paused at the door and smiled again at Jason's sweet aunt. "I won't," she promised.

Once in her own room, Mary hastily poured a large glass of water from the pitcher on the ebony stand by the bed and drank without stopping.

The horrible taste still lingered.

She drank some more, swirling the water around in her mouth. Slowly the foulness diminished. She repeated the process several times. The taste dwindled, then disappeared. With a sigh of relief, she put down the glass.

Turning away from the stand, she unbuttoned her dress. She hoped Aunt Sally hadn't guessed that she'd disliked the tea—she would hate to hurt the woman's feelings when she seemed so lonely, so vulnerable. More than ever she hoped that Jason would not take Lady Weldon's advice to shun Aunt Sally. Isolation was the last thing the poor woman needed. She would have to tell Jason so.

Mary folded her dress slowly and put it in the wardrobe. The only question was, would he listen to her?

Her petticoats followed the dress as she wondered what his reaction would be if she offered her opinion about his aunt. Would he be happy to hear her thoughts? Indifferent? Offended? She fumbled with a knot in her corset strings. It was difficult to predict how he would respond. She couldn't tell what he was thinking any more, the way she once had.

The knot in her corset string loosened. Mary untied it and tugged at the other strings.

She wished she still had that ability. He had seemed to be watching her very closely in the parlor, and she wasn't quite sure why. She didn't remember him looking at her like that before. Before, at the Coopers' house, his eyes had always been warm and friendly. In the few hours since she'd arrived here, his gaze had mostly seemed cool and distant. But in the parlor, when he'd been watching her sew, she'd seen a different expression in his eyes—a dark intensity that did strange things to her insides.

She pulled the last string on her corset. As it fell open, she heard an odd noise. She grabbed the edge of the garment as it started to fall and held it in front of her, listening.

She heard the noise again.

She stared at the heavy blue satin drapes covering the window. She couldn't identify the noise—a rustling, scratching sound—but it seemed to be coming from outside.

The noise grew louder.

Mary draped her corset over a chair and picked up a

candle. Slowly, she walked toward the window. What could be out there?

Perhaps it was the ghost.

She smiled at the ridiculous thought. But in spite of herself, a small shiver coursed down her spine. What if it were Vincent out there, scratching at her window pane, waiting to take her in his cold embrace . . . ?

Shaking her head at the fanciful thoughts, Mary pushed back the drapes. She pressed her forehead against the cold glass, trying to see outside, but the reflection of the candle thwarted her. She pushed open the window, shivering as the cool night air blew over her bare arms and neck and penetrated the thin cotton of her chemise. Directly below her was the rustling noise, loud and clear now. Holding the candle high, she leaned out over the sill. She couldn't see anything, so she leaned out still farther—

A pair of black eyes stared up at her.

Mary jumped and squealed.

The prickly hedgehog climbing the drainpipe squealed, too. Pointed nose quivering, claws scrabbling on the metal pipe, it turned tail and scurried away.

Laughing at the small intruder and at herself as well, Mary closed the window, let the drapes fall back into place, and put the candle on the dressing table. How foolish of her to be frightened by a hedgehog. The stories about ghosts were definitely addling her brain. She would be seeing leprechauns next.

Still smiling, she returned to the wardrobe and stripped off her chemise. Shivering in earnest now, she pulled on her warm flannel nightgown and sat down at the dressing table.

She had picked up the brush and raised it to her hair when a huge yawn caught her by surprise. She shook herself and tried again, but another enormous yawn overwhelmed her.

She put down the brush and lifted her arms to braid her hair, but they felt like lead weights.

She lowered her arms. Perhaps if she rested them for a moment or two . . .

Her eyes drifted shut. She swayed forward, almost falling off the chair. Her eyes flew open. She lifted her arms again, but they seemed heavier than ever. Lowering them, she tried to decide what to do, but her brain was unusually fuzzy, making it difficult for her to think.

Her eyelids were drooping shut again when she heard a loud rapping noise.

She sat up straight, momentarily confused. She looked around the room, trying to determine where the sound had come from. Had the hedgehog returned?

The noise came again, and she realized someone was knocking at her door.

She stood up, her head swimming as she walked across the room and opened the door.

Jason, his hand poised to knock again, stood there.

She blinked up at him owlishly. "Jason?"

Slowly, he lowered his hand. "Did I awaken you?"

"No, I was braiding my hair. But my arms are tired. I mean *I'm* tired." Her tongue was as sluggish as her brain. "Did you want something?"

His gaze flickered over her. "Mary . . ." He paused and cleared his throat. "Mary, don't you have a wrapper?"

She frowned, trying to think. "I don't believe so. Jason, do you mind if I sit down?" She yawned. "I am extra . . . extraordi . . . I am very sleepy."

Swaying, she turned and took an unsteady step forward.

With an exclamation, Jason caught her arm. "You're asleep on your feet," he muttered. Kicking the door shut, he swung her up in his arms.

The hard muscles of his arms pressed against her back and the bottoms of her thighs. He was very strong, she thought hazily. Stronger than she remembered.

With a sigh, she wrapped her arms around his neck. As he carried her over to the bed, her fingers curled into the hair at the nape of his neck. It was amazingly soft—not at all like she'd expected.

He set her down on the mattress, and she made a small noise of protest, even as her eyes closed. "I can't go to bed until I've braided my hair. It will be all knots in the morning."

He didn't answer for a moment. Then he said, "I'll braid it for you."

She opened her eyes a fraction and smiled sleepily at him. "Would you, Jason? You're so kind."

He muttered something under his breath that she didn't quite understand, then strong hands pulled her upright and turned her so her back was to him. Then she felt his fingers in her hair. They lingered there. She heard him inhale deeply, then he gently separated the strands into three sections and began braiding.

She sighed in blissful contentment. This was the Jason she knew . . . thoughtful and kind. How foolish she'd been to think that he had changed. His hands were so warm, so gentle in her hair. . . .

His fingers brushed against her neck, and a tingle traipsed down her spine. She closed her eyes and leaned back against him, turning her head so that her cheek was resting against the slightly rough fabric of his coat. She inhaled the scent of wool and soap that was becoming pleasantly familiar. . . .

His fingers grew still in her hair. "Mary . . ." His voice sounded husky. His breath rippled over her skin in warm waves, and she wriggled against him with pleasure.

His hands slid down and gripped her arms tightly. "I must talk to you, Mary."

She liked the feel of his hands on her arms. She wanted to cuddle against the warmth of him, to enjoy the enticing scent of him. She tried to snuggle closer.

He made an odd noise, something like a groan, and turned her, pushing her back. She sank into a soft cloud. She wrapped her arms around Jason's neck to keep from falling through.

"Mary . . . "

His voice sounded strained. Was he angry at her again?

She tried to open her eyes, but it was too much effort. She decided to settle for telling him to continue, but all that came out of her mouth was, "Mmmm?"

He gently tugged her hands from around his neck. "This house . . . it sometimes makes odd noises."

"Mmmm?" She ran her hands down his chest, feeling hardness under the textures of wool and silk. She could feel the rhythm of his heart, beating strong and oddly fast. She felt him lean down until his breath was warm against her lips.

His voice was a whisper of sound. "I don't want you to be frightened."

I'm not, she tried to say, but her mouth wouldn't form the words. A smile on her lips, she drifted away on the cloud, unspoken words forming in her head.

She would never be afraid as long as he was there. . . .

Hearing her soft, even breathing, Jason pulled back. Mary's arms fell limply from around his neck. He stared down at her in disbelief. She was asleep.

With a groan, he sat up, raking his hands through his hair.

He should not have come here. He had wanted to warn her about the ghost—just in case Vincent did not keep his word—but that was all. He certainly hadn't intended to be beset by a surge of lust.

Again.

He pressed his hand against his forehead. It was all the fault of her damned sewing. Watching her in the parlor had brought back a nearly forgotten memory of doing the same at the Coopers' house. He'd often sat with her in the evening while she sewed. Her nimble fingers had fascinated him. They'd flown over the material, rhythmically thrusting the needle in and out of the fabric. He'd watched, mesmerized, imagining those fingers doing forbidden, erotic things to his body—

He rose to his feet and turned away from the bed, struggling to regain control. He was the earl of Helsbury now—he had to rein in his natural impulses and let logic, not emotion, dictate his actions. He must maintain an appearance of complete strength and self-command if he was to be master of this house—and *every*one in it.

The wedding was only a week away. He could wait to make love to Mary. . . .

His gaze was drawn to her once more. In sleep, a slight smile curved her lips upward. Her dark gold lashes lay against her flushed cheeks. Her silky hair was slipping from its braid. He walked over to her dressing table, stopping when he saw a pink corset draped haphazardly over the chair.

He averted his gaze, trying not to imagine what she would look like wearing it and nothing else. He picked up a thin ribbon from the dressing table and returned to her side. Sitting on the edge of the bed, he carefully tied the end of her braid, his fingers lingering in her hair again. Almost compulsively, he stroked the soft length, then traced the line of her jaw to her chin. His finger moved up over the soft roundness, down the slight dip and up to the fullness of her lips. Soft and warm, they parted at his touch, allowing him to insert his finger into her mouth and feel the moistness there—

Blood pulsed in his groin. With an oath, he pulled his hand away. Shoving his tightly clenched fist into his pocket, he rose to his feet and left the room, taking great care not to look again at the corset hanging on the chair.

The house was very dark. From somewhere within, the muted chimes of a clock struck three.

A dim glow appeared outside the Blue Room and pulsed and flared. Hovering, it grew brighter and brighter. It grew taller and wider and took shape until the figure of a man stood in the corridor—Vincent Parsell.

He stood there a moment, allowing the particles of light that made up his form to settle and align themselves. He made sure they were all in place before turning to face the familiar ebony-paneled door.

He was later than he would have liked. He had not wanted to begin his task until Jason was asleep—he didn't want to risk the boy's interference—but when he'd peeked into the master bedchamber, Jason had been tossing and turning restlessly in the bed. Vincent had waited what seemed like an eternity for him to fall asleep.

But Jason had finally succumbed, and now all Vincent had to do was open the door before him, go into the Blue Room, and groan a few times. Mary would be scared witless, and then he could leave. He would be in the room no more than a minute or two at the most. He wouldn't even have time to think of Elizabeth. . . .

Vincent muttered a curse under his breath. Why the devil had Jason put his fiancée here? Vincent didn't believe for a minute that lame excuse about Mary hating yellow. None of the other earls would have dreamed of opening up this room—so why had Jason?

Vincent shook his head impatiently. The reason really didn't matter. All that mattered was the imminent departure of Miss Mary Goodwin.

Taking a deep breath, he stepped through the ebony door.

Immediately, a force pulled at him, draining him. Fighting a nearly overwhelming urge to return to his painting, he glanced around the room. It had not changed at all. The ebony furniture gleamed in the light from his aura, and the drapes and bedcurtains were still the same deep, rich blue. He remembered sending the bolts of satin back to the upholsterers three times until they got the shade exactly right. . . .

The draining force increased.

God, it was worse than he'd expected. Fighting an impulse to flee, he forced himself not to glance around as he walked over to the bed and looked down at the woman sleeping there.

She was surprisingly plain. He wondered what Jason had seen in her. She was hardly the sort to incite lust in a man. Her hair was mousy brown, her lips an innocent shade of pink, and her breasts rather small. She was nothing like Elizabeth.

An image flashed before him: of dark, sweet-smelling curls and seductively smiling red lips; of full, rose-tipped breasts and soft, incredibly white skin; of pleasure and passion so intense that the memory was still fresh though it had been over twenty-five years ago.

He turned away from the bed, cursing silently. There was no purpose in torturing himself with memories of a pleasure he could no longer experience. And there was no point in indulging in an irrational anger over Mary's presence in this room—she would soon be gone. If he ever stopped dawdling and attended to the matter at hand.

Closing his eyes, he concentrated on aligning his particles again. Slowly, strength and energy flowed through him.

In control again, he smiled and opened his eyes. The room's power had definitely lessened.

His smile widening, he turned back to the bed. This would be simple—almost too simple. After years of practice, he had turned the science of focusing and directing energy into an art. It would require almost no effort on his part to scare Miss Mary Goodwin out of Jason's life.

Focusing his concentration inward, he gathered the necessary energy and opened his mouth to release it. "OOOOOOOOOhhhh."

The sound rolled through the room, full of ominous foreboding.

Not a bad effort, he congratulated himself. Subtle, yet eerie.

Smiling, he glanced over at the bed.

Mary lay still under the covers, her breasts rising and falling with the slow, untroubled breathing of sleep.

Vincent's brows rose. The room's draining force tugged at him, but he ignored it. Perhaps he'd been a touch too subtle. He would have to try for a little more volume. He focused and concentrated and emitted a long, moaning sigh.

"OOOoooooooooooooooooohhhhhhh."

The moan rose with satisfying eeriness. In the distance, he heard a dog howl in response. Well satisfied, he looked at Mary.

She slept on undisturbed.

Vincent frowned. She must be a heavy sleeper. Perhaps this would be more difficult than he'd thought. He would just have to make his best effort. It seemed a shame to waste it on the likes of Miss Mary Goodwin, but there was no help for it.

He concentrated once more, focusing inward with a fierce intensity that counteracted the pull of the room. He allowed the energy to build and expand and intensify. When it reached a critical level, he released it.

"OOOOOOOOOOOOOOOOOOOooooooooooooooooo OOOOOOOOHHHHHH."

It was a sound to make hair stand on end and flesh creep and crawl. It was a lament to make one's blood run cold and petrify one's bones. It was a wail of sorrow, the cry of a tormented soul, an unearthly requiem for the dead. The eerie sound echoed around the room. It rose and fell and then rose again to a shrieking sob before dying away to a sighing moan.

Truly, he had outdone himself. Proudly, expectantly, he looked at Mary.

She emitted a small snore.

His eyes widened, then narrowed. He clenched his fists, angry disbelief pulsing through him. He stomped over to the fireplace and rattled the poker and tongs. They clashed together like swords, sparks flying. The sound of clamoring iron was as thunderous as in a blacksmith's shop.

Mary rolled over and slept on.

Gritting his teeth, Vincent gazed at a china pitcher and bowl, sending them flying across the room to crash against the wall. He stomped across the floor, his footsteps ringing out loudly. And he blew a draft of cold air toward the bed.

Mary snuggled deeper into the covers.

Vincent stormed around the room, glaring as he went. The wardrobe doors opened and slammed shut. The desk and commode drawers banged in and out. The windows flew open against the wall and smashed back against their frames. The din was loud enough to wake the dead.

But not loud enough to wake Miss Mary Goodwin. She continued to sleep, undisturbed by all the racket.

Vincent turned red—literally. A crimson glow filled the room as he paced furiously about.

This was ridiculous. He had never known a woman to sleep so heavily. Obviously, it would take more than noise to awaken her. Which meant that he would have to use . . . the Bed Maneuver.

He stopped abruptly by the fireplace. He really would rather not do something so extreme. He had felt a trifle guilty when Timothy's fiancée had run screaming out of the house in the middle of the night. The woman hadn't stopped running until she reached Sir Dudley's house, almost five miles away.

Vincent glanced at Mary. She slept peacefully, her hands folded under her cheek.

He could feel his strength ebbing, his edges growing hazy. He could not stay in here much longer. His lips tightened. Plainly, he had no choice. He had to do it.

Hardening his heart, he walked over to the bed and placed his hands on one of the bedposts. Closing his eyes, he concentrated with all his will, blocking out the room's draining force. He concentrated harder and harder until he could feel the energy pulsing within him. The energy built and built until he could barely contain it. Then he focused on the bed.

The four-poster trembled. Then it shook. It shook and shook, rocking back and forth like a ship on a stormy ocean, bucking like a wild horse, jolting and swaying like a runaway carriage. The bed rose several inches into the air and then thumped back to the ground like a boulder crashing down from a cliff.

Releasing the bedpost, Vincent's hands fell to his sides.

He inhaled deeply, steadying himself. Opening his eyes, he looked at Mary.

Cocooned in the soft, deep mattress, she rolled over and mumbled something in her sleep.

He stared down at her in disbelief. What the devil did it take to wake the woman? She slept like the dead! No, he took it back. Even the dead didn't sleep so soundly. He knew that from experience.

He stood there, inhaling heavily, his aura brightening and dimming with each breath, trying to summon the energy to continue.

It was impossible. He was as weak as a new-dead ghost. Worse, he could feel the room sucking at him, weakening him even more. He had to leave immediately or he might be completely drained.

Exhausted, he glared at her. "Very well, Miss Mary Goodwin," he snarled through clenched teeth. "You may have won this round . . . but tomorrow you won't be so lucky."

With a furious flash of light, he disappeared.

Once again, the room was dark and silent.

Mary, lost in a pleasant dream, smiled in her sleep and murmured a single word.

"Jason . . ."

7

Sunlight stabbed at Mary's eyelids. Groaning, she turned her face into her pillow, trying to regain the oblivion of sleep, but it was useless. Her head ached, her mouth was sour, and her thoughts so fuzzy she couldn't even remember what had happened last night. She recalled drinking Aunt Sally's vile camomile tea, but everything after that was a little hazy. She remembered undressing and hearing the hedgehog and then suddenly feeling very tired, too tired to braid her hair. So Jason had . . .

Jason!

She sat straight up. The sudden motion made her head swim. Groaning again, she cradled her pounding head in her hands and tried to think. Jason had been here—in her room! Why had he come? It really wasn't proper of him to have done so. Had he wanted to say good night, perhaps?

She couldn't really remember—she had only a vague memory of gentle hands in her hair, braiding the tresses with exquisite care. . . .

A lovely, warm glow filled her. He must have seen how sleepy she was and realized she was too tired to braid her hair. How kind of him. How thoughtful.

Perhaps her fears that he had changed were unfounded.

A tap at the door interrupted her pleasant thoughts and heralded the arrival of a maid. The girl's bony knuckles protruded as she clutched a tray that appeared to weigh more than she did. "I have breakfast for you, miss."

Astonished, Mary stared at the servant. She had never had breakfast in bed in her life. "Why, thank you . . . what is your name?"

"Peggy, miss." The girl set the tray on a table by Mary's bed and asked, "Would you like me to pour you some tea?"

Mary started to nod, then hesitated. "It's not Aunt Sally's tea, is it?"

"Oh, no, miss." The ruffles on Peggy's mobcap fluttered as she shook her head emphatically. "Cook purchased this tea in the village."

Mary accepted a cup and, without adding sugar or milk, drank thirstily. The strong, hot tea washed away the sour taste in her mouth and helped clear her head, but it didn't help her remember any more of what had happened last night. She truly had been tired. She had slept deeply, dreaming strange dreams. About ghosts and fire irons and floating beds. . . .

"My goodness, miss! Did you have an accident?"

Mary looked over to see Peggy staring at the smashed pitcher and bowl on the floor.

"I . . . I don't know." She must have bumped against it last night and forgotten. Or maybe Jason had knocked it over. She glanced around the room to see if anything else was out of place and spied her corset hanging on a chair. Heat warmed her cheeks. She hoped Jason hadn't seen *that*. How could she have forgotten to put it away? She wasn't normally so untidy.

"Is the food not to your liking, miss?"

Mary looked at the maid, who was sweeping up the shards of china, then down at the tray. There were scones with fresh cream and strawberry jam. "It looks wonderful, Peggy." To prove her words, she picked up a scone, spread it with jam, and took a bite.

The textures and tastes of sweet fruit, rich smooth cream, and floury scones revived her immeasurably. She ate slowly, enjoying each bite.

"That was delicious!" she said to the maid when she had finished. "Please tell the cook."

"Yes, miss." Peggy took the tray and smiled, revealing slightly crooked teeth and a dimple in one cheek. "Would you like me to help you dress now?"

In the act of throwing back the bedcovers, Mary paused, again startled. "I don't need any help, thank you."

"Oh, but his lordship said I was to be your maid, miss."

"He did?" Mary's heart fluttered. "That was considerate of him."

"Yes, indeed, miss. He was very concerned that his fiancée have a proper maid and all. He said it didn't look right that you didn't."

Mary's heart stopped fluttering, and she frowned a little. But then she pushed back the bedcovers and stood up. It *had* been kind of him, whatever his reason. "I shall have to thank him as soon as I see him."

"That you will, miss. He told me to tell you that he wants you to meet him in the parlor in half an hour."

"Oh?" Mary laughed, happiness erasing all of yesterday's doubts. "I must hurry, then."

Peggy helped her dress very quickly indeed. Within a few minutes, Mary was standing outside the parlor door, wearing her brown dress and smoothing her hair. A smile on her lips, she entered the room.

Her smile faltered when she saw not only Jason, but Lady Weldon and Beatrice too, talking in low voices by the fireplace. They all turned and stared at her, growing silent.

"Good morning," she said.

Jason stepped forward. "Good morning. I hope you slept well."

Again, he was immaculately dressed in a dark blue coat with a velvet collar, trousers with a fashionable thin stripe, and a patterned neckcloth. She looked up into his gray-blue eyes. An odd image flashed through her brain, of those eyes very close to hers and his breath warm on her face as he whispered something against her lips. . . .

"Mary? Are you all right?"

The image vanished and Mary blushed. She must have dreamed it. "Yes, I'm fine. And I slept very well, thank you. After I routed the ghost."

"You saw the ghost?" Jason asked sharply.

Mary nodded solemnly. "I heard some very strange sounds last night. I looked out the window, and there he was—a hedgehog!"

The tense lines of Jason's face eased and he looked amused. "It was only a hedgehog?"

"Yes, crawling up the drainpipe. I think I scared him more than he scared me."

Beatrice smiled coolly. "You're fortunate the real ghost didn't visit you."

"Oh, he did—but only in my dreams," Mary said, laughing a little. "I think there was something in Aunt Sally's tea that didn't agree with me."

"Aunt Sally's tea," Jason murmured, a smile curving his lips.

Lady Weldon sniffed disapprovingly, her face as stiff as the skirts of her purple and black bombazine dress. "It's a miracle Sarah hasn't killed someone with her noxious concoctions. I suspect she puts liquor in them."

Jason's smile vanished. "I don't think that's all she puts in them." Frowning, he turned to Mary. "You'd better not drink any more of her tea."

"I won't," Mary said ruefully. "I woke up with a headache of sizable proportions. But I liked Aunt Sally. She seemed very lonely."

"Lonely!" Lady Weldon said. "That woman is an embarrassment beyond belief. It is fortunate for all of us that she chooses to stay in her room." She turned to Jason. "In fact, I've been meaning to speak to you about her. Are you available this morning? There are some other things I must discuss with you as well—the entertainments especially. I'm concerned there won't be enough chairs for the musicale, and the housekeeper told me she will need additional help even beyond the ten extra servants we've hired, and the invitations for the masquerade arrived only just this morning—"

Jason's frown deepened. "Whatever arrangements you wish to make will be fine, Aunt Weldon. I have to go to the village. I have business to discuss with Blevins."

"Hmmph. I hope you don't intend to take Mary with you," Lady Weldon said. "I need her to address the invitations. I cannot do everything by myself."

Mary clasped her hands tightly. Usually she would have been glad to help. But she had been so looking forward to spending some time with Jason. A drive sounded heavenly.

She sighed. She knew she could not selfishly abandon Lady Weldon to the task of preparing for the parties—especially when the parties were in *her* honor. Forcing herself to smile, she said, "I'll be glad to assist you, Lady Weldon."

Jason shook his head. "I'm afraid Mary will be unable to help."

Mary looked at him, a flicker of hope burgeoning in her heart. Would he insist she accompany him?

"I've arranged for a dressmaker to come this morning. Mrs. French will be fitting Mary for several new gowns."

Mary's hope was drowned under a flood of surprised embarrassment. Had he guessed that she didn't have any suitable gowns for the parties? She'd been foolish to think that her two simple dresses were enough. But then, the Jason she remembered had always had simple tastes. He hadn't cared a fig about clothes.

She glanced at his immaculate attire. A flush rose in her cheeks, and unconsciously she fingered a small darned patch on one of her sleeves. "Thank you," she managed to say.

"Order whatever you need," Jason said. "Be sure to choose something suitable for the masquerade ball also."

Mary nodded and tried to smile.

Beatrice stepped forward, adjusting the drape of her blue-and-green paisley shawl. "May I come with you to the village, Jason?" she asked, smiling prettily. "I must purchase some new gloves before tomorrow night." She glanced at her mother. "That is, if you don't need me to help you with the invitations, Mama."

"No, you run along, dear." Lady Weldon's thin lips stretched in a smile that did not reveal her teeth. "We don't want to risk getting ink stains on your hands, since you will be singing at the musicale tomorrow night. I am certain I can manage."

That settled, Beatrice tucked her arm into Jason's. "Shall we go?"

"In a moment." Disengaging himself, he turned to Mary. "I will talk to you when I return," he said in a low voice.

A flush of pleasure tingled over Mary's skin. She nodded and watched as he escorted Beatrice out of the room. The sight did not bother her as much as it had yesterday. Smiling, she met Lady Weldon's cold gaze. Mary swallowed. Curtsying, she murmured, "Excuse me, Lady Weldon," and hurried out of the room.

In the hall, she discovered Mrs. French and four seamstresses had just arrived. The dressmaker was small and plump and wore the most stylish bonnet Mary had ever seen. "Mrs. French? I am Miss Goodwin. Shall we go upstairs?"

Mrs. French nodded, causing the ribbons and feathers on her bonnet to flutter. "Yes, of course." She turned to the butler and, in spite of her short stature, managed to lift her chin to lofty heights. "Have a servant take the two trunks from the carriage upstairs, if you please."

Wilmott returned an equally haughty stare before turning to Mary. "To the Blue Room, miss?"

"Yes." Mary smiled at Mrs. French and the seamstresses. "Come along, ladies."

They were passing Aunt Sally's room when an idea occurred to Mary. "Wait here a moment," she said and tapped lightly at the door.

"Come in," a despondent voice called.

Mary entered. Aunt Sally, still wearing her frilly pink bedgown and smock, was sitting by the window between two potted plants, staring out. Mary glanced over the older woman's shoulder. Off in the distance, she saw Jason and Beatrice driving down the road, then into the trees and out of sight.

"Why aren't you out there with him instead of *her?*"

Mary turned to see Sally observing her closely. "Because I am to have some new dresses made. But I don't know much about fashion. Would you mind coming to my room and helping me select some fabrics and styles?"

Aunt Sally shook her head. "I cannot."

"Please?" Mary asked. "I truly need your help."

Aunt Sally touched the small purple flowers on one plant. "I wish I could, Mary, but I just can't. Unless . . ." Her face brightened. "Why don't you come in here? There's plenty of room."

Mary hesitated, glancing around the plant-filled room. She looked back at Aunt Sally. The older woman's eyes were almost pathetically hopeful. Mary smiled gently. "Very well," she said, then went to the door to summon the dressmaker and her assistants.

The next several hours were some of the most pleasant Mary had ever spent. Since her interest in fashion was minimal at best, she occupied herself by investigating the contents of one of Mrs. French's trunks. It contained bolt after bolt of beautiful fabrics, and Mary ran her fingers along each one, reveling in the exotic materials—batiste de soie, organdy, crepe, and tulle; Ottoman satin, velvet, moiré, and gauze.

Aunt Sally, however, turned out to be quite interested in the latest modes—indeed, she seemed starved for them. She pored over the pattern books and fashion magazines with intense interest and a remarkably astute eye. She debated the merits of several different styles with Mrs. French and showed Mary various plates of ball gowns, morning gowns, walking dresses, and evening dresses. She also showed Mary pictures of riding, carriage, and hunting dresses; mantles, shawls, and pelerines; and bonnets, hats, and caps.

"Stop," Mary laughingly protested after several hours of this. "How shall I ever choose from amongst so many? My head is spinning. Why don't you order something for yourself, Aunt Sally?"

"A dress for me? No, no, it would be a waste. There's no need for me to have stylish gowns." Wistfully, the older woman gazed at a bolt of green velvet sticking out of the trunk.

"If it would give you pleasure, that's reason enough." Mary picked up the bolt and put it on the older woman's lap. "You seem to have a eye for fashion."

Stroking the rich velvet, Aunt Sally smiled reminiscently. "Actually, I *was* quite fashionable when I was younger. I used to spend hours studying the various magazines. Elizabeth always said I had a talent for being à la mode."

Mary smiled at the pride in the older woman's voice. Kneeling by the trunk to pull out another bolt, this one of gold cloth, she asked idly, "Who is Elizabeth?"

Aunt Sally hesitated, then said, "She was the sixth earl's fiancée."

Mary glanced up from the trunk. "The ghost's fiancée?"

Aunt Sally peered around nervously, then nodded. "I really shouldn't be talking about her. Vincent becomes very upset whenever he hears her name. Everyone avoids mentioning her."

"Was she really so terrible?"

"Oh, no! At least, I didn't think so. I met her during my first Season. She was so dashing, so exciting. The first time Vincent saw her, Elizabeth was wearing a gold gown, and he couldn't keep his eyes off of her. Later, when they were engaged, he had a portrait of her painted wearing that same dress." Aunt Sally's lip quivered. "I know Vincent blames me for his death because I introduced him to her."

Sympathy welled up in Mary. No wonder Aunt Sally was suffering delusions of ghosts—the poor woman thought she was somehow responsible for Vincent's death. "He could not possibly blame you," she said gently.

Aunt Sally clutched the bolt of velvet to her chest. "You don't know Vincent."

Mary smiled a little. "I wouldn't want to know him. He sounds like he was a thoroughly unpleasant man."

"Oh, no, he wasn't. He was . . . oh, I don't know how to describe him. Fascinating. Women were always falling in love with him—even Eugenia, and she had already decided to marry Weldon. But Vincent never paid the slightest attention to any of them. Because of the family history, you know."

Mary looked at her curiously. "Cecil mentioned something about the Helsbury earls all being betrayed by women."

Aunt Sally nodded sadly. "Nearly all of them have had miserable marriages. The first earl received his title for being so accommodating as to marry the king's mistress after the Royal Interest had faded—they despised and distrusted each other nearly the whole time of their marriage. The second earl arranged to marry his neighbor's daughter only to discover that her parents had forced her into the marriage—she wound up in a convent. The third earl—the second earl's brother—had an uneventful marriage, but the next one, Vincent's grandfather, married an heiress, then spent half his fortune trying to divorce her after she ran off with her lover."

"Good heavens!" Mary said. "It does sound as though they've been remarkably unlucky with women. Although . . ." Her voice trailed off, and she fingered a length of the gold cloth.

"Although what?" Aunt Sally asked.

Mary started and looked up from the cloth. "Oh, nothing." She began unwinding the gold cloth from the bolt. "Only . . . did any of them marry for love?"

"Oh, heavens no," Aunt Sally said. "The Helsbury earls marry for convenience, not love."

Mary stopped unwinding the cloth. "Convenience?" she asked in a small voice.

Aunt Sally nodded, then paused, looking at Mary. "Not that I mean to imply that Jason would. I'm sure he loves you."

Mary forced herself to smile, but made no reply.

Aunt Sally didn't appear to notice Mary's silence. "Well, perhaps Vincent had feelings for Elizabeth," she mused, a frown creasing her forehead. "But I think it was more his pride that was involved. When a messenger brought the news that she planned to marry another man, Vincent was enraged. It was the same day she was supposed to have married him, you see. There was a terrible storm that night, but he rode off like a madman into the rain. The bridge at the end of the drive had been washed away and he drowned in the river."

"Oh!" In spite of Mary's growing dislike for Vincent, his untimely end made her breast swell with sympathy. "The poor man."

"Yes. Now he haunts this house, determined to prevent all the other Helsbury earls from marrying. You must be careful, Mary, or he will frighten you away like the others."

"I'm not afraid of ghosts," Mary repeated for the umpteenth time since arriving at Helsbury House. Ghosts didn't concern her—but Jason and his feelings for her did. Was she a mere "convenience" to him?

No, she couldn't be. A plain, dowerless almost-spinster with only three dresses to her name was hardly a convenience.

Cheered by the thought, she glanced at the dressmaker and seamstresses who were listening with wide eyes. "Shall we proceed, Mrs. French?"

Snapping out of her trance, the dressmaker bustled forward and opened the other trunk. "Certainly, Miss Goodwin. You must try on these dresses. A client ordered them for her daughter. Unfortunately, her account was overdrawn." She lifted out a pink gown with double-bouffante sleeves and a deep flounce of ribbons and lace at the hem. "Fortunately, the daughter was just about your size."

"Hmm," Aunt Sally said, studying the dress. "Since time is so short, I suppose it will have to do."

Mary put down the bolt of gold cloth and reached out to touch one of the huge sleeves reverently. "Oh, it's beautiful!" she breathed. "I can wear it to the musicale."

Mrs. French pulled out a second dress, a thin white cotton with a profusion of lilac bows and a matching pelisse, trimmed with an abundance of ribbon.

Aunt Sally eyed it doubtfully. "I think a simpler style would become Mary better."

"Oh, no," Mary protested. "It will be perfect for the breakfast."

Mrs. French beamed. "I have another trunk in the wagon with eight other gowns. Would you care to see them, also?"

"No, thank you," Mary said, tracing the fine stitches on the white dress with her finger.

Aunt Sally looked up from a pattern book in surprise. "But of course you must look at them, Mary. You must have them all."

"Oh, no, I couldn't." Mary's hand fell to her side. "Jason told me to order only what I need."

"Goose!" Aunt Sally said affectionately. "You do need all of them."

Mary shook her head firmly. "No, I only need three for the parties. I couldn't accept any more than that. It wouldn't be right."

"You will be married in less than a week," Aunt Sally said. "What difference can it make?"

Mary shook her head again. She didn't feel comfortable ordering so many dresses—especially without Jason's knowledge. "I prefer to wait. These two will do for now. Although I still need a costume for the masquerade."

Mary picked up the bolt of gold cloth and began rewinding the material. "Do you have any ideas, Aunt Sally?"

"Something simple might be best. There is not much time." She tapped her finger against her chin, then smiled. "I know! You must go as Empress Josephine! It will be easier to make an Empire dress. And it will become you very well."

"An Empire gown?" Mary asked doubtfully. "They are very revealing."

"Nonsense. I wore them all the time when I was younger and they were much more sensible than the clothes everyone wears now. At least we didn't weigh ourselves down with monstrous bustles and a stone's worth of petticoats and padding." Aunt Sally glanced at the bolt Mary was holding. "That gold cloth will be perfect."

"It is decided, then," Mrs. French said briskly. "Now, we must take your measurements and try on these two dresses. Giselle, Babette, help Miss Goodwin with the pink gown."

Unfortunately, the waist on the dress was several inches smaller than Mary's. Mrs. French tsk'd and hmm'd as the dress was removed. "It is your corset," she finally decided. "It is all wrong."

Startled, Mary glanced in the mirror. Her corset, although a bit worn, seemed perfectly adequate to her. The lightly boned fabric gave definition to her waist and support to her breasts. "What is wrong with my corset?" she asked.

"The fashion is for tight lacing and small waists. You need a corset to nip you in and push you up."

Mary frowned. "I don't think I want to be pushed up."

The seamstresses giggled.

Mrs. French ignored them and Mary. She pulled a new corset out of the trunk. "Ah, here we are. Try this on."

Reluctantly, Mary complied. The seamstresses helped her remove the old one and tied the new one in place over her chemise.

"That is much better," Mrs. French said.

Mary regarded her image in the mirror doubtfully. "I don't know. I look rather ridiculous."

"That is the fashion," Mrs. French said.

"The fashion is to look ridiculous?" Mary asked.

The seamstresses giggled again.

Mrs. French frowned at them sternly. "You look fine, Miss Goodwin."

Mary glanced at the mirror again. "But don't you think I look like a—"

"A strumpet?" Sally interjected helpfully.

"Aunt Sally . . ." Mary said, trying not to laugh. "You shouldn't say such things."

Mrs. French ignored their silliness. Quickly and efficiently, she measured Mary in the new corset. "There. Do you wish to keep this corset on?"

"No, thank you." Mary could barely breathe. "I think I prefer to change back into my old one."

Still giggling and whispering amongst themselves, the seamstresses helped her take off the new corset and put her own back on. Babette had just tied the last string when the door opened.

Mary turned and saw Jason standing in the doorway.

She froze. He stood very still, his gaze wandering down over her barely covered breasts, to her waist and hips, and to her legs in the lace-edged drawers. Then back up again to her breasts.

"Jason!" Aunt Sally clucked. "You should know better than to enter a room without knocking."

The sound of the older woman's voice brought Mary to her senses. Blushing furiously, she grabbed her dress from the bed and held it in front of herself.

"Jason?" Aunt Sally repeated.

For a moment, Mary thought he wouldn't respond. She looked into his eyes and saw that they were very blue. She clutched the dress against her breasts.

He stared at her a moment longer, then turned his back. "I beg your pardon," he said, his voice cool. "I did knock. You ladies were giggling so much you must not have heard me. I couldn't imagine what was going on, Aunt Sally. I thought maybe you were entertaining a gentleman friend."

Mary gasped again at his words, but Aunt Sally chuckled. "You are such a rascal, Jason. Mary, go into the dressing room and put on your dress."

Mary hurriedly complied. Babette came with her. As the seamstress helped her into her gown, Mary tried to calm the rapid beating of her heart. She felt hot and flushed and as breathless as if she had the new corset on again. He had looked at her so strangely. . . .

She concentrated on breathing deeply. She was imagining things. He had probably just been shocked to see her in her corset.

Her heartbeat slowed, and she moved to the doorway, pausing to take one last deep breath. She could hear the murmur of voices from the other room, but couldn't make out what they were saying. She stepped into the bedroom.

The seamstresses were returning the bolts of cloth to the trunk, and Mrs. French was gathering up her books and patterns. Aunt Sally was smiling at Jason. "I've always liked you better than my other relatives."

"Thank you," Jason said, a trifle dryly.

Aunt Sally laughed, then glanced up and saw Mary. "Ah, here she is, Jason. You must take your fiancée for a walk in the garden. She has been cooped up inside all day."

Jason turned and looked at her, his gaze unreadable.

"I would like to talk to Mary," he murmured, "but it can wait until after my visit with you, Aunt Sally."

Aunt Sally shook her head. "It's time for my nap."

Jason arched a brow. "I visit you every day at this time, Aunt Sally. I thought you didn't take your nap until later."

"I'm tired today," Sally said. "You two run along."

Giving in to Sally's insistence, Jason escorted Mary out into the corridor. Mary stole a glance at his rigid jaw. He did not look pleased. She swallowed.

"I'm looking forward to seeing the gardens," she said brightly.

"If you don't mind, there is something I would like to discuss with you in the library," he said.

He sounded very grim, and Mary's heart sank to her slippers as she followed him down the stairs. Had something happened? Was he upset about something? Perhaps he was shocked by her behavior. When he had walked into Aunt Sally's room, she had just stood there, letting him look at her. Everywhere his gaze touched, she'd felt a warmth, almost as if it were his hands running over her, not his eyes. . . .

Her cheeks grew hot. Definitely she had behaved in an uncountesslike manner. Being a countess was going to be much more difficult than she had thought. Not only did she have to dress differently, she also had to act, talk, and even think differently. She only hoped Jason loved her enough to be patient with her.

The Helsbury earls marry for convenience, not love.

Aunt Sally's words echoed in Mary's ears, and a horrible suspicion entered her brain. Perhaps Jason had changed his mind. Perhaps, like his forebears, he had decided to make a more convenient, more advantageous marriage. Perhaps he wanted to break off their engagement—

No. It couldn't be true.

But as she followed him into the library, she was very much afraid that it might be. She felt a burning sensation behind her eyes.

If he does break the engagement, I won't cry, she promised herself.

She walked over to a chessboard and pretended to study the game in progress, waiting for him to speak.

He cleared his throat. "I want to apologize for my behavior last night."

His words were so unexpected, so different from what she had thought he would say, that for a moment she could do nothing but stare at him.

"Apologize for what?" she finally managed to say.

He glanced at her sharply, studying her face for what seemed like a long time. "Mary," he said slowly, "how much do you remember?"

"Not much," she admitted. "I was very tired, and I think Aunt Sally's tea had an odd effect on me."

"Very odd," he murmured.

"I do remember you braiding my hair, though," she continued. "I've been wanting to thank you. That was very kind of you."

He made an odd choking noise. "You're welcome."

Mary smiled in relief. "Is that what you wanted to see me about?"

"Yes, but there is something else, also," he said, his gaze meeting hers.

Her heart sank. *He had saved the bad news for last,* she thought.

But to her surprise, he did not speak. Instead, he strode over to a painting hanging on the wall and pulled it aside. Behind it was a safe. He turned the dial, pushed the door open, and took out a small case. With a slight bow, he handed it to her.

She stared at it stupidly. "What is this?"

"Open it and see," he said, a trifle impatiently.

She obeyed. Inside was a ring. In an elaborate gold setting, a huge ruby was surrounded by small emeralds and diamonds. Mary stared at it. It looked like something a Byzantine princess would wear.

"What is this?" she whispered.

He smiled then. "An engagement ring, of course." He took it from the case and slid it on her finger.

The ring was a bit tight, but Mary didn't care. It was the most beautiful thing she'd ever seen. Her heart swelled with happiness. The tears she had sworn she wouldn't shed trembled on her eyelashes. "Thank you, Jason," she whispered.

He stared down into her face. "You're welcome." His voice sounded husky.

He was looking at her the way he had in Aunt Sally's bedroom, and suddenly she wanted him to kiss her. A kiss was a harmless thing, she thought. If he would just kiss her the way he had kissed her when he proposed, she would know everything was all right. She would know that nothing had changed. She would feel that wonderful warm glow that would reassure and comfort her. . . .

He bent toward her. Her breath caught in her throat. His face came closer. She could see the black pupils of his eyes surrounded by a band of bright blue. Her heart pounded. He leaned closer. . . .

His mouth a whisper away from hers, he stopped, staring at something behind her.

She glanced over her shoulder. Nothing was there. "Is something wrong?"

"No." He straightened and turned away. "I forgot to tell you that the ring is very valuable. Charles the Second gave it to the first earl's wife as a wedding present. You must take great care not to lose it. After we are wed, it will have to be kept locked in the vault most of the time."

Mary stared at his averted face, then looked down at the ring. Charles II had given this ring to the first earl's wife? She remembered Aunt Sally's story of the first earl marrying the king's mistress, a woman he despised and distrusted, in return for a title and fortune. A slight nausea rose in her throat. "You'd best put it away, then." She tugged at the ring, but it wouldn't come off.

Jason frowned. "I want you to wear it this week."

Still tugging at the ring, she shook her head. "I really can't. I might lose it."

His hands closed over hers. Startled, she looked up into his eyes. "Leave the ring on," he said.

She opened her mouth to argue, but before she could get the words out, the door opened and the butler entered.

Blushing, Mary tugged at her hands. Jason did not release them. "Yes?" he said coolly to Wilmott.

"I beg your pardon, my lord," the butler said, fixing his

gaze on the wall, "but Lady Weldon desired me to inform you that they are waiting tea on you."

"Thank you, Wilmott." Finally, Jason released her hands and held out his arm.

Mary hesitated. She really did not want to wear the ring. She wanted to pry it off her finger and have him lock it away in the safe.

But somehow, under his compelling gaze, she found herself placing her hand on his sleeve, the heavy weight of the ring still on her finger, the jewels sparkling tauntingly against the dark material of his sleeve.

8

Vincent groaned as a shaft of morning light shone through the dining room windows and struck his portrait. He had a headache the size of which he'd never experienced before—in life or death. This was worse than any hangover. This felt as though all substance had been sucked out of him, beaten with a stick, and shoved back in.

It was all the woman's fault.

He opened one bleary eye and saw the family gathered at the table. At one end sat Miss Mary Goodwin, quietly eating her breakfast. He glared at her, then closed his eye.

He'd been too drained by his visit to the Blue Room to make any attempts to frighten her off yesterday—he'd barely had the energy to appear and stop Jason from kissing her in the library—but today he was determined to rid Helsbury House of her unsettling presence.

The only question was how.

He cracked his eyes open just far enough to be able to peer at the people at the table. They were seated in the same order as they had been at dinner the night before last, although everyone was less formal. Cecil Parsell, apparently uninterested in the cold mutton pie on his plate, spoke across the table to Horace Quimby, who was wolfing down his own pie with blatant enjoyment. Sourfaced Lady Weldon was addressing some comment to her slyboots daughter. And Jason . . .

He glanced at Jason and saw the boy was staring straight at him—or at least at the portrait.

Vincent frowned. The boy had an uncanny knack for knowing when Vincent was lurking in the room—even if he didn't materialize. He'd made several attempts to trick Jason, without success.

It really didn't matter, of course, but it was irritating at times. He'd had to listen at the library keyhole yesterday, an activity beneath his dignity, to prevent Jason's sensing his presence until the proper moment—

A bright flash caught Vincent's eye. He scowled as he looked at the Helsbury ring adorning Mary's finger. He wished he'd had the strength to prevent Jason's giving the heirloom to her. Maybe he would have been able to if he hadn't been so caught off guard. He still couldn't quite believe Jason had given the ring to Mary before the wedding. The tradition was for the earl to present it to the Helsbury bride *after* their wedding night—none of the earls had been fool enough to trust a woman with the valuable jewel before the ceremony.

Vincent glared at Mary, wondering what cunning wiles she'd used to convince Jason to give her the ring early. She sat quietly, eating a scone, looking as though she'd never had a mean or calculating thought in her entire life.

The little hussy.

Lady Weldon laid her napkin on the table. "Jason," she said, her voice carrying easily across the length of the table, "what are your plans for today? The musicale is tonight, and I need to consult with you on a few more matters."

Jason looked up from his plate. "Will later be convenient? I had intended to take Mary on a tour of the house this morning."

Vincent frowned. He didn't want Jason to spend time alone with his little fiancée—it was too dangerous. By giving her the ring, Jason had proven himself susceptible to her scheming ways. Vincent would have to keep a sharp eye on the boy to prevent him from committing further follies.

Lady Weldon glanced at her daughter. Whatever she saw in Beatrice's face made her smile and nod. "This afternoon will be fine. A tour of the house sounds like an excellent idea. Beatrice will accompany you and tell Mary the history of the house." To Mary, she said, "Beatrice has made a study of Helsbury House and its occupants and will be able to answer any questions you might have."

In spite of his aching head, Vincent grinned. Although he had never liked Lady Weldon, he suddenly perceived that she might have her uses. She was a very distant relation to the Parsells, but she had managed to play upon the relationship to snag herself the earl of Weldon. After her husband died, she had appeared on the doorstep, her daughter in tow. Roger had been the earl of Helsbury at the time, and Lady Weldon had tried to push herself first on him, then on Timothy. Now, for the last six months, she'd been trying to push her daughter on Jason.

"Jason, you must be sure to take Mary to the West Gallery," Lady Weldon continued. "I am sure she will want to see the watercolors Beatrice has painted." To Mary, she said, "Beatrice is an extraordinarily fine landscape artist."

Beatrice took a dainty sip of her tea. "Do you paint, Mary?"

Mary shook her head. "No, I never had the opportunity to learn."

"No? Dear me, Jason, you will have to hire an art tutor as well as a music instructor for Mary. There are certain accomplishments that a lady with any pretensions to gentility simply must have."

Vincent gazed at Beatrice with fascinated dislike. She looked so sincerely concerned that Mary could not be offended. But it was apparent from Mary's expression that the words pricked at her. He knew Beatrice's sort well—pretty as a picture on the outside, greedy and manipulative on the inside. Plainly, she had set her sights on Jason, and no trifle like a fiancée was going to stand in her way.

An unpleasant smile curled his lips. Between Beatrice, Lady Weldon, and him, Miss Mary Goodwin didn't stand a chance.

Cecil laid down his fork. "I say, Jason, Mary doesn't want to spend the morning looking at boring old landscapes. You must show her something more interesting. Like the dungeon."

Mary perked up. "Dungeon?"

Vincent, his satisfaction ebbing away, glared at Cecil. What was the puppy thinking, to suggest such a thing?

Horace Quimby stopped shoveling buttered eggs and smoked salmon in his mouth long enough to say, "I doubt you would want to see the nether regions of the house, Miss Goodwin. You will find them very dark and dirty."

Vincent nodded in agreement. *Very* dark and dirty. He had always avoided the dungeon, even when he was alive. He had ventured down there once after his death. He'd only stayed a few seconds, but that had been enough— more than enough.

"It sounds fascinating. I don't mind a little dirt." She turned to Jason. "Please, may we see it?" she enquired, smiling up at him.

Vincent was taken a little off guard by that smile. For all her plainness, she had a remarkably enticing smile.

Jason was no proof against it. His gaze lingering on her mouth, he said, "If that's what you wish, Mary."

Vincent cursed silently.

Lady Weldon's sharp voice interrupted him in the middle of a particularly colorful oath. "Jason, what are you thinking? The dungeon is not a suitable place to take a lady."

Jason shrugged. "She must see it sometime."

"Now, Mama," Beatrice said, her smile looking even more false than usual. "We must try to accommodate our guest."

"I think I will come, too," Cecil said. "It's been forever since I saw the dungeon. Whenever we came here for one of the earls' funerals, Jason and I would always play in it." He smiled reminiscently. "Remember, Jason, how we used to dare each other to go into the Pit?"

"The Pit?" Mary repeated.

Vincent groaned.

"A small, dark cell in the dungeon," Jason explained. He rose to his feet. "Quimby, will you join us?"

Quimby, slathering a scone with jam and cream, shook his head. "No, I must tend to my flock. Besides, I do not care for the dungeon. Especially the Pit. There is something eerie about it."

Involuntarily, Vincent shuddered. Ever since he was a child and one of his brothers had "accidentally" locked him in it, he'd hated the Pit. He didn't want to go anywhere near the cell. He would have to wait to scare Mary away—

Mary stood up also. "Perhaps I shall find the ghost there," she said in a joking voice.

Vincent stiffened. Why, the impudent little—

"I doubt any self-respecting phantom would lurk in such an unpleasant place," Jason said, taking Mary's arm.

He escorted her and Cecil and Beatrice out of the room, Lady Weldon following a short while later. Quimby, after finishing off the plate of scones, belched loudly and left also. As soon as Vincent was alone, he stepped down from his portrait and began pacing about the room.

Very well, he thought, rounding the corner of the table. He might not like the dungeon, but if Mary insisted on going there, then he would go too. He would just stay out of the Pit.

He paused and inhaled deeply. Really, it wouldn't be difficult to scare the devil out of her. It would be even easier if she was alone. If possible, he would try to isolate her from the others. But even if he couldn't, he refused to wait any longer.

Mary Goodwin would be out of Helsbury House before noon.

* * *

Tense and wary, Jason held the torch high in the air as he led the small group down the steep wooden steps into the bowels of Helsbury House. He knew Vincent had been listening that morning, and he had no doubt that the ghost had some nefarious purpose planned. He half expected a disembodied head to pop out of the wall or unearthly hands to grab at their feet. But so far, he'd seen no sign of the ghost, and Mary, smiling and excited, was tugging at his arm to urge him to go faster.

He glanced down at the gold-brown head at his side. He was aware of all the drawbacks to marrying her— Beatrice and Vincent had pointed them out often enough. Mary would have difficulty fitting in. He was giving up his freedom. Her accomplishments were lacking, her clothes atrocious. The earls of Helsbury were unlucky—sometimes tragically so—in love.

He knew all of this. So why, as the narrowness of the stairs forced her close against him, was he so conscious of the warmth of her, of the sweet scent of her hair, of the side of her breast pressed against his arm—

The rickety wooden steps groaned under his weight, and Jason groaned silently along with them. She was intruding more on his thoughts than he would have believed possible. Yesterday, when he should have been discussing final payments and dates of departure with Blevins, images of her had kept popping into his head. He kept remembering how she'd appeared when he'd gone to her room the night before last—all soft and sleepy-eyed; how her hair had looked—long and thick and shining; and how her mouth had felt—warm and sweet and moist. . . .

Jason's grip on the torch tightened. He'd spent most of yesterday trying to banish the images. And he had almost succeeded. Until he had arrived home and walked into Aunt Sally's room.

Closing his eyes, he paused on the stairs.

"Is something wrong, Jason?" Mary asked.

He opened his eyes. "No, not at all," he managed to

say, before continuing down the stairs. That corset. That damned corset. It had been bad enough seeing it on her chair, teasing him to imagine what she would look like in it, but that had been nothing compared to the reality.

He was certain the picture of her in her stays and drawers was burned into his brain for all eternity.

Her delicate ankles and calves beneath the lace-edged drawers had made the blood rush through his veins. Her waist and hips, sweetly emphasized by the stays, had sent the pulsing blood up to his head. But it was her breasts, gently cupped by the corset, that had sent the pounding blood straight to his groin. He'd wanted to unlace the corset and replace its hold with his own—

"Jason, could you please hold the torch a little higher?" Beatrice asked. "The smoke is blowing directly into my face."

Jason jerked the torch up. He was really going to have to exert more self-control. As it was, he had nearly lost it when he'd almost kissed her in the library. Part of him was actually thankful Vincent had appeared, bringing him to his senses.

But that didn't mean that he was going to concede to the ghost. Vincent had had his way for entirely too long. Jason was determined to make his own decisions about marriage. Yet at the same time, he had no intention of being ruled by lust. He'd make love to Mary at the proper time and place—after the wedding.

They reached the bottom of the stairs. Mary stopped and clasped her hands. "How wonderful!" she breathed.

Jason glanced around at the long, narrow, windowless chamber with its rack and headscrew, dirt floor, stone walls, and low wooden-beamed ceilings. "Nearly as fine as Windsor Castle," he said dryly.

Mary laughed. "I'm serious. How many people can boast that they have a dungeon in their home? You're very lucky."

Jason's gaze lingered on her sparkling eyes and smiling

lips, before he forced himself to look away. Very lucky indeed. He might need to lock himself down here every night until their wedding.

Beatrice stepped to the front of the small group. "Have you noticed the torture instruments, Mary? They are real—although of course the Parsells never used them. They were used only to intimidate prisoners."

Mary went over to the chair with the head screw and sat on it. She bounced on the seat, sending a stream of dust floating up into the air.

Beatrice sneezed. "Really, Mary. Must you be so . . . enthusiastic?"

"I'm sorry." Mary stopped bouncing and stretched her neck up instead, trying to put her head between the screws.

"You're not tall enough," Cecil said. "Come over to the rack. I'll shackle you in if you like."

"Oh, yes!" Laughing, she started to cross the room.

Jason caught her arm. "I don't think that would be a good idea," he said through tight lips.

She blinked up at him.

"The table is filthy," he said. "Your dress would be ruined."

"Oh," Mary said.

"You already have dust all along the back of your dress from sitting in that repulsive chair," Beatrice said, twitching her skirts away from Mary's.

"Oh, dear." Frowning, Mary craned her head over her shoulder, trying to see, then brushed off her backside.

Jason bit back an impulse to offer to help her.

Beatrice cleared her throat. "A hundred years ago, these cells were used to house traitorous Jacobites until they could be transported to London."

Jason released Mary's arm. He knew he'd overreacted a bit. But somehow he couldn't tolerate the idea of her allowing Cecil to touch her wrists and ankles—

The flame of his torch dimmed, nearly going out. Then it flared, radiating out in a brilliant circle of light, before dimming again to glow a trifle less brightly than before.

Jason stiffened and glanced around. Everything was still and quiet, and there was no visible sign of another presence in the dungeon—and yet he detected the faint scent of autumn leaves.

He stepped closer to Mary and forced his tone to lightness. "One of those traitors was my great-grand-uncle, who had the poor judgment to support the Pretender."

Beatrice frowned. "There's no need to mention him, Jason. He was a disgrace to the Parsell name."

"He certainly was," Jason murmured, scanning the shadows of the room. "He managed to escape from the Pit and fought with the rebels, before fleeing for his life to America. Personally, I think Cynric was much more interesting."

"Who was he?" Mary asked, wandering over to inspect a pair of rusted shackles hanging from the wall.

Jason followed close behind. "Another family reprobate. A Saxon. When the Normans first conquered England, a soldier named Arnaux was charged with building a castle here. Cynric, who owned the land before the invasion, did not approve. He made life miserable for Arnaux and was eventually imprisoned in the Pit. But he, too, escaped and kidnapped Arnaux's daughter."

"Oh, the poor girl!" Mary dropped the shackle. "What happened to her?"

"She was, er, compromised, and the two married." Jason stared hard at the far corner. Had he seen a flicker of light there? "As the story goes, the Saxon ended up ruling the castle, and Arnaux's daughter ended up ruling the Saxon."

Mary smiled. "How clever of her." She peered around. "Where is the Pit? I would like to see it."

Jason hesitated. He glanced under the rack and up at the ceiling. Everything looked normal. Taking Mary's arm, he led her to the shadowed corner and opened a small door of splintering wood.

She had to bend over to look in. "How frightful," she said, her eyes bright. "I want to go in."

"Don't be foolish, Mary." Beatrice shuddered. "Surely you've seen enough."

Mary shrugged and smiled and took a step forward.

"Wait!" Jason said sharply.

She stopped, turning to stare at him with a surprised expression.

Jason ignored her questioning look. "Let me go first," he said. Crouching down, he entered the cell. Once inside, he could stand up straight again. He glanced around. It had been years since he'd been in here, but it hadn't changed. In one corner there was still a broken rocking horse, some canvas-covered paintings, and a chair without any seat. The room was damp, with black mold growing on the walls, but surprisingly warm.

He held out his hand to help Mary through the door.

As soon as she was inside, her nose wrinkled. "It smells." She straightened and looked around, her gaze falling on the items in the corner. "What—"

A loud crash made her jump and turn. Jason turned also, although he already knew what he would find. The door had slammed closed. He stepped over and tried to open it. It was locked.

Cecil's bewildered voice floated through the thick wood. "I don't know what happened, Jason, but we can't open the door."

Jason knew exactly what had happened. He glanced around. Vincent was not in the cell, but Jason had no doubt the ghost was lurking outside. He cursed silently. What did Vincent hope to gain by this trick? "Go ask the housekeeper for the key, Cecil."

"Very well," Cecil said.

"Wait," Jason heard Beatrice say. "You can't take the torch."

"I have to take the torch," Cecil said. "I won't be able to see the stairs if I don't."

"Surely you don't expect me to stand here in the dark?"

"Cecil . . ." Jason said, gritting his teeth. "The key."

"Yes, Jason, I'm going. Lady Beatrice, you may come with me or not, but I am going."

"Well!" The sound of two pairs of footsteps faded away.

Silence fell over the Pit. The torchlight flickered and ghostly shadows danced on the stone walls. In the quiet, small noises could be heard—an odd creaking, a low whistling sound, and the faint scratching of some unknown creature behind the wall.

Jason turned back to Mary, prepared to reassure her. But to his surprise, she didn't appear at all frightened. She looked up at him, her clear blue eyes sparkling in the torchlight, and smiled. His breath caught in his throat.

"Isn't this exciting, Jason? I can almost imagine that we're prisoners, waiting to be ransomed."

He stared down at her smiling face. He wouldn't mind being a prisoner. As long as he was in a cell with her. . . .

A cold draft blew through the Pit. It seemed to come from the keyhole, as if someone were blowing through it. The torch flickered. The draft blew through again, stronger this time. Jason tried to shield the torch, but it was too late.

The light flickered again, then went out.

9

Mary stared through the inky blackness, trying to discern where Jason was. She could see nothing, not even a dark outline. But she could smell the fragrance of the soap and tobacco he used.

"Jason?" she asked.

She heard him set down the torch and step toward her. "I'm sorry, Mary," he said in a low voice. "I hope you're not afraid of the dark."

"No," she said, squinting in the direction of his voice. "I like the dark."

"You do?" He sounded surprised. "Why?"

"Oh, I don't know," she said, laughing a little. "I suppose because everything seems more intense."

"More intense?"

"Yes," she said. "Sounds are clearer and more distinct. Smells richer and fuller. And touch is much more sensitive, don't you think? There's something elemental about the dark. Something primitive—"

Suddenly aware of what she was saying, she stopped. Jason didn't speak.

The rich, black darkness seemed to flow around them. She felt warm suddenly, and she could almost smell something in the air. Something vague and unidentifiable. Her heart began to pound, an odd mix of emotions filling her—wariness, fear. Anticipation. . . .

"Your voice does sound different," he murmured huskily.

"Warm, melodic, as if each syllable is the note of a beautiful song. And you do smell incredibly sweet . . . like flowers and honey and mint. As for touch . . . "

She felt, rather than saw, him reach out toward her. His hand brushed against her hip.

She gasped and jumped back, but he only stepped closer, one hand encircling her waist, while the other moved up her side, along the edge of her corset to the prim lace collar at her neck. He fingered the lace, then moved on to the sensitive skin in the hollow of her throat. Her pulse leapt under his fingers.

"Ahh." His voice was a bare whisper of sound. "You feel soft, Mary. Warm and soft." His fingers continued up, tracing a tingling trail up her neck to her jaw, and then up to her ear. He explored its shape, then moved his fingers along her hairline, around and down until he cupped her chin in his hand, tilting her face up toward his.

"But you forgot to mention one thing, Mary." Their breaths mingled, became one. "You forgot about taste. . . ."

His mouth touched hers. Gently. As gently as she remembered from that day when he'd kissed her in the garden so long ago. Her heart melted, and her body relaxed. There was no reason to be afraid. This was Jason—

His tongue touched her lips. She gasped again, but he paid no attention. He traced the curve of her lips, sending small darts of fire from her lips to her neck and shoulders, and down to the tips of her breasts, and down farther still to curl in her belly and gather at the juncture of her thighs. . . .

She tried to pull back, to slow down the overwhelming sensations assaulting her, but the strong hand encircling her waist tightened, pressing her against him. Her breasts were flattened against the wall of his chest. She felt the serration of his ribs, the ridges of knotted muscles. Heat radiated from him, and overlying the aroma of wool and soap was another smell—a musky scent that seemed to rise from his very pores.

His tongue pressed at the crease of her mouth, and his leg pressed between hers. His tongue stroked her lips, and his thigh rubbed gently against the most intimate part of her. His tongue entered her mouth, and his hand slipped inside her dress, pressing against her breast—

With a small cry, she wrenched herself away and stumbled back a few steps, breathing hard.

"Mary? Come back, Mary."

His voice was soft and persuasive, urgent and compelling. Her heart pounded in her chest. She was frightened. Not from being locked in the dark pit, but from the sound of Jason's voice. It sounded strange—demanding . . . pleading. . . .

She heard him step toward her. Her breathing harsh and ragged, she backed away, feeling along the wall, but he continued forward. "Mary? Don't be frightened. I just want to hold you."

She heard him stumble over the torch. He cursed, then stepped forward again. "Mary . . . "

His voice, so gentle and beseeching, tugged at her heart. She knew she should step away, but her feet wouldn't move. All of her senses responded to the ache in his voice, urging her to go to him, to let him soothe the corresponding ache in her. . . .

Without conscious volition, she stepped toward him—

"OOOOOOOOOOooooooohhhhhhhh."

The eerie groan echoed through the dungeon, stopping Mary in her tracks. "What was that?"

She heard Jason mutter a curse. "Nothing," he said, his voice urgent. "The wind. Come here, Mary."

Outside the Pit, dragging footsteps sounded.

Startled, she stepped back, bumping into the rocking horse. "Jason, who is that?"

He made a noise something between a laugh and a groan. "It must be the ghost. Come here, Mary, and I will protect you from him."

But the interruption had enabled her to gain control of her senses again. She laughed, albeit a little breathlessly. "I think I need protection from you, not the ghost."

"Mary . . . "

More footsteps sounded outside the cell . . . but these were definitely human.

Mary circled the spot where Jason's frustrated voice had come from and stopped by the door. "Cecil, is that you?"

"Yes, and I have the key!" Cecil announced through the door.

The lock rattled. Then there was a click, and the door swung open. Torchlight streamed into the cell.

Cecil peered in. "Come out, you two."

Mary blinked, her eyes adjusting to the light, then glanced at Jason. His face was all tight angles and planes, his eyes dark with some intense emotion. Swallowing, she scurried out. Jason picked up the torch and followed more slowly.

"Sorry it took so long," Cecil said cheerfully, relighting Jason's torch from his. "I had to search for the key. It had fallen off the housekeeper's ring and we had to retrace her steps."

"Where's Beatrice?" Mary asked.

"She decided she needed to practice for the musicale tonight."

"Oh. Well, I think I've seen enough of the dungeon. I'd better go see if Mrs. French has delivered my dress yet." Pretending not to see Jason's proffered arm, she ascended the narrow wooden stairs with dangerous haste. Jason followed close behind. She was conscious of his burning gaze on the back of her neck.

At the top of the stairs, Cecil and Jason stopped to extinguish the torches, and put them in their brackets. Mary didn't pause, however. She continued on into the hall and was about to go upstairs, when Jason caught up to her.

He grasped her arm. "Mary . . . "

His gaze was dark and probing. Averting her eyes, she

pulled away. "I must go upstairs," she mumbled and hurried up the stairs.

Her heart was pounding by the time she reached her room. She closed the door and leaned back against it, her eyes closed. He had changed. She knew it now. She knew it, because before he had seemed like a friend.

And now, he seemed like something entirely different.

10

His footsteps echoing on the polished floorboards, Jason advanced swiftly, his rapier slashing through the air with little regard for the science or art of fencing. Instead of the elegant, disciplined cuts and thrusts that were customary, he swung the sword in high sweeping arcs, attacking like some ancient Viking berserker. Sweat rolled down his face, and his shirt clung to his back, but he did not slow his pace. The exercise distracted him from, even if it did not alleviate, the raging desire inside him.

"Your form is deplorable, nephew," a mocking voice drawled from behind him. "You appear sadly out of practice."

Jason swung around, lowering the sword to his side. Vincent, his aura dulled by sunlight, lounged carelessly against the door, casually dressed in dark green and brown hunting attire.

Jason glared at him. "Is that an invitation, uncle?"

Vincent lifted one straight black brow. "I had not intended it as such, but I would be glad to oblige." A glowing sword appeared in his hand. "You appear a trifle . . . tense, nephew."

Jason choked back a sound that was half a groan, half a laugh. Tense didn't begin to describe the frustration he felt. His insides were in knots. His body ached. And Vincent, if not the direct cause, was at least partially to blame. "Being locked in a dungeon sometimes has that effect on me."

"Oh, really? Perhaps you should avoid such places in the future." Vincent raised his blade. "*En garde.*"

"Perhaps you are right." Jason saluted the ghost with his sword. As his blade touched Vincent's glowing rapier, he heard a slight buzzing sound. Accustomed to the noise, Jason ignored it and moved his sword to a high ward position, circling the point of his blade around Vincent's. "There's a matter I wish to speak to you about, uncle."

"Oh? Have you come to your senses and decided you want my help in getting rid of your fiancée after all?" Vincent made a quick forward thrust.

Taking a step to the left, Jason parried to the right. The swords met, the volume of the buzzing increasing. "Not exactly," he said with a cold smile. "I thought we agreed to let me handle Mary in my own way." He made his own thrust.

Vincent's parry was smoothly executed. "So we did."

Jason followed with a cutting attack from the outside. "I'm surprised you felt it necessary to make an appearance in the library yesterday afternoon, then."

Again, Vincent parried. "Ah, that was ill-timed of me. But purely unintentional, I assure you. I had merely intended to ask you if you wished to continue our chess game. Seeing your little fiancée was there, I left immediately."

Jason stepped back to wipe the sweat from his eyes. "How discreet of you. Your sensitivity astounds me." Moving back into range, he made a feinting motion with his left hand. "She said she had strange dreams the other night."

Vincent ignored the ploy. "I'm not surprised. The Blue Room is enough to give anyone nightmares. You should move her to another room."

"She said she dreamed about *you.*"

"Did she?" Vincent held his sword at an innocent angle, then made a swift circular motion with his wrist. "Well, don't be jealous, nephew. I can't help it if I'm the man of her dreams."

Vincent's blade slipped through Jason's guard and nicked his left hand. A shock of electricity coursed up Jason's arm, and a red, burnlike spot appeared on the back of his hand. Familiar with the sensation from previous bouts with Vincent, Jason did not withdraw or even wince.

"Very amusing," Jason said, watching for an opening. "And I suppose that wasn't you moaning and carrying on in the dungeon this morning."

"Must have been some other ghost concerned about your choice of a bride," Vincent agreed, circling casually to the left.

Jason narrowed his eyes and kept pace with Vincent's movements. "Whoever it was, then I can only assume that Mary passed the 'test.' She wasn't at all frightened by that theatrical moaning."

"Theatrical!" Unwarily, Vincent dropped the point of his sword.

Jason, his mouth curling upward, made no move to take advantage of Vincent's lowered guard.

Vincent's brows drew together. Without warning, he thrust his sword upward in a vicious, lethal move.

Jason beat the thrust inward, turned his hand, and made a reverse cut to the ghost's face.

Vincent's hand flew to his cheek, covering the dark line of the slice that had appeared in his aura. He stepped back, the glow around him flickering a bit. "So perhaps she isn't as fainthearted as she appears," he said coldly. "That still doesn't mean she's worthy of the Helsbury title. I have no doubt she is as greedy and grasping as all women are—"

The door to the fencing room opened. Jason, his sword still in a ward position, turned to see Beatrice standing in the doorway.

"Ah, there you are," she said, twirling a red ringlet around her finger. "Mother sent me to tell you that it's almost time for dinner."

"Thank you, Beatrice," Jason said politely, lowering

the point of his sword to the floor. "I will be along in a few minutes."

She did not take the hint and leave. Her gaze flickered over his chest, covered only by his linen shirt. "I hope you have recovered from your ordeal in the dungeon this morning."

"Yes, I have, thank you," Jason said curtly.

Beatrice gave a little trill of laughter. "But of course you have. You are a man. Ladies are more sensitive to these things."

"Mary has suffered no ill effects either, I assure you."

"Oh, but she is less . . . delicate than most ladies. She seems so . . . robust. I like her very much, of course. I am certain she will do well at the musicale tonight. I doubt anyone will guess her background." She hesitated, then said, "I don't mean to interfere, but I am concerned about a small matter. I spoke to Mrs. French when she delivered Mary's gowns today, and she told me that she was going to be making upward of ten dresses. I realize Mary probably doesn't understand how it looks for her to be accepting clothes from you before you are married—especially such an excessive amount—but I thought you should know."

"Ha!" Vincent said. "I knew it! She's spending your money like water. Ten dresses! She's even greedier than Elizabeth was."

Ignoring Vincent, Jason said to Beatrice, "Mary doesn't know about the additional dresses. In fact, you will be glad to hear, she refused to take them. They are to be a wedding present from me." Jason took her arm and escorted her to the door. "Now, if you will excuse me, I have a few things to finish up here. I will see you at dinner."

Ignoring her pouting face, he closed the door firmly behind her and turned to face Vincent once more. "Mary is not timid, nor is she greedy or grasping. She has more than passed your test. Now, leave her alone."

Vincent looked down at his sword. "As you wish," he said, his gaze on the blade.

Jason returned his rapier to the brackets on the wall and picked up his coat and waistcoat. "Thank you, uncle."

Vincent did not look up as the door closed softly. Idly, he drew his finger along the dark line in his cheek. The boy had defended himself well—and his fiancée too. But Jason was wrong when he said Mary had passed Vincent's test. The incident in the dungeon was not a fair measure.

He had been unpardonably clumsy this morning. Although he had been unable to avoid it, locking Jason in the cell with Mary had not been a good idea. Also, it had been a mistake to leave them while he hurried upstairs to slip the key off the housekeeper's ring. He wasn't quite sure what had happened in that dark cell while he was upstairs—although he could venture an excellent guess— but one thing was certain. Jason now seemed much more emphatic about his intention to wed Mary.

She was clever. More clever than he'd realized. The incident with the clothes proved that. By pretending not to want the dresses, she had no doubt induced Jason to buy even more. She obviously had Jason fooled into thinking she was two breaths away from sainthood.

Well, she hadn't fooled *him*. He knew that under that angelic surface she was exactly like all other women. She only needed a little prodding to make her show her true colors, and he knew just how to do it. After all, no woman was immune to the demon of jealousy.

He raised the sword and saluted an imaginary opponent. With a flourish, he made a thrust, confident that tonight at the musicale his new plan would enable him to slip through Miss Mary Goodwin's guard—and vanquish her once and for all.

11

Mary tapped on Aunt Sally's door.

"Come in!" Aunt Sally, lying in bed reading *Culpepper's Complete Herbal*, looked up as Mary entered. Her mouth fell open. "My dear, you look splendid!"

Mary held her arms a little away from her sides so she wouldn't crush the double-bouffante sleeves of the pink dress. "You don't think it's a bit . . . overwhelming on me?"

"Not at all," Aunt Sally said kindly. "Jason will be pleased."

Mary lowered her eyelashes, her heart suddenly beating against the tight cinching of her new corset. "You think so?"

"I am certain of it. Turn around and let me see the back."

She complied, and Aunt Sally oohed and aahed over the gown, but Mary's thoughts were elsewhere.

She was uneasy about facing Jason tonight. After what had happened in the Pit, she felt embarrassed and confused. She felt as though she no longer knew him. Before, he had always treated her with courtesy and respect—he had always been a gentleman. But this morning, in the darkness of the Pit, he had been a stranger. A sweet, seductive stranger, who had whispered entreatingly in her ear and touched gentle lips to hers. A compelling, sensual stranger, who had pushed his tongue into her mouth, pressed his leg against the ache between her thighs, and slipped his hand inside her dress to rub his thumb across the peak of her breast. . . .

Mary closed her eyes and tried to take a deep breath. Unfortunately, the corset prevented her. She forced herself to take small, even breaths until her racing pulse slowed.

"I believe you're ready to pass the gantlet, my dear."

Mary's eyes flew open and she stared at Jason's aunt. "The gantlet?"

"Yes, the gantlet. I'm certain Eugenia will have invited the most important and influential families in the district to the musicale tonight. I expect Sir Dudley, Lord and Lady Bosfield, and of course the duke of Stafford will all attend." Aunt Sally's gaze searched her face. "Are you nervous?"

Mary shrugged as nonchalantly as possible. "A trifle, I suppose. But my brother and his wife often entertained. I have attended many parties. I'm looking forward to this one," she lied. "Why don't you come, too? It will be fun."

The older woman averted her gaze. "No, it's impossible."

Mary sat on the edge of the bed and took the older woman's hands in hers. "Aunt Sally, I doubt anyone would hold a grudge against you this long. Even Vincent."

"You don't understand!" Tears brimmed in Aunt Sally's eyes. "I . . . I *planned* for them to meet."

Mary was confused. "You planned for whom to meet?"

"Vincent and Elizabeth, of course! She was my best friend, and he was my cousin." Aunt Sally's voice was wretched. "I thought they would be perfect for each other. So I contrived to invite Elizabeth to a party I knew Vincent would be attending. I was certain they would fall in love."

Mary tightened her clasp on Aunt Sally's hands. "But they didn't?"

"No. Oh, he paid all sorts of attentions to her, but she

was very cool toward him. She told me she thought he was very arrogant and in need of a set-down."

Mary frowned. "So she led him on, then married another man?"

"Well . . . it didn't happen exactly like that. At first, when he proposed to her, I thought everything had worked out as I planned. She seemed happy and excited. And so did he. He ordered her portrait painted, and she insisted he have one of himself done also. He took her portrait with him when he came to Helsbury House to prepare for her arrival and hung it in the dining room, saying he wanted to be able to look at her whenever he wished. He even had the Blue Room decorated for her— ebony and blue satin to match her hair and eyes."

"How romantic," Mary exclaimed involuntarily. "So what happened?"

"I'm not sure. I think they argued the night of the musicale, because after that she became very cool toward him again—even colder than before their engagement. She seemed to avoid him, and he was tense and angry all the time."

"And she broke the engagement?"

Aunt Sally nodded. "The night of the Helsbury masquerade. I've never seen him so furious. I thought his anger toward her would cool, but it didn't. The day he learned she was to marry Haversham, he ordered the portrait of her burned. He died that same night."

"How sad." It *was* a sad story. In spite of Aunt Sally's avowal that the Helsbury earls married only for convenience, Mary wondered if perhaps Vincent hadn't loved Elizabeth after all.

"So you see," Aunt Sally finished morosely, "Vincent has every reason to be angry at me, and I must stay in my room."

Looking into Aunt Sally's tearful brown eyes, Mary gripped the older woman's hands more tightly. "No, I don't see. Your part in the whole affair was minor. I'm sure if Vincent had lived, he would have forgiven you long ago."

Aunt Sally shook her head. "That's kind of you to say, Mary, but you don't know Vincent." Her gaze softened. "You're a sweet child. You'll be good for Jason. If the ghost doesn't frighten you off, that is. Has he tried?"

Mary couldn't help smiling. "No, Aunt Sally."

"Hmm. That's not like him. Well, before you go downstairs, I have something I want to lend you for tonight." She picked up the pink-and-white plumed fan resting on the table by her bed and handed it to Mary.

"Why, thank you!" Impulsively, Mary gave the older woman a hug. "I will take good care of it, I promise."

Aunt Sally dabbed at her eyes with a handkerchief. "You'd better run along now. You don't want to be late. Eugenia wouldn't like it, and you don't want to upset her."

Obediently, Mary left and went downstairs, plying the fan experimentally. She'd almost reached the bottom step when she noticed Jason, Beatrice, and Lady Weldon standing in the hall, staring at her.

Hastily, Mary closed the fan and looked at Jason, her heart thumping in her chest.

He looked remarkably handsome in his dark blue coat and snowy white waistcoat and cravat. His dark brown hair curled against his collar, and his gray-blue eyes met hers for a heart-stopping instant before sweeping over her new gown.

A faint frown creased his brow.

She paused on the bottom stair. "Is something wrong?"

"Where is your ring?"

His voice was harsh. Instinctively, Mary buried her gloved, ringless hand in the folds of her dress. "It's in my room. It wouldn't fit over my glove and it was too bulky to go underneath."

Beatrice, smiling as usual, intervened. "A ring can be awkward with gloves. It's better that you don't wear it. You look very nice, Mary. Although that dress is a trifle outdated. But I'm certain no one will notice."

Mary's fingers tightened on Aunt Sally's fan. But before

she could reply, Jason stepped forward. "I didn't notice." Bowing, he kissed her hand, his lips skimming the back of her glove. "You look lovely, Mary."

His manner was exquisitely polite now. Mary could almost believe that she'd imagined what had happened in the Pit this morning.

"Thank you, Jason. You look very handsome also."

He smiled at her reply and, relieved, she smiled back. She wished he would smile more often—when he smiled, he was the Jason she knew and loved. The Jason she trusted and felt comfortable with—

His expression altered, and he stared at her, his gaze dark and intent.

A memory floated through her brain of his urgent, pleading, demanding voice whispering, *Come here, Mary. . . .*

She glanced away, her corset suddenly feeling too tight again. A knock sounded at the door.

Lady Weldon marched forward. "Come along," she commanded. "The first guests have arrived."

"I'm sure you'll do fine," Beatrice said kindly. "You needn't be nervous."

Mary took a deep breath.

Jason glanced at her. "If you aren't sure what to do, watch Beatrice," he ordered. "She is familiar with all the ways of society."

Jason's advice did not make Mary feel better. She took her place in the receiving line, praying that she wouldn't make some terrible faux pas.

Please, God, she entreated silently, *don't let me do anything stupid.*

God must have heard her prayer, because over the next hour, as Mary greeted each guest, she didn't faint, she didn't lose her voice, and she didn't trip. But her spirits sank lower and lower as each new person arrived and the hall filled with people who were as well dressed as they were well born.

She had never met so many lords and ladies in her life.

In the past, she'd never been too awed by the aristocracy, but now she felt the silent assessment in their eyes, the weight of their expectations. She smiled and held her head high, but she felt like an impostor and was afraid everyone who looked at her knew it.

She was relieved when the receiving line broke up some time later. She didn't know which ached more—her face from smiling, her knees from curtsying, or her brain from trying to remember all the guests' names.

She was looking forward to sneaking a few moments' respite in the ladies' cloakroom, but before she could slip away, Jason took her arm and escorted her over to a small group that included Lord and Lady Bosfield, Cecil, Beatrice, and the duke of Stafford. Stout and bald as an egg, with jug-handled ears, the duke nodded to them, then continued pontificating on the evils of the proposed Reform Bill.

Mary listened with interest. Last year when the bill was first introduced, she had often discussed the issue with Jason. They had both been in complete agreement on its necessity.

"This bill is too radical, too far-reaching," the duke said. "No one knows what the consequences will be. It's not that I'm opposed to reform—it's just that we need to accomplish it in a careful fashion, considering every aspect of what the changes will mean. The people must be patient."

Lord and Lady Bosfield, both of whom had rather vacant expressions on their faces, nodded. "People must be patient," Lord Bosfield echoed.

Cecil, his silver-blonde hair set off by the dark blue of his coat, shook his head. "The people lost much of their patience when the House of Commons refused to do something about the East Retford situation."

Lord and Lady Bosfield looked confused, but Mary nodded her head in agreement. The corruption in East Retford was a disgrace. If the House of Commons had allowed representation to be transferred from there to Birmingham, all might have been well.

"The rights of all Englishmen will remain in jeopardy," Cecil continued, "so long as the rotten boroughs exist and seats in Parliament can be purchased."

"I don't deny that something has to be done about the rotten boroughs," the duke argued. "But if you study the system, you will see that it actually works very well and that all the major public interests are well represented in Parliament—law, commerce, banking, shipping and industry—"

"Everyone and everything except the agricultural laborers," Cecil remarked. "And many of them are starving."

"True, there have been cases of extreme hardship," Jason said, entering the fray, "but those are more often caused by crop failures and trade depressions than any piece of legislature. It is unrealistic to blame the government for matters beyond its control."

Mary stared at him in astonishment, unable to believe her ears. "Are you saying we should stand by and let people starve?" she blurted out. "Don't you think we have a moral duty to help those in need?"

Jason looked at her. "Yes, we have a moral duty. That is why we participate in philanthropic efforts and pay poor rates."

"But people still starve," Mary pointed out. "And they have no one to speak up for them."

Beatrice gave a tinkling laugh. "Except *you,* apparently."

Mary flushed a little. "Have I spoken out of place? I did not mean to do so. I only meant to express my concern for those who are often ignored or overlooked."

"La, how you do worry." Beatrice fluttered her eyelashes at Jason and the duke. "I have no head for politics, I'm afraid."

The duke smiled at her. "That's what makes you so charming, Lady Beatrice."

Mary's flush deepened.

Beatrice laughed. "You are such a flatterer, your grace.

I think I will dedicate the song I am singing tonight especially to you."

"Ah, it is *you* who are the flatterer, Lady Beatrice." The duke glanced at Mary. Apparently taking pity on her, he said kindly, "I am looking forward to your performance, also, Miss Goodwin."

"I will not be performing tonight, your grace," Mary said quietly.

"Mary is a trifle . . . shy about performing in public," Beatrice explained. "That is why I am taking her place."

Mary gave a strained smile. "Lady Beatrice is being kind. The truth is, I don't sing or play."

Lord and Lady Bosfield gasped as if she'd confessed she never wore drawers. The duke's bushy eyebrows rose to where his hair used to be, and Beatrice smiled. Jason frowned.

Cecil cleared his throat. "Ah, I see Mrs. St. Paul beckoning. Mary, will you accompany me?"

Jason's brows drew together as Mary nodded, but she was too upset to notice. Gratefully, she allowed Cecil to escort her away.

"Have I put myself beyond the pale?" she asked when they were some distance away.

Cecil laughed. "Not at all. There are many ladies who can't sing or play. It's only too bad more of them won't admit it instead of torturing us poor fellows."

Mary couldn't restrain a small smile, but she was still troubled. "Why did everyone stare at me when I talked about the Reform Bill?"

Cecil patted her hand. "You surprised them, that's all."

"But why? I didn't say anything so terrible, did I?"

"Of course not. They're just not used to young, beautiful women caring about anyone or anything except themselves. Debutantes are generally an empty-headed lot."

"But what about Jason? I could not believe my ears when he spoke against the bill."

"Jason doesn't oppose the bill. He is very logical, however, and likes to examine both sides of the issue."

"I see." Mary gave Cecil a strained smile. "Thank you for whisking me away before I made a complete fool of myself."

He looked at her with gentle hazel eyes. "There was no danger of that."

"You're very kind," she murmured. But in spite of his kindness, she still longed to escape the crowded hall. "Will you please excuse me? I would like to pay a visit to the cloakroom."

"Of course." He escorted her to the door of the small room set aside for the ladies' convenience, bowed, and departed. Mary went inside and glanced around.

To her relief, the room was empty. She sat on a stool and studied her face in the mirror. Her cheeks were a trifle pink, but otherwise, no sign of her inner turmoil showed.

Sighing, she stroked one of the soft plumes on her fan. She was more confused than ever. She didn't understand this new world she had blundered into. She didn't understand the people or the rules. She didn't understand Jason either. She didn't know what he was thinking or feeling. But even worse, she no longer understood herself. She was plagued by uncertainties and strange emotions she'd never experienced before. Everything seemed so complicated. She wished everything could just be simple again.

The door opened behind her. Mary leaned forward and pretended to smooth her hair. In the mirror, she saw a young girl enter, of perhaps seventeen or eighteen, with thick mahogany hair and blue eyes.

"Hello, Miss Goodwin," a pretty contralto voice said.

Mary turned, scanning her memory. Adams. Miss Cynthia Adams. Jason had introduced her as a distant relative, Mary recalled. "Hello, Miss Adams. Are you enjoying the party?"

"Oh, yes!" The girl sat down next to Mary and pulled several pins out of her reticule. Positioning a torn bit of lace on her skirt, she began to pin it in place. "Although it's a bit intimidating meeting so many grand people. My knees quaked when I was introduced to the duke," she mumbled around a mouthful of pins. "I wish I had your poise."

"My poise?" Mary repeated in astonishment.

"Yes, I saw you talking to him, and you looked so at ease. But in spite of the duke, I'm having a splendid time. So is Peregrine, and I didn't think he would. He doesn't like parties much."

Mary couldn't help smiling at the girl's candor. "Who is Peregrine?"

"Peregrine Benedict is my fiancé. Almost."

"Almost?"

Cynthia sighed and stuck another pin into place. "My parents won't allow us to become engaged until he has some means of supporting himself. He's trying to obtain a position with a shipping firm, but so far he hasn't had any luck. What he would *like* to do, though, is join the army. He wants to be a captain."

Mary eyed her curiously. "Would you like to be a soldier's wife?"

"Oh, yes. I think it would be very exciting. Even Mama and Papa said they would be willing to approve our marriage if he had a commission. Unfortunately, he can't afford the purchase price."

"So what will you do?"

Cynthia stuck the final pin into her hem. "Hope he finds a position at a shipping firm, I suppose." She rose to her feet. "I must return now. I'm sure Peregrine is becoming uncomfortable without me. I'm glad I had a chance to talk to you." With a cheerful smile, the girl left.

Mary waited a minute before following her. What a sweet girl. She wished she could help her.

She entered the hall, only to find it deserted. Surprised, she glanced around, wondering where everyone had gone.

"There you are!"

Mary turned to find Beatrice bearing down on her.

"Where have you been?" the other girl demanded. "The glove game is about to begin."

"I'm sorry," Mary said. "I was talking to Miss Adams and I lost track of the time."

"Miss Adams? Oh, yes, I remember—her mother claims that her grandfather was a cousin of the fourth earl's wife. Personally, I don't believe it. Mrs. Adams is nothing but a shopgirl." Beatrice's eyes widened, and she glanced at Mary. "Oh, dear. I did not mean to imply . . . please don't misunderstand."

"I didn't," Mary said stiffly. "I thought Miss Adams was charming. She is engaged to a Mr. Benedict."

"I've met him. His birth is respectable enough. But his family is as poor as church mice."

"If he had a commission in the army, he and Miss Adams could be married."

Beatrice looked bored. "Oh?"

"I was thinking of asking Jason to help them," Mary said impulsively.

"You cannot be serious."

"Why not?"

"Jason is inundated with requests from charity cases who claim some form of kinship. If he sets a precedent, it will be doubly difficult for him to refuse the next request." Beatrice paused by the door of the music room. "Ah, here we are. Oh, good, Mama hasn't started yet."

The music room was crowded. Mary sat in the last row. Beatrice sat next to her. A moment later, Cynthia slipped into the seat on the other side of Beatrice.

"Hullo!" the girl whispered to Mary. Her smile fading a bit, she said, "Good evening, Lady Beatrice."

Beatrice nodded coolly.

At the front of the room, Lady Weldon cleared her throat. "As most of you know, it's a tradition that we play a special game at the Helsbury musicale. It's been over twenty-five years since we last played this game, but I am sure some of you here remember it. The rules are simple. First, a servant will come around with a tray and all the ladies must put one of their gloves on it. The servant will then summon the gentlemen from the library and take the tray around to them. Each must put his card on one of the gloves. Then, we will all listen to the performances of our talented young ladies. After the music, each of the ladies will retrieve her glove and the card. The lady may then ask whatever favor she wishes of the gentleman whose card she holds."

A great deal of giggling and laughing ensued as the ladies stripped off one of their gloves and laid them on the tray.

"If my husband chooses my glove—and he'd better— I'm going to demand that he rub my feet," Mrs. St. Paul announced.

"I'm going to insist that mine buys me a new bonnet," Lady Bosfield said.

When the servant reached the last row, Cynthia placed her glove on the tray. "I think I will make Peregrine take me to the theater. He hates the theater."

"What if he doesn't choose your glove?" Mary teased.

"He will," Cynthia said with utter conviction. "He loves me very much."

Mary's smile faltered a bit. She wished she felt as certain of Jason's love. She wished she didn't feel so confused whenever she was with him.

Beatrice stripped off her glove and placed it next to Cynthia's. "What will you ask for, Mary?"

"I thought perhaps a dance at the masquerade ball," Mary said. There was a buzz of voices as the gentlemen entered and stood along the wall at the back of the room. Hastily, Mary put her elbow-length glove at the end of the tray.

"How unimaginative of you," Beatrice whispered as Lady Barbara and Miss Bruce took their respective places at the pianoforte and the front of the room. "I feel sorry for the poor gentleman who receives such a dull request." A smile curled her lips. "I plan to make the gentleman who chooses my glove be my servant for a day. I will order him to take me on a picnic to a very secluded spot I know where he will have to do whatever I wish. I know which gentleman I want, too."

Mary turned, following Beatrice's gaze to the back of the room. There, leaning against the wall, stood Jason.

Mary stiffened. Surely Beatrice didn't mean—

Lady Barbara brought her hands down on the pianoforte in a crash of chords. Miss Bruce opened her mouth and sang.

The music was beautiful. The ladies all sighed. Even the gentlemen stopped fidgeting to listen.

And Mary, pasting a smile on her face, tried to listen as well, doing her best to ignore the suspicion that had suddenly reared its ugly head.

Vincent, hovering in the shadows at the back of the music room, stared at the servant walking out with the tray, not really seeing him. He was fighting a tide of memories, memories that he didn't want to remember.

He should have stayed away. He should have known how the evening would affect him. Twenty-five years had passed since the musicale for Elizabeth and him, but in some bizarre way, as he looked at the assembled crowd, nothing seemed to have changed.

Oh, the ladies' dresses were full and fussy instead of slim and classical, and their hair was arranged in long, tortuous braids instead of short, simple curls. The men wore trousers instead of breeches, and they had odd little tufts of hair on their chins or whiskers that circled the lower halves of their faces instead of being clean-shaven. But the smiling faces, the gossiping, the laughter, even the conversations had changed very little. Everything was the same—the gathering of friends and neighbors, the music, and, of course, the glove game.

At that long-ago party, he had watched so that he would be able to pick out Elizabeth's glove. And when the servant brought the trayful of gloves to the waiting circle of men, he'd known instantly which one was Elizabeth's. He'd waited impatiently as the servant moved slowly around the circle, anticipating putting his card on the small pale ivory glove with pearl buttons.

So it had been something of a shock when Haversham—Haversham!—put his card on Elizabeth's glove. Vincent's shock had given way to white-hot fury. Fixing the other man with a lethal gaze, he'd advised him to move his card or step up to the fencing room. Haversham, the cowardly fop, had grown pale and complied immediately.

Vincent had still been simmering at the end of the game when Elizabeth whispered in his ear the "favor" she wanted of him—a kiss.

His anger had been forgotten. He tried several times to maneuver her into a secluded place. But eager, friendly, incredibly *stupid* guests obstructed him time and time again. He went to his room that night, angry, frustrated, and swearing to discontinue the tradition of the musicale.

Only, after he'd reached his room, he heard a small tapping at his door. And when he opened it, there stood Elizabeth, smiling, blushing a little, looking up at him with those beautiful blue eyes, asking, "Don't you want your kiss?"

He had drawn her into his room and kissed her. And the kiss had gone on and on. And on—

Applause broke out, startling Vincent from his reverie. Glancing at the front of the room, he saw that Miss Bruce had finished her song. Smiling and blushing, she returned to her seat and Miss Adams took her place. She began a song even more poignant than Miss Bruce's.

Vincent muttered an oath. He could not allow these maudlin memories to distract him from his purpose. He had to pay attention to business, to the task of ridding Helsbury House of Miss Mary Goodwin's presence. Otherwise, the legacy of a woman inflicting pain on a Helsbury earl would continue—and Jason would be the newest victim.

Turning away from the assembly, he forced himself to concentrate on his plan.

He had decided last night that the glove game would be the perfect opportunity to make Mary jealous. After overhearing the little conversation between her and Beatrice, he knew that his plan would work even better than he had hoped.

Closing his mind—and his heart—to the music, he smiled unpleasantly and floated out into the hall.

12

In the hall, Vincent found the tray on a table between two marble pillars. A servant—a youth in full scarlet and gold livery and a powdered wig—stood in front of one of the pillars, his spine rigid, arms held stiffly at his sides. Vincent frowned a little when he saw him, then shrugged. The servant's presence was a nuisance, but nothing more. Positioning himself in front of the other pillar, Vincent turned his attention to the tray.

The gloves were a variety of styles and colors and sizes. Some were black lace, some were worked with gold, some had a fringe below the elbow. Most of the young ladies had worn plain white gloves, however, which were not easily distinguishable from one another. Fortunately, he had seen Mary put her glove at the end of the tray—right next to Beatrice's.

The cards were face down on the gloves. Vincent motioned with his hand, and the card on Mary's flipped over. He wasn't surprised to see Jason's name. He had seen Jason unerringly place his card on the glove without so much as a hint from anyone.

The servant glanced over and stared at the upturned card on Mary's glove. Frowning, he stepped over and returned the card to its proper position, then resumed his place, once again standing at rigid attention.

Vincent glanced at him thoughtfully, then turned his gaze back to the tray and concentrated. The card on

Mary's glove rose and switched places with the one on the glove next to it. Vincent smiled in satisfaction.

The servant's bewigged head swiveled around and he stared at the now-still cards. Shaking his head, he faced forward again.

The door to the music room opened, allowing the rippling notes of a harp to float into the hall. Beatrice came out, fanning herself. She looked around the room, then casually walked over to the servant.

"Hello, Kendall," she said, smiling prettily.

Kendall gaped. Then a violent surge of color rushed to his face. "G-good evening, my lady."

It was probably the first time Beatrice had ever deigned to address a servant by name, Vincent thought sardonically.

"I'm so glad you're here." She closed her fan and tapped Kendall's arm with it. "Lord Helsbury told me that he was worried he might have chosen the wrong glove. It would be terrible if he did."

"You needn't worry, my lady," Kendall said, his prominent Adam's apple bobbing above his tight collar. "Lord Helsbury picked Miss Goodwin's glove all right 'n' tight. I saw him myself."

"Ah, excellent, Kendall. I suppose I should return to the music room now . . . oh!"

The exclamation flew from her mouth as her fan slipped through her fingers.

"Please, my lady, allow me!" Kendall dropped to his knees.

Quick as a wink, Beatrice switched the cards on the two gloves at the end of the tray.

Kendall stood up, the fan in his hands. "Thank you, Kendall," she said, smiling, then strolled back to the music room.

Vincent had to laugh at her performance. The little minx! He could have saved his efforts. He should have known she would pull a stunt like this. She was quite the schemer.

Swiftly, while the servant stared after her with a moon-struck expression, Vincent switched the cards again.

No sooner had he done so than the door to the music room opened and Cecil came out, a frown on his narrow face. He stopped by the table. "I say, Kendall, didn't I see Lady Beatrice come out here?"

"Yes, Mr. Parsell." Kendall's head bobbed along with his Adam's apple. "She wanted to make sure that his lordship had chosen Miss Goodwin's glove."

"Oh, did she?" Cecil turned slightly away, and Vincent heard him say softly under his breath, "Not bloody likely."

Kendall pointed to the small white glove at the end of the tray. "I told Lady Beatrice that I saw Lord Helsbury put his card there myself."

"I see," Cecil said. "Well, I'm glad to hear it." He glanced at the servant. "Oh, by the way, Kendall, you'd better check your wig in the mirror. It's a trifle askew."

Kendall grew pale and his hands flew to his wig. "Thank you for telling me, Mr. Parsell. Lady Weldon would skewer me if she saw my wig on crooked." He hurried over to the mirror hanging on the opposite wall.

Cecil quickly checked the names on the cards at the end of the tray. "Ha, I knew it," he muttered. He moved them back to their original positions.

The servant returned, and Cecil glanced at the wig. "Much better, Kendall. I suppose I'd better return now, before Lady Weldon catches me dodging the harp play-ing."

He sauntered back into the music room.

Vincent scowled after him, before turning to the tray. He could feel that his energy had diminished a bit—not enough to matter, but enough for him to be annoyed to have to switch the cards again. He concentrated. It was a little more difficult this time, but the cards moved easily enough.

Kendall's head whipped around.

He was still staring at the cards when the door opened

again, and Lady Weldon came out. She walked directly over to the servant. "Ah, Kendall, there you are. Is everything well?"

The servant dragged his gaze away from the cards. "Yes, my lady."

"Excellent, excellent." Lady Weldon glanced at the tray. "Tell me, do you know which glove my nephew chose? It would be quite embarrassing if he chose someone besides Miss Goodwin."

"You needn't worry, my lady. He chose the correct glove."

"Did he?" Lady Weldon smiled thinly. "How fortunate." Her sharp brown eyes inspected the servant. He almost trembled under her gaze. Apparently satisfied that nothing was amiss with his appearance, she said, "Please bring a tray of lemonade to the music room. Make certain that you offer some to Mrs. St. Paul. She has been imbibing a little too freely of the wine."

"Yes, my lady." Visibly relieved, Kendall bowed and hastened away. As soon as he was out of sight, Lady Weldon moved to the tray and began peeking at the names on the cards.

Vincent watched with trepidation.

She had started at the opposite end of the tray from where Mary's and Beatrice's gloves were. Methodically, she looked at the name on each card, then replaced it, until she reached a card in the middle of the tray. With a grunt of satisfaction, she quickly switched it with the one on a large gray glove.

Vincent breathed a sigh of relief. Thank heaven she hadn't—

From behind her, the music room door opened. Applause could be heard from inside. She stiffened, then hastily switched the two cards at the end of the tray.

Quimby's voice interrupted Vincent's long, vicious string of oaths. "Ah, there you are, Lady Weldon!"

Lady Weldon turned and smiled coldly. "Good evening, Mr. Quimby. Is there a problem?"

"No, not at all. I only wanted to congratulate you on a wonderful party. I am most impressed, most impressed!" The vicar beamed. With his round cheeks, tufts of white hair, and the ever-present Bible tucked under his arm, he looked like an elderly cherub.

"I enjoyed Miss Sanders's harp-playing tremendously," Quimby continued. "Such attention to phrasing and tone and voice! Her mischords were hardly noticeable. And Miss Adams! What finesse! Her singing is amazingly evocative. It's difficult to believe that this is only her second public performance, don't you agree?"

The vicar continued to ramble on and Vincent gritted his teeth. If Quimby enjoyed the music so much, why didn't he return to the music room and listen to it?

"Miss Bruce is quite exceptional also. . . ."

Vincent began to wonder if the music would finish before the vicar. He glanced from Quimby to Lady Weldon. She stood by the table, Quimby in front of her, blocking her view of the music room. And also blocking Quimby's view of the tray.

Vincent straightened. He glanced at the two mortals once more, before looking at the tray. He concentrated, trying to focus so that instead of arching up in the air, the cards would move quickly and low against the tray. It was a tricky maneuver, and he could definitely feel the strain this time. He concentrated harder, and the two cards switched.

"And Lady Barbara! I've heard her play many times before. What a repertoire! A true virtuoso! But I must confess, the one I'm looking forward to the most is Lady Beatrice."

"Beatrice will be delighted to hear that, Mr. Quimby," Lady Weldon said frostily. "Now if you will excuse me, I must return to the guests."

She brushed by him and entered the music room.

Quimby stared after her, looking rather surprised. He frowned, glanced at the tray, then peered after Lady Weldon again. Moving over to the tray, he glanced quickly about, then picked up the card on Beatrice's glove.

"By George!" he exclaimed. He peeked at the card to the right, then the one to the left. "Aha!" Quickly, he exchanged the two cards.

Vincent clenched his fists.

Quimby stepped away, then hesitated. He turned back and picked up Beatrice's glove. Pressing it to his face, he inhaled deeply and sighed rapturously. He replaced the glove and hurried back to the music room.

Vincent glared after him. The lovesick old fool! He stalked over to the tray and stared at the card on Mary's glove.

It didn't move.

Hell and damnation!

Taking a deep breath, he held out his hands and focused. He imagined beams of light going from his fingers to the gloves. With agonizing slowness, the two cards rose in the air. Carefully, painstakingly, not even breathing, he directed them past each other. He exhaled on a sigh of relief.

As Jason's card floated down on Beatrice's glove, the music room door opened again. Lowering his hands, Vincent glanced over, and saw Jason gazing at the settling card. Then he looked up and stared hard at Vincent.

Vincent hastily arranged his features in an expression of blank innocence.

Jason closed the door quietly and crossed his arms over his chest. "You decided to attend the musicale, uncle?"

Vincent pulled out his snuffbox. "A ghost's life is dull—what else is there for me to do?"

"You could devote yourself to prayer—and ask God to forgive you for your sins."

Vincent took a pinch of snuff. "It would take decades of prayer to accomplish that. What are you doing out here, nephew? Does the music not agree with you?"

"It's very fine." Jason strolled forward until he was standing by the table. Casually, he rested a hand on it—

right next to the tray of gloves. "Why don't you go in and listen?"

"Perhaps I will. Will you join me?"

"I prefer to remain out here for a moment. Lady Beatrice's high notes can be a bit shrill at times."

"Then I shall eschew her performance. My ears are very sensitive."

The two men stared at each other, their gazes unwavering.

The door at the other end of the hall opened, and Kendall entered with the tray of lemonade. He paused when he saw Jason. "My lord, is something wrong?"

"Not at all, Kendall," Jason said. "I needed a respite from the music."

The servant nodded and continued forward, passing close by Jason. At an inopportune moment, Jason turned, somehow knocking against the tray. It crashed to the floor, glass and lemonade flying everywhere.

"Oh, my lord, I am so sorry!" Kendall exclaimed. "I don't know how I came to be so clumsy."

Vincent looked up from the mess on the floor, a half smile on his lips, just in time to see Jason lowering his hand to his side. Vincent's eyes narrowed.

Jason casually brushed a spot of lemonade from his trousers. "It wasn't your fault, Kendall." From inside the music room a burst of applause rang out. "Hmm. It would appear the music is over. I will ring for a maid to clean up this mess so that you may take the tray of gloves into the music room."

"Very well, my lord." Kendall picked up the tray.

Jason nodded and strode over to the bellpull.

Vincent stared after him thoughtfully, then followed the servant as he walked toward the music room. Looking over Kendall's shoulder, Vincent studied the gloves.

The card on Beatrice's was on the wrist of the glove. Before it had been on the palm.

Vincent cursed. He glanced at Kendall and saw the servant was watching the tray with an eagle eye as he opened the music room door. Vincent cursed again, but he knew there was no help for it. He concentrated and focused, drawing on all his reserves. The last vestiges of his energy gathered, and without pause he released it. The cards switched places.

In the doorway of the music room, Kendall froze, staring down at the tray, all color draining from his face.

At the front of the room, Lady Weldon faced the crowd, smiling. "And now it's time for the ladies to retrieve their gloves. Kendall, bring the tray up here, please. Kendall? Kendall!"

Pale and shaking, Kendall tottered a step forward, set the tray on a table by the door, and bolted from the room.

Smiling, Vincent lounged against the back wall as Lady Weldon swelled like a bullfrog.

"Well!" she huffed.

A murmur floated through the room.

Mary rose to her feet and walked over to the door, staring after the servant with a worried expression on her face. She shut the door, then turned to the tray.

Grinning with satisfaction, Vincent watched her, wondering if Jason's apparent choice of Beatrice would make Mary break off the engagement. He glanced at Beatrice. The girl was gazing at Jason, a smug look on her face.

Vincent laughed softly. Of course Mary would break off the engagement. No woman could tolerate the insult of her fiancé's choosing another—especially not when that other was the beauteous Beatrice.

His gaze flickered back to Mary as she picked up the tray and carried it over to the servant who stood by Lady Weldon, then resumed her seat at the back of the room. She sat there, looking so unsuspecting, so unaware of the humiliation she was about to experience, that Vincent actually felt sorry for her. But it was truly for the best, he told himself. She was way out of her depth in these circles. Once she broke off her engagement to Jason, she could find a nice stolid banker whom she could marry and have a dozen children with. Really, he was doing her a favor.

His conscience clear, he leaned back against the wall and prepared to enjoy his victory.

Great bursts of laughter rang through the room as each lady picked up her glove and the card thereon. Mrs. St. Paul, who had definitely partaken a bit too freely of the wine, kicked off her huge slippers and demanded that her husband rub her feet right then and there.

Lady Weldon smiled coyly as she picked up her large gray glove. "Let us see which gentleman will be doing a favor for me. Why, it's the duke of Stafford!"

Finally, the servant moved to the back row. There were only four gloves left on the tray. Vincent glanced at Jason, who stood at the side of the room. As if sensing his gaze, Jason turned and met Vincent's stare.

Vincent smiled.

The corner of Jason's mouth curled upward, and a mocking gleam entered his eyes.

Vincent laughed inwardly. The boy had no idea that Vincent had guessed what he had done.

Miss Bruce picked up her glove. "Mr. Cecil Parsell! How wonderful. I wish you to teach me to drive your curricle."

Cecil groaned, and everyone laughed.

Vincent smiled absently. Jason had made a fatal mistake in turning his back to ring the bell. If Vincent had been in his place, he would have carried the tray into the music room himself. Foolish of the boy. Uncharacteristically foolish, actually.

A sudden suspicion rose in Vincent's breast. He watched tensely as the last three ladies picked up their gloves. Smiling, Beatrice announced, "I will be asking a very special and very private favor of—" She glanced at the card. Her smile froze.

Quimby looked over her shoulder. "Ah, I see I'm the lucky fellow, Lady Beatrice! I cannot wait to hear what this very special favor is. I will, of course, be delighted to do whatever you ask of me."

Vincent stared at Quimby, then turned his disbelieving gaze to Jason. Jason laughed.

The rest of the room laughed, too, giggling and chuckling over the odd match of Quimby and Lady Beatrice.

Vincent glared at Jason. So the cub had outwitted him after all—

Cynthia Adams smiled at Peregrine Benedict and looked down at her card. She gasped, her smile fading. "Lord Helsbury!"

It was Jason's turn to freeze.

Gasps rose throughout the room.

Jason looked at the girl, then at Mary, who was smiling widely.

Peregrine stepped forward furiously. "That can't be! I am certain I—"

Mary put her hand on his arm, stopping his impetuous words. "Ah, I see I have your card, Mr. Benedict. I would very much like to have a dance at the masquerade ball." She turned to Cynthia. "What will you ask of Helsbury?"

"I don't know," she mumbled, looking perfectly wretched.

"I think a captain's commission for Mr. Benedict would be a good idea."

Cynthia's eyes widened. "Oh, no, I couldn't!" She glanced at Jason, hope dawning in her eyes. "Could I?"

"Of course you could," Mary encouraged her.

Jason, who had been watching Mary with an inscrutable expression on his face, turned to Cynthia and bowed deeply. "I would be delighted to purchase a commission for Mr. Benedict."

With much laughter, everyone settled in their seats again to listen to Lady Barbara give an encore. Liquid notes rolled from the pianoforte out over the room, and everyone grew quiet, but Vincent barely heard the exquisite music.

He could not quite believe what had happened. The

outcome had not been what he wished. But then, neither
had it been what Jason wanted.

Suddenly, he laughed. "A draw, definitely a draw," he
murmured. He took a pinch of snuff, still smiling. Miss
Mary Goodwin had surprised him. It wasn't often that a
woman could surprise him.

It was a shame—almost—that she must be made to
leave.

But leave she must.

He glanced at her sitting in the front row. He expected
to see her cheerful and victorious, but instead her forehead was slightly wrinkled as she gazed at Beatrice standing next to Jason, her hand resting upon his arm.

Ahh.

So the evening hadn't been a complete failure after all.
A seed of doubt had been planted. Tomorrow, with a little
encouragement, he should be able to coax it into sprout-
ing quite nicely.

Quite nicely indeed.

13

Mary tossed and turned in her bed that night, and a question twisted and turned in her brain. She woke the next morning with heavy eyes and a knot in her stomach, no closer to an answer than she had been the night before. Burying her face in her pillow, she tried not to think about it, but it was no use.

What was between Jason and Beatrice?

She supposed she should have wondered about them before—Beatrice was very lovely and had lived under the same roof with Jason for almost a year. But Mary had always been so sure of Jason's love. And she still was. He couldn't have fallen in love with someone else.

At least, not the Jason she knew.

Restlessly, she rose from the bed and went over to the window. It was a bright, sunny day, and looking out, she saw the preparations for the breakfast were under way. Four menservants were struggling with a scarlet-and-gold canopy that appeared to be on the verge of collapsing. Under another canopy near the kitchens, a steady stream of maids loaded tables with covered dishes. And on a flat, grassy spot near the woods, Quimby directed a footman who was roping off an area for the fencing contest.

Mary turned away from the window. It was very odd to think of Jason entertaining on such a grand scale. But then, for a long time it had been odd for her to think of him as an earl. After meeting all of his august friends last night, it was no longer so odd. . . .

Mary pressed her hands to her temples. She desperately needed to distract herself from her thoughts.

Her glance fell on the pink ostrich-feather fan on her dressing table.

Aunt Sally. Mary picked up the fan. A visit to the older woman might be just the thing. . . .

A short while later, dressed in the lilac-trimmed dress and fingerless knit gloves, Mary entered Aunt Sally's room and found the older woman staring out the window.

Aunt Sally turned. "Good morning, dear. Are you ready for—why, good heavens! What happened to your dress?"

"I cut off most of the ribbons and bows." Mary glanced down at the denuded white gown. "Does it look terrible?"

"No, not at all. In fact, I think it's greatly improved. How clever of you, dear. The gentlemen will appreciate it, I'm sure." Her gaze strayed back to the window. "You will have a wonderful time at the breakfast."

Hearing the wistful note in the older woman's voice, Mary forgot about her own troubles. "You could come, too," she said gently.

"Oh, no. No, I couldn't. The breakfast will remind Vincent of how angry he is at me. At the last one, he glared at me every time I looked at him."

"How rude of him." Seeing the fear in Aunt Sally's eyes, Mary felt a spurt of anger. How had the cad dared to frighten this poor woman so? She wished he were still alive so she could give him a piece of her mind—

"I think he wanted to be alone with Elizabeth, but she insisted that I accompany her everywhere she went that day."

"That wasn't your fault. Vincent has no reason to be angry at you. Please come, Aunt Sally." Mary placed her hand on the older woman's arm.

Shaking her head, Aunt Sally started to pat Mary's

hand, then stopped, gasping. "Good heavens! What is that ring you're wearing?"

"It's the Helsbury ring." Mary glanced down at it. "Jason gave it to me."

"How extraordinary." Aunt Sally appeared thunderstruck.

Mary frowned. "I thought all the Helsbury fiancées wore this ring."

"No, no, my dear. Traditionally, the earl gives it to his bride after their wedding night."

"Oh? Well, I suppose Jason must have decided not to wait."

"Perhaps, but I think there was another reason. Mary, don't you see?" Aunt Sally's eyes sparkled. "Jason gave you the ring to send a message to Vincent! So that the ghost wouldn't try to frighten you away."

Mary, at a loss how to respond to this flight of fancy, smiled weakly. "You think so?"

"Yes, of course. I'm sure of it." Aunt Sally paused. "Unless he was sending a message to Eugenia." Picking up a small pair of scissors, she snipped a dead leaf off her valerian plant. "Either way, Jason has shown how much he honors you. What did everyone say when they saw it last night at the musicale?"

"I didn't wear it. It wouldn't fit under my glove." Remembering the fan she was carrying, she set it on a table. "Thank you for lending me your fan."

Aunt Sally waved her scissors, dismissing Mary's thanks. "It's a shame you weren't wearing the ring. Everyone would have been most impressed." She cut off another dead leaf. "Did you enjoy the musicale?"

"Yes, of course. It was very pleasant," Mary lied.

Aunt Sally didn't appear to notice. "That's nice. What favor did you ask of Jason?"

"None. That is, Jason didn't choose my glove."

"He didn't! Oh, you poor girl!" Aunt Sally's face was full of sympathy. "How embarrassing for you."

"Oh, no!" Mary said. "I wasn't embarrassed. He chose

a Miss Cynthia Adams, which turned out to be a fortunate thing. She asked him to purchase a captain's commission for her fiancé. Now the two of them can be married. I'm very happy at how things turned out."

"Hmmph. That's very generous of you, but I would think . . . oh, well. I suppose it isn't important now. At least he didn't choose that Beatrice." Aunt Sally snipped off another leaf—a perfectly healthy leaf— then glanced out the window. "You'd better go, dear. There's a line of carriages coming up the drive. Jason must be wondering where you are."

Must he? Mary wondered, then immediately scolded herself silently. She kissed Aunt Sally's cheek and left, still admonishing herself for her suspicious thoughts. She was becoming irrational, she told herself as she walked down the corridor to the stairs. She had no reason to suspect Jason of anything. Or Beatrice either, really. The younger girl had probably been looking at someone else last night.

But even if Beatrice *had* been looking at Jason, Mary thought as she descended the stairs, that didn't mean Jason was interested in the younger girl. It was mean and suspicious of Mary to think otherwise. He probably thought of the younger girl as nothing more than a sister. . . .

Reaching the foot of the stairs, Mary glanced up and saw Jason and Beatrice standing near the doorway of the dining room across the hall. She stopped, staring at them. Jason, in his perfectly tailored forest green coat and buff-colored trousers, looked incredibly handsome. Beatrice, with her red hair and pale yellow dress, complemented his dark good looks beautifully.

For a moment, Mary's breath caught in her throat. Then, with a determined smile, she stepped forward to call out.

Suddenly, Jason stumbled forward and threw his arms around Beatrice.

"Oh, please, Jason!" Beatrice cried, flinging her arms around his neck and pressing against him. "We must control ourselves!"

Mary froze.

Jason, his mouth tight, glanced over his shoulder. As he did so, his gaze met Mary's.

She expected him to apologize. Or at least look guilty. But he didn't. Instead, he looked annoyed—angry even. And then his face smoothed out and even those emotions were gone. She couldn't read his expression at all.

He stepped away from Beatrice. As if nothing had happened, he said to Mary, "Shall we go outside? I believe the guests are arriving."

Barely noticing Beatrice slipping away with an odd little smile on her lips, Mary took his arm and allowed him to escort her outside, her emotions in a turmoil. He drew her to a group of people who had been at the musicale last night, and she greeted them perfunctorily, then fell silent, unable to concentrate on the conversation.

Dear heaven, what had happened between Jason and Beatrice? He had embraced her, right in the hall, and Beatrice . . . Beatrice had sounded so *agonized*.

Becoming aware that her hands were trembling, Mary tightened her grip on her parasol.

Perhaps there was some other explanation. But what?

She glanced sideways at Jason. He appeared perfectly composed, as if nothing out of the ordinary had occurred. Could he truly be so unmoved? She would think he would at least be worried enough about what she was thinking to offer some explanation.

But perhaps the explanation was one he couldn't give. Perhaps he had fallen in love with Beatrice—

No! She couldn't believe it. She *wouldn't* believe it. There must be some innocent explanation of what had occurred.

But then why didn't he tell her what it was?

Oh, it was insane to torment herself like this! The sensible thing to do would be to ask Jason. And she would. Calmly. Coolly. Rationally.

As soon as they were alone. . . .

Unfortunately, there was no sign of that happening

soon. She continued to fret as guests milled about the lawn, joining and leaving their group. The duke of Stafford stopped for a moment to report on the progress of the fencing contest. Peregrine Benedict and Cynthia Adams, on their way to the food tables, thanked Jason and her for their part in enabling the young man to purchase his commission. Mr. and Mrs. St. Paul wandered by, arguing over whether or not she had cheated at battledore and shuttlecock. Tenants and villagers waited to be introduced to Mary, and a man named Blevins asked to speak to Jason privately. Jason refused, and the man slunk away, leaving Mary and Jason alone, finally.

She was about to speak when a stout, red-faced man rushed up to Jason.

"Eh, good afternoon, your lordship! I just wanted to thank you for hosting this magnificent feast. And to thank you for inviting me and the missus. We are truly honored, and I wanted to make sure that I told you so. Your condescension is as deep as the ocean. Your consideration is as lofty as the sky. Your generosity is as vast as the desert—"

Mary, distracted from her worries, stared at the man in astonishment.

"Thank you, Trumball," Jason murmured. "Where is your wife? I haven't seen her."

Trumball hitched his trousers up over his protruding belly. "She's a bit shy, unfortunately. I told her it was only polite to thank you, but she wouldn't listen."

"I see. I hope you will convey my regards to her."

"Eh, of course I will! She will be honored and thrilled, I assure you. I'd better go tell her right away."

With a deep, flourishing bow that would have been suitable for the Sun King, Trumball waddled off.

" 'Condescension as deep as the ocean'?" Mary said, when Trumball was out of earshot.

Jason shifted his feet. "Trumball is sometimes a trifle effusive."

"A *trifle*? I've never met anyone before whose 'consideration is as lofty as the sky.'"

He looked at her suspiciously. "Mary . . . "

"Or whose 'generosity is as vast as a *desert*'—"

His lips twitched. "Mary, I'm warning you—"

She struggled to keep a straight face. "I had no idea you were so admired—"

"Jason! There you are!" a familiar voice interrupted.

Mary's teasing mood vanished. How could she have forgotten, even for a moment? She turned slowly to see Beatrice glide up to Jason and tuck her arm into his.

"When will it be your turn in the fencing contest?" the younger girl cooed. "I'm dying from anticipation."

"Not for another half hour or so," Jason said.

"You must accompany me to the food tables, then," Beatrice said with a beguiling smile. "I want to try the plovers' eggs. Mr. Quimby told me they are delicious."

Jason turned to Mary. "Mary?"

"I'm not hungry, thank you." In truth, watching Beatrice cling to Jason, Mary felt slightly ill. Averting her gaze, she saw Cecil approaching.

"Good morning!" he said, swinging a paddle through the air. "Would anyone be interested in a game of battledore and shuttlecock?"

"Cecil!" Mary restrained an urge to hug him, she was so glad to see him. "I would love to play!"

Beatrice sniffed. "Battledore and shuttlecock is a game for children and commoners. Besides, Jason and I were about to go eat."

"Oh?" Cecil tapped the paddle against his open palm. "Mary and I will have to play by ourselves, then. It's just as well. I never could beat Jason."

Jason, his narrowed gaze on Cecil's face, shrugged off Beatrice's clinging hold and took a step closer to Mary. "Actually, I wouldn't mind playing a game or two."

"Well, if Jason is going to play, I suppose I will, too," Beatrice said as they all walked toward a flat grassy field. "Shall we play partners?"

"An excellent idea," Jason said, glancing at Mary.

"The most skilled and the least must be partners to

make the game fair." Beatrice picked up a paddle from a basket at the edge of the field. "Mary, you are so strapping, you are bound to be better than I am. Since Jason is the best, he and I will have to play together."

Mary's enthusiasm suddenly dwindled.

"That means you're my partner, Mary." Cecil handed her a paddle. "Come on, we'll show them a thing or two."

Cecil's good humor restoring her spirits somewhat, Mary leaned her parasol against a stump and took her place on the field. She stood a little in front of Cecil, determined to enjoy herself.

Jason batted the shuttlecock, and it flew to a spot to the right of Mary. She ran over, but missed.

"Nice try, Mary," Cecil said.

Mary picked up the shuttlecock and lobbed it toward Jason. He hit it easily and it flew to the left of her. She dashed across the field, but missed again.

The third volley was the same.

Panting, she positioned herself in the middle of the field, determined not to miss another one.

The shuttlecock flew to her right. She sprinted in that direction and swung.

The shuttlecock sailed back through the air.

"I hit it!" she crowed.

Unfortunately, while she was standing there crowing, Jason hit the shuttlecock to the left. Mary ran back to hit it, only to collide headlong with Cecil.

Knocked off balance, she felt herself falling backward, just as a strong arm slid around her waist to steady her.

Laughing, Mary looked up at Cecil. "Thank you! You saved my dignity, if not the point."

Grinning, Cecil released her and made an elaborate bow. "No sacrifice is too great, if I may serve my lady."

A harsh voice interrupted their nonsense. "Shall we continue?" Jason asked, his face wintry.

Surprised by his tone, Mary nodded and took her position. Jason served and the shuttlecock whizzed toward her. She ran for it, but missed. A sheen of perspiration on her forehead and her heart hammering against the constriction of her stays, she glared at the shuttlecock.

Beatrice—calm, cool and immaculate—looked down her nose. "You are supposed to stand still, and let the gentlemen hit the shuttlecock."

Mary, her new corset squeezing her lungs, decided to follow the younger girl's advice. When the next shuttlecock came in Mary's direction, she didn't move. Cecil ran forward and lobbed it back to Jason.

Jason returned it with surprising fierceness.

The volley continued, the play becoming more and more intense. The shuttlecock flew faster and faster as the two men ran back and forth, battling to win the point. Finally, after almost a full minute of play, Cecil missed.

"You see," Beatrice smiled. "It's much easier this way."

Another volley began. The shuttlecock sailed back and forth over her head, and Mary watched it wistfully. Perhaps it was easier, but it wasn't as much fun.

"Mary," Beatrice said in a low voice, during another fierce volley, "I hope you don't think there is anything between Jason and me. We are just friends—nothing more."

Beatrice sounded so earnest, so sincere, it was impossible not to believe her. "Thank you, Beatrice. I appreciate your telling me."

Beatrice lowered her lashes and sighed in relief. "I am so glad. I was afraid that with your background you wouldn't understand that an earl is allowed certain . . . pleasures. And that it is your duty, as his wife, to overlook them. Not that Jason would—oh, dear, how I do jumble my words. Please forgive me."

Mary stared at her, unable to believe any longer that the girl's malice was unintentional. A slow, unaccustomed anger rose in her. She opened her mouth to say something—anything—when suddenly, she saw the shuttlecock flying straight at her.

Instinctively, she held up her paddle in front of her

face. The shuttlecock bounced off, shot through the air—and hit Beatrice right on the nose.

Screaming, Beatrice clapped her hands to her face.

Horrified, Mary hurried to the girl's side. Between Beatrice's fingers, Mary could see a tiny trickle of blood from her nose.

"Lady Beatrice! I'm so sorry!"

Tears running down her face, her eyes red and squinty, Beatrice screamed, "Get away from me, you—you commoner, you!"

Appalled, Mary stepped back, almost bumping into Cecil, who had approached from behind.

He clucked his tongue. "Be careful what you say, Beatrice. People are listening."

Beatrice abruptly stopped sobbing and glanced around at the crowd that had gathered, before looking at Jason. Her lower lip quivered. "I . . . I'm sorry, Jason. I didn't mean to call your fiancée names. The excruciating pain caused by Mary's vicious action made me speak without thinking."

"I'm sure Mary didn't intend to hit you," Jason said, his face impassive.

Before Beatrice could say anything else, Lady Weldon rushed up. "My dear child, what happened?"

"Mary hit me in the nose with the shuttlecock." She pressed a handkerchief to her nose and tears filled her eyes. "Oh, Mama, I may be disfigured for life!"

"There, there, my dear, come with me. I'm sure the housekeeper has something that will stop the bleeding." Her arm around Beatrice's shoulders, Lady Weldon started to lead her daughter away.

Mary touched Lady Weldon's sleeve. "Is there anything I can do to help?" she asked hesitantly.

Lady Weldon froze her with a single glance. "You've done quite enough already, thank you." She hustled Beatrice away.

Mary watched their retreating figures helplessly, feeling like a murderer. She never would have thought an innocent little shuttlecock could hurt anyone.

"Nice shot," Cecil whispered in her ear.

Choking back a horrified laugh, Mary opened her mouth to scold him, but before she could do so, Jason strode over and stepped between them.

"Cecil," he said, his voice cold, "isn't it about time for your turn in the ring?"

Cecil's brows rose. "Why, yes, I believe it is." Tossing his paddle in the basket, he turned back to Mary. "Thank you for being an excellent partner, Miss Goodwin."

He strolled off, whistling. Clutching her own paddle, Mary glanced at Jason.

He was glaring after Cecil, his lips a thin white line.

Mary, her emotions in a turmoil, asked a bit sharply, "Was it necessary to be so rude?"

"Yes, I believe it was. I protect what's mine."

Mary's mouth dropped open. "You call being horribly rude protecting me?"

He shrugged. "It is sometimes effective."

"Effective against what?" she asked indignantly. "What exactly are you protecting me from?"

He gave her a sardonic look. "Don't pretend you haven't noticed Cecil is becoming overly friendly."

"Overly friendly!" Outrage burned in her breast. But before she could find the words to express it, a hesitant voice interrupted.

"Your lordship?"

Mary turned and saw a man standing a short distance away, his hat in his hands. He had a drawn, melancholy face and stooped shoulders. She recognized him as the man who had approached Jason earlier—Blevins, she remembered.

"What is it, Blevins?" Jason asked impatiently.

The man made an awkward bow. "Begging your pardon, your lordship, but I was wondering if I could have a few words in private?"

"There's nothing to say."

Blevins drew himself up. "Yes, there is. I want to ask you one last time to give me that job at the mill. I swear I'll do a good job for you, your lordship."

"I'm sorry, Blevins, but your history speaks for itself." Jason pulled out his watch and glanced at it. "I must go. I was supposed to be at the ring for the fencing contest several minutes ago."

"Please wait, your lordship," the man pleaded. "I've changed—I swear I have. I won't ever touch a drop of the devil's brew again. I haven't this last six months and more—my wife will vouch for that. Please, I'm begging you to reconsider. I have two young girls—what will become of them if I can't find work?"

"You may inquire about positions for them with my aunt, Lady Weldon. But I expect you to be off my property by the end of the week." Jason snapped his watch closed and returned it to his pocket.

"You would take my girls away from me?"

"It would probably be for the best," Jason said cruelly.

Blevins turned pale. An expression of defeat crossed his features. His shoulders hunched, he shuffled away.

Mary stared after him, then looked at Jason, unable to believe what she had just heard. How could he be so cold, so heartless, in the face of such desperation?

A small boy ran up. "Your lordship! Your lordship! Everyone's waiting. You must come at once!"

"Jason," Mary said quietly, "I would like to talk to you."

He gave a curt nod. "I will be at your disposal after the fencing match." With a slight bow, he strode off toward the ring.

Mary retrieved her parasol and followed at a slower pace. A few minutes later, she arrived at the edge of the crowd. She couldn't see the ring itself, but she could hear the loud clang of steel striking steel. The spectators were laughing, placing wagers, and shouting encouragement to the combatants.

She squeezed through the mass of bodies until she reached the rope that formed the ring's boundary. She noticed Quimby sitting on a high seat, gnawing on a leg of mutton as he observed the contest. Every once in a while, he made a note in a small, leather-bound book.

Mary turned her attention to the ring. Jason and Cecil, in white padded vests and protective masks, circled each other, long, dangerous-looking swords in their hands. As she watched, Jason made a thrust. Cecil jumped back, avoiding the blade, but Jason immediately jabbed at him again. Cecil barely managed to block it. Jason's blow struck near the tip of Cecil's blade, causing Cecil's grip on the hilt to falter.

There was a clear opening for Jason to score his point and end the contest, but instead of doing so, he swung his blade around, allowing Cecil time to regain his grip. However, the force of Jason's new blow, with all the strength of his shoulder behind it, was stunning. Cecil parried gamely, but Mary could see the muscles in the smaller man's arm quivering with the effort.

The contest continued, Jason advancing mercilessly, Cecil parrying and retreating helplessly under the onslaught of Jason's thrusts. Against Jason's expertise, Cecil seemed almost clumsy. He simply couldn't match the skill and elegance of Jason's swordplay.

Mary clutched her parasol. Despite the protective gear they wore and the buttons on the tips of the swords, the contest looked exceedingly dangerous. She noticed two spectators with bloody bandages on their arms—apparently losers from earlier matches. She turned her gaze back to the ring. The swords moved quickly—impossibly, frighteningly quickly.

Suddenly, Cecil made a daring thrust at Jason. The deadly blade flashed toward Jason's chest.

The crowd gasped. For an endless moment, Mary's heart stopped beating and every muscle in her body froze.

Then, in a move quicker than she could follow, Jason stepped forward, blocking the blade and making his own thrust. His sword flickered out, tapped Cecil's chest, and withdrew.

"I concede!" Cecil lowered his sword and pulled off his mask. Laughing, he said, "You've convinced me never to challenge you to a duel."

Pulling his own mask off, Jason gazed unsmilingly at Cecil. "How wise of you, cousin."

Cecil paused, an arrested look on his face, but Mary didn't wait to hear the rest of the conversation. She turned and pushed her way through the crowd.

Once free, she hurried across the lawn to the edge of the trees bordering the lawn. She plunged down a path, going deeper and deeper into the forest until the sounds of the party had faded. She stopped, panting, her corset cutting into her side, looking for a place to sit down.

Hearing a murmur of water, she pushed through some bushes until she came to a small, grassy clearing by a shallow brook. She sank down beside it and put her parasol on her lap. She felt sick. She wanted to rest her head on her knees and catch her breath, but the rigid corset prevented her from bending or even from drawing in more than a thimbleful of oxygen. She wished she could take it off. It was uncomfortable, ugly, and barbaric. She hated it more than she'd ever hated anything in her life—

The underbrush rustled behind her.

Startled, she looked over her shoulder.

Cecil was pushing his way through the bushes. Reaching the edge of the clearing, he straightened. "Mary! Are you all right?"

She averted her gaze. "Yes, I'm fine."

She heard footsteps crossing to her side. From the corner of her eye, she saw him crouch down beside her. "Are you sure? I saw you leave the ring. You looked upset. Did something happen?"

Still refusing to look at him, she shook her head.

"Mary, we're friends, aren't we? Please tell me what's wrong."

"Nothing's wrong. Only . . . how *could* you play such a dangerous game?" she blurted out, glaring at him. "You could have killed Jason!"

Cecil stared at her in astonishment. "Is that what you're upset about?" His eyes began to twinkle. "There was little chance of that. The reverse was much more likely to be true, I assure you."

Cecil's words didn't make her feel much better. She still felt sick remembering that moment when she had thought Jason would be killed. What if he hadn't blocked the blade in time? Would the frail button on the tip of the sword have prevented injury? "I don't know why men must engage in such stupid sports," she muttered.

"We enjoy having pretty ladies worry over us."

Mary gave a reluctant smile. "I suppose you think I am being foolish."

Cecil seated himself on the grass, resting his elbow on one bent knee, the other leg stretched out before him. "Not at all."

"I feel foolish. This has been a terrible day." She looked down at a spider crawling across the grass. "Cecil . . . "

"Yes?"

Mary picked a blade of grass and poked at the spider, not looking at him. "Do you think there's anything between Jason and Beatrice?"

"Jason and Beatrice?" He sounded incredulous. "Good God, no!"

Mary glanced up. "You don't think Jason is attracted to her?"

"No, I don't," he said bluntly. "A man would have to be an idiot to find her attractive. She is the slyest, greediest, most cunning little troublemaker I have ever seen."

"She can't be that bad," Mary protested halfheartedly.

Cecil snorted. "That only shows how little you know her. She deserved that bloody nose, believe me."

"Please don't say that." Mary dropped the blade of grass. "I already feel terrible about hitting her with the shuttlecock."

Cecil muttered under his breath.

Mary frowned at him, but he only shrugged. "Why would you think Jason has any interest in Beatrice?" he asked.

"He seems to admire her very much." Mary looked

down at the spider again. "At the musicale, he said I should watch her if I wasn't sure how to behave—"

"He said *what?*"

Cecil sounded so aghast, Mary couldn't help smiling. "You're a good friend, Cecil. I'm glad you're here." Her smile dimmed. "I used to think Jason was my friend, but now I'm not sure any more. I don't understand him. He's changed."

"No, he hasn't." Cecil leaned toward her as if to emphasize what he was saying. "Not really. It's just this damned earldom that makes it seem so. He's still your friend. He needs you, Mary."

In spite of everything that had happened that day, she felt a spark of hope. "Do you truly think so?"

Cecil took her hand in his and nodded. "You're kind and generous, beautiful and compassionate. Why, any man would consider himself lucky to—"

"To what?" a cold voice enquired from behind them.

14

Mary looked up, startled. "Oh, it's you, Jason." She pulled her hand away from Cecil's and rose to her feet.

"Yes." He approached them. "Am I interrupting?"

"Not at all," Cecil said, rising also. "In fact, I'm glad you're here. I think Mary would like to talk to you."

"Oh, would she?" His voice had a cynical edge.

Mary stared at him, surprised by Cecil's words, but more by Jason's. From his hostile tone, one would think that *she* had done something wrong. She lifted her chin a little. "Yes, I would, actually."

"Fine. I want to talk to you, too."

"Ahem." Cecil, looking amused, brushed the grass off his trousers. "I can see my presence here is superfluous. I'd best return to the party." With a smile at Mary, he sauntered off.

Jason watched him go, then turned back to Mary. "Well?"

She lifted her chin higher. "Well?"

He moved closer so that he was looming over her. "I don't think it's appropriate behavior for you and Cecil to steal away into the woods."

Mary gasped. "I suppose it would have been better if we embraced in the dining room doorway."

Jason had the grace to flush, but his gaze did not waver. "The dining room doorway would have been better than the shuttlecock field, in full view of the entire county."

Mary gaped at him. "Are you insane? I bumped into Cecil during the course of the game. It was completely innocent."

"Nevertheless, I think it would be wise for you avoid him in the future."

Anger burned in Mary. "What do you want me to do? Stay in my room and never come out, like Aunt Sally?"

"Don't be ridiculous."

"I'm not being ridiculous. What's ridiculous is your unreasonable jealousy of Cecil."

"I am not jealous of Cecil," Jason snapped.

"Oh? What do you call it, then?"

"I call it . . ." He paused, and appeared to search for words. "I call it *reasonable* concern."

"I think you would be better off expending your concern on someone who needs it—like Aunt Sally."

"Aunt Sally!" He looked dumbfounded. "Why should I be concerned about Aunt Sally?"

"Because she is sad and lonely and virtually ignored by her family, that's why!"

He frowned. "She likes her solitude."

"You can't truly believe that."

"What do you want me to do? Force her from her room?"

"No, but you could try to help her. You could tell her that there is no ghost. She might believe you."

"I don't think it's my place to question her beliefs."

Mary, seeing the faint curve of his lips, glared at him. "How can you be so flippant? Why don't you do something to help her?"

"There is nothing I can do right now—"

"You are terrible! You are a cold, unfeeling man!"

His face hardened. "Because I won't tell Aunt Sally to leave her room?"

"Because of that, and because of that man—Blevins."

"Blevins!" Jason stared down at her in astonishment. "What does he have to do with anything?"

"He seemed so desperate." Mary shivered a little,

remembering the man's despair. "All he was asking for was a job. Couldn't you have given him one?"

"You don't understand, Mary. The man is a drunkard. He hasn't been able to keep any job due to his drinking."

"Can't you afford to give him a chance? There must be something he can do. Perhaps Mr. Quimby could keep an eye on him. I am sure a vicar could keep him on the straight and narrow path."

"I think you overestimate Quimby," Jason said dryly.

Mary waved her hand impatiently. "The point is that Mr. Blevins needs a job. What will he do if you won't give him one?"

"I have no idea."

She stared at him. "How can you be so uncaring?"

"What is it you want me to do, Mary? Buy him a commission, too? I have to do what I think is right."

"Is it right to deprive a man of his livelihood?"

"It is his own behavior that has brought on his problems. If he can show me that he will be responsible for himself, then I might reconsider."

"That's not what you told him. You told him to be off your property by the end of the week. You didn't care at all about him or his family."

Jason's jaw tightened. "Perhaps I care more about the safety and well-being of the other workers and their families."

"I don't believe you care about anyone but yourself," she said sharply. "I am beginning to think you are like all the others."

His brows drew together. "What others?"

"The duke and his ilk. A haughty, selfish aristocrat. With an overinflated opinion of himself." She turned away.

A hand seized her arm and swung her around. Gasping, she looked up to meet Jason's furious gaze. She glared at him. "Take your hands off—"

Before she could finish, he suddenly stumbled forward, falling hard against her and knocking her off balance. She fell back, and his arms encircled her waist as they plunged down, down, down—right into the shallow water on the bank of the brook.

Mary hit the ground with a thump that left her gasping for air.

Water splashed up, then rained down on her.

She squeezed her eyes closed as the droplets sprayed her face. She lay motionless, the breath knocked out of her by the fall.

A hand pushed her hair away from her face. "Mary! Oh my God, Mary! Are you all right?"

She didn't answer—she couldn't. Her new corset was making it difficult for her to draw in air.

"Mary! Can you hear me? Open your eyes, Mary."

She breathed in, and oxygen expanded her lungs. She became aware of an ache in her hip where a rock was pressing against it, and of the cold water lapping at her hair, and Jason's weight above her. Opening her eyes, she looked up at him.

"Mary! Thank God! Are you hurt?"

He was staring down at her, his eyes no longer cold with anger, but warm with concern. Mud was smeared across his cheek and dribbling down the side of his nose. His hair was caked with the gooey substance. His damp cravat sagged limply against his chest, and his once-pristine shirt was covered with brown splotches.

She blinked at his sodden, dripping, mud-streaked appearance. Her lips twitched.

"Mary?"

The sight of a blob of mud sliding down his chin was too much for her. She burst into laughter.

He scowled down at her. "What are you laughing at?"

"I . . . I'm sorry," she gasped. "It's just that you don't look at all like a . . . a haughty aristocrat anymore!"

"Don't I?" His arms tightened around her, the scowl disappearing, but Mary barely noticed, she was laughing so hard.

"I'm sorry," she said again, wiping the tears from her

eyes and trying to control herself. "I don't mean to laugh at you."

"I don't mind."

His voice sounded oddly husky, and Mary looked at him, her laughter fading.

"I like to hear you laugh," he said, his gaze on her mouth.

A warm flush spread over her. She became aware of the lengths of their bodies pressed tightly together. She tried to get up, but his weight prevented her.

"Mary . . . "

His mouth closed over hers. He pushed her back onto the bank, the wet, cool water lapping against her suddenly heated skin.

She tried to protest, but when her lips parted, his tongue slipped between and caressed the inside of her mouth. A hundred sweet sensations raced through her, flashing and sparkling through her blood.

His hand cupped her jaw, angling her head so that he could deepen the kiss. Pleasure snaked through her, and she curled her fingers into the soft mud of the riverbank.

She felt him undo the top few buttons at the front of her dress, laying her neck and throat bare. Still kissing her, he placed two mud-laden fingers against the hollow of her shoulder. The combination of the slow, circular movements of his fingers and the smooth texture of the mud sent a flaring, prickling heat across her skin. She moaned against his mouth in shock and protest. And pleasure. . . .

His fingers moved to her buttons again. With an incoherent murmur, she reached up and gripped his hand, stopping him.

His lips moved to her ear. "Mary," he whispered, "let me undo your dress."

"No, you mustn't." Her voice sounded odd, even to her own ears. "Jason, you mustn't."

"Yes, I must, Mary. I must." He kissed the corner of her mouth and her chin and her neck.

Her skin tingled everywhere his mouth touched. There was a buzzing in her ears. She couldn't seem to breathe, or think. A strange languor spread throughout her limbs, lulling her and pacifying her.

"Please, Mary." He kissed her mouth again, slowly, seductively, persuasively. "Let me touch your breasts."

Her hand tightened on his. She knew she should say no. But she couldn't think why. Her heart was pounding and her skin quivering at the thought of the slick mud and his warm fingers sliding across her breasts. She wanted to let him. She wanted to let him do whatever he wanted.

Her grip on his hand loosened. . . .

KA-BOOM!

Jason's fingers grew still on her buttons as the crack of the thunder echoed through the sky.

Another boom sounded. The sky turned strangely dark, and a cold wind whistled through the trees.

Jason raised his head. A third thunderclap rang out. He looked up at the black clouds boiling in the sky above them.

He gripped Mary's shoulders.

An instant later, a torrent of rain hurtled down like a tidal wave, drenching what few parts of them were still dry.

Cursing, Jason leapt to his feet, pulling Mary up with him.

She stood there a moment, swaying, blinking at him through the downpour. Then her hand crept up to her throat.

What had she been thinking? One minute, she had been standing on the riverbank, furiously angry and arguing with Jason. The next moment, she had been lying in the brook, breathless with passion, kissing him and letting him smear mud over her skin.

Mud!

Clasping her hands to her suddenly burning cheeks, she wrenched away from him.

"Mary . . ." he said, reaching out toward her.

But she didn't stop to listen. Eluding his grasp, she turned on her heel and ran across the clearing and through the bushes as if all the hounds of hell were after her.

Rain pouring down on him, Jason stared after her, then looked up at the sky.

Moments ago there had been bright sunshine and blue skies. Now, there was only a thick, dark blanket of black clouds. He shook his fist up at the heavens. "Damn you, Vincent!"

KA-BOOM! the sky replied.

With another curse, Jason strode after Mary.

He entered the house a few minutes later. Brushing by the huddled groups of drenched guests, he went into the dining room and slammed the door shut. Stopping in front of the portrait of Vincent, he glared up at it. "I wish to speak to you, uncle!" he snapped.

The painted eyes smiled down at him mockingly.

Long minutes passed. Water dripped from Jason's clothes onto the floor, forming a small pool around his feet, but there was no sign of life from the portrait. Still, Jason didn't move.

The door opened behind him. He turned to see a rain-soaked Cecil stroll into the room, a slight frown on his face. "There you are, Jason! I saw Mary bolt up the stairs a few minutes ago, looking very upset. Is everything all right? Is there anything I can do to help?"

"Yes, there is," Jason said icily. "You can mind your own business and leave Mary to me."

Cecil stiffened. "I beg your pardon."

"You heard me."

Cecil gave an incredulous, angry laugh. "Oh yes, I heard you. I just can't believe my ears. Don't be a fool, Jason."

Jason gave him a cold stare. "I hate to be rude, but it might be better for all concerned if you cut short your visit and returned to your own home."

"I'll leave—after your wedding. Until then, I'm staying right here. Mary might need a friend. One who isn't trying to change her into something she's not."

"What nonsense is this? I'm not trying to change her."

"Aren't you? You're a fool, cousin. A blind fool, too stupid to realize what you have." Cecil stormed out of the room.

Jason made no effort to stop him. His temper still raging, he glanced back at the portrait.

The mocking glint in Vincent's eyes seemed brighter.

Jason stepped closer, clenching his fists at his sides. In a low, menacing voice, he said, "Don't think to hide forever, uncle. I'll discuss this with you later." He strode out of the room.

Painted eyes watched him go, the mocking glint vanishing.

Frowning, Vincent stepped down from the portrait and lounged against the wall, more disturbed than he liked to admit by Jason's anger.

But perhaps he should have expected it—Jason's fury was only one more setback in a day of plans gone awry. It had started out not too badly—pushing Jason into Beatrice's arms just as Mary came down the stairs had been a masterstroke—but things had deteriorated from that point on.

His frown deepening, he tapped a finger on his snuffbox. Mary had not reacted quite the way he'd expected. Oh, she'd been angry, but over ridiculous, unimportant things. Even worse, she had somehow managed to end up at the one place on the estate that he least wanted to visit—the bank of the brook in the woods. The very place he'd drawn Elizabeth after finally managing to separate her from the crowd at the breakfast twenty-five years ago.

Vincent took a pinch of snuff and inhaled deeply.

He'd been half-insane with frustrated desire at the time—after giving him a taste of incredible pleasure the night of the musicale, Elizabeth had inexplicably turned into an ice maiden, avoiding him whenever possible. He

had been confused, alternately begging and demanding
that she explain. But she had only laughed, a cold, artificial laugh, and sent him away.

He'd been desperate when the day of the breakfast
arrived—desperate and hopeful. Surely he would be able
to lure her off to a secluded spot. And surely, once there,
he would be able to discover why she'd become so cold.

Only it hadn't worked out quite that way.

Once they were alone, he hadn't been able to keep
from kissing her. And once he kissed her, he hadn't been
able to keep from touching her, and caressing her, and
making love to her. . . .

In spite of her initial resistance, she had soon begun to
respond—passionately. More passionately than he could
have hoped for. Afterward, thinking that everything was
resolved between them, he'd told her he was going to purchase a special license and marry her the next day.

But to his shock, she had refused. She'd become even
colder than before, not speaking to him for an entire
month after that.

Vincent snapped his snuffbox closed and glared at the
vase of roses someone had put on the table. They withered
instantly. He hated roses. And he hated these damned
melancholy memories that made him aware of exactly
how weak, how powerless, he'd been. They made him
aware of something else, too.

He'd been wrong about Mary. She wasn't the greedy,
selfish woman he had thought. He remembered her pleading on behalf of Sally and Blevins. Then, when he'd pushed
them into the brook, she had laughed—laughed, when any
other woman would have been furious! Even when Jason
had kissed her, she had pleaded with him to stop.

Mary was different from Elizabeth. She was something
he'd had no experience of—something more dangerous
than he would have dreamed possible.

She was a *good* woman.

More than ever, he felt the urgency to come up with a
plan to make her leave.

It wouldn't be easy. She had proved that already. And a good woman would be more difficult to get rid of than a selfish, vain, or greedy one.

Difficult, yes. But not impossible. Especially not if he used her goodness against her.

Vincent stopped by a delicate china teapot resting on the sideboard, an unpleasant smile curling his lips.

If Miss Goody-Goody Goodwin knew what men were really like—what *Jason* was really like—she would be shocked.

Shocked right out of her prim flannel drawers. . . .

15

The next day was Sunday, and Jason, walking down the corridor, was glad. He was looking forward to going to church. He needed a day of peace. Especially after yesterday.

The breakfast had been an unmitigated disaster. It had started off badly, when Vincent had pushed him into Beatrice's clinging embrace. Fortunately, Jason had managed to counter the ghost by behaving as though nothing had happened. But he'd been less successful at keeping a level head when Cecil put his arms around Mary. He'd wanted to beat Cecil to a pulp. Or throttle him. Or run him through. Still, he'd been able to curb the impulses.

With Mary, however, he seemed unable to curb anything.

Turning into the corridor where the Blue Room was, he saw Aunt Sally's door was open. As he approached, he heard voices.

"Aunt Sally, isn't there anything I can do to convince you that this silly ghost doesn't exist?"

"Hush!" Reaching the open door, Jason saw Aunt Sally glance nervously around. "He might hear you!"

Jason frowned at the older woman's remark. Mary's words from yesterday echoed in his head. *Why don't you do something to help her?*

He shook off a niggling unease. He was working on the situation—there wasn't any more that he could do. Mary didn't realize everything that was involved. She should trust him.

"Surely a ghost couldn't do anything on Sunday at church?" he heard Mary ask his aunt. "It wouldn't dare."

Jason stepped into the room. Mary was sitting on a chair with her back to the door. His pulse quickened when he saw her.

"Vincent would dare anything," Aunt Sally said darkly. She glanced up and caught sight of Jason. "Good morning, Jason."

He was conscious of the way Mary's back stiffened. "Good morning, Aunt Sally. Good morning, Mary. Are you ready to go?"

She rose to her feet. "Yes, of course. I was just trying to convince Aunt Sally to come with us."

Jason looked at the older woman. "You're always welcome, you know that, Aunt Sally."

She smiled and shook her head. "I prefer to stay here. Give my regards to Cousin Horace."

Jason escorted Mary out into the corridor, then paused. "Mary . . ." He cleared his throat. "Mary, I'm sorry about yesterday."

She darted a quick glance at him. "Thank you, Jason."

"It won't happen again," he said.

Her lashes swept up, then down. "I'm glad to hear that. I accept your apology. Shall we go?"

Jason studied her a moment, wishing he knew what she was thinking. She looked pale this morning, as if she hadn't slept well. He hadn't slept well either. He'd tossed and turned all night, his groin aching, remembering how it had felt to kiss her and touch her. . . .

Stifling a groan, Jason offered Mary his arm.

A short while later, he was ensconced in the carriage with Mary, as well as Lady Weldon and Beatrice. Lady Weldon and Beatrice were both quiet, to Jason's relief. Yesterday, he'd spent the afternoon and evening listening to Beatrice cry about her injured nose and Aunt Weldon moan about the ruined breakfast and worry about whether the rain would play havoc with the masquerade and wedding also.

Fortunately, her fears appeared to have no foundation. The day was warm—so warm, he could feel his shirt clinging to his back under his coat. He glanced out the window at Cecil, who had announced earlier with a cold stare at Jason that he preferred to ride. Jason had felt a twinge of regret for their argument—but not enough to apologize. He didn't like the growing intimacy between Mary and Cecil. It was better to nip it in the bud now. After the wedding, he wouldn't have to worry about her friendship with his cousin. But until then, he preferred that Cecil keep his distance.

Jason returned his gaze to Mary's averted profile. She was wearing her old blue dress—her white one must still be wet, he realized. But he was beginning to like the blue gown—he'd always liked her in blue. The simplicity of the dress made Beatrice's puffs and feathers and bows look rather ridiculous.

He wondered what Mary was thinking. Although she had accepted his apology, he knew that his relationship with her was on shaky ground. She had been angry yesterday—angrier than he'd ever seen her. All because of the way he'd dealt with Aunt Sally and Cecil—and Blevins!

She didn't understand. She had no idea what it was like to be an earl. He sometimes had to make hard decisions, decisions that might seem cold and cruel, but he had reasons—reasons Mary didn't know. She didn't know that Blevins's drinking could endanger everyone in the mill, that his poor work habits made the other men resentful. He had to consider the interests of everyone—not just a single individual.

He could explain it to her, and she might understand—if Vincent would only stop making trouble. And if he, Jason, could only exercise some self-control. He was sure he could do so—if he didn't have to look at her too much. And if he didn't have to touch her. And if he didn't have to smell her sweet scent—

She shifted on the seat next to him, her leg brushing against his. His blood immediately rushed faster. Swallowing, he looked out the window. This was becoming dangerous. If he wasn't careful, Vincent would notice his weakness—and then the ghost would undoubtedly find a way to exploit it.

He had to be more careful. Attending church should help. What better way to turn his thoughts in a more pious direction than to listen to the word of God?

The carriage arrived at the church, and Jason spent the next several minutes greeting the people gathered out front and chatting about the sudden rainfall yesterday, while Mary stood quietly by his side. Inside, he escorted her to the front pew and seated her beside him. Lady Weldon, Beatrice, and Cecil filled up the rest of the row. When everyone was seated, Quimby took his place at the pulpit. He made several announcements, including proclaiming the final banns for Mary and Jason. Finished with that, he cleared his throat in preparation of starting his sermon.

"Beware the demon of lust," he intoned.

Immediately, Jason was acutely aware of Mary sitting beside him.

"It is a trap to snare the unwary," Quimby warned.

Jason remembered Mary lying trapped beneath him on the riverbank. Her body had been soft and yielding against his. . . .

"You must beware lust's sinful kiss."

He had wanted to keep kissing her. Her mouth had tasted incredibly sweet, and the scent of her had wound its way into his senses until he felt drugged with desire. . . .

"You must beware lust's pernicious influence."

How maddening the buttons of her dress had been. But once they were undone, how sweet to hear her nearly soundless moans of pleasure as he spread mud over her soft, smooth skin. . . .

"It will drag down the virtuous!"

If only the wedding weren't still three days away. Three

days seemed like an eternity. He didn't think he could wait that long. He didn't *want* to wait that long.

"It will divert the pure and holy from the path of righteousness!"

He wanted to claim her and kiss away that slight frown that sometimes wrinkled her forehead when she looked at him. He knew she was upset by some of the things that had happened, but he was certain she would be happy once they were married and on their way to Paris—away from Vincent and his pranks. . . .

A smell like autumn leaves wafted through the air.

Jason tensed. He gazed around the church, searching for the source of the smell. Everything appeared normal. The ladies sat in their seats, waving their fans, their gazes wandering. The men shifted and yawned. A few had nodded off. The children squirmed and played with the prayer books.

"Lust will bring you nothing! Nothing, I tell you!"

Relaxing, Jason sank bank against his seat. He must have imagined the smell—

"Nothing, that is, but incredible pleasure."

Jason whipped his head around. The rustling and swaying of fans grew still as the congregation stared at Quimby in astonishment.

Quimby coughed. "I mean, nothing but incredible misery."

An almost audible sigh went around the church. The fans and the rustling resumed.

"Of course," Quimby continued. "One can't deny that there's pleasure involved, also."

Gasps reverberated throughout the church. Jason clutched the railing at his side.

Quimby looked confused. "I didn't mean to say that. I meant to say that sin can be seductive. I speak from experience."

Beatrice tittered. Other chuckles and giggles throughout the church were quickly stifled.

"I don't condone this, of course," Quimby said hastily.

"This all occurred before I became vicar here. Before I came here last year, I lived in London. There are some quite excellent entertainments in London—wouldn't you agree, Jason? Wild parties, gaming hells, and, of course, Madame Fleur's House of Heavenly Delights. . . ."

Jason clenched his jaw. He glanced at Mary and saw she was sitting very still, her face pale.

The vicar tried once again to correct himself. "Not that Jason, er, his lordship ever indulged in any of those vices. He would never intentionally do anything sinful. . . . I'm sure that at the time he thought drinking and gambling and associating with loose women was perfectly acceptable behavior."

Jason heard Mary inhale sharply. Surging to his feet, he said forcefully, "Mr. Quimby, I am afraid you are not feeling well."

Quimby, gazing off toward one of the windows, appeared not to hear him. "If only Jason hadn't insisted that I become vicar here, I would still be in London, enjoying the pleasures of Madame Fleur's delightful establishment. Now the only pleasure left to me is eating—"

Jason strode up to the pulpit and took Quimby's arm. "You had better lie down at once."

Quimby blinked, glancing about in confusion. Then an expression of horror crept over his face. "Good heavens! Did I say . . . ?"

"Dr. Scott, will you please join us in the vestibule?" Jason asked, looking at a thin, dark-haired man seated in the pew behind Mary. The doctor nodded and rose to his feet.

Pale and trembling, Quimby mopped his brow. "Yes, yes, you're right. I'm not feeling well. Not well at all. I don't know what came over me. Everything I thought, I said—"

Jason hustled him off the pulpit and out through a door at the front of the church before he could say anything more. The doctor joined them, and Cecil, jumping up from the pew, followed.

For a moment, there was an astonished silence in the church. Then Lady Weldon said in a low voice, "Well, I *never!*"

A hum of conversation broke out. Murmurs of "Astonishing!" and "Never seen the like!" could be heard all over the church.

Beatrice, her eyes bright with malice, turned to Mary. "You must not mind what Mr. Quimby says. I am sure he is . . . mistaken about Jason doing all those terrible things."

Mary, averting her gaze, did not reply.

A few moments later, Jason reentered the church. He stepped up to the pulpit and faced the congregation. Everyone looked at him expectantly.

"The heat of the day has made Mr. Quimby a trifle light-headed," he announced. "The doctor says he will recover soon, but thinks the vicar should rest. Therefore, the rest of the service is canceled."

The crowd rose to their feet, the hum of voices increasing to a roar.

Jason, keeping his expression impassive, stepped off the pulpit.

"Where is Cecil?" Lady Weldon asked.

"He offered to stay with Quimby," Jason said shortly. "The doctor thinks he shouldn't be moved for a while. Come, let us go home." Without stopping to talk to anyone, he led the ladies through the murmuring crowd to the carriage and handed them in. As he was about to climb in himself, he heard a voice call, "Your lordship! I say, your lordship!"

Pausing, he turned to see Trumball, huffing and puffing, hurrying up to the carriage.

"So glad I caught you!" he gasped, hitching his breeches up over his protruding belly. "I'm sorry to detain you, my lord, but I wanted to ask you a question." He glanced around, then said in a booming whisper that could no doubt be heard fifty feet away, "Could you give me the address of Madame Fleur's establishment?"

"I do not know it, sir," Jason said in freezing accents. Ignoring Trumball's skeptical look, he turned on his heel and said to the coachman, "Take us home—fast."

He barely was seated before the carriage took off.

Jason glanced at Mary. Her eyes were downcast, her hands folded in her lap. Mentally, he cursed Vincent for the trick.

Lady Weldon broke the stunned silence. "I am shocked," she said, gripping her purple shawl against her bosom. "Utterly shocked. I could not believe my ears. I would never have thought that Mr. Quimby, a man of the cloth, could be so crude, so disgusting, so revolting." She paused, then added, "Although I suppose I shouldn't be surprised. Nothing a man could do surprises me. Beasts, the lot of them. Including *you*, Jason."

Jason stiffened. "I beg your pardon?"

"And so you should! It hasn't been easy managing Helsbury House, catering to your selfish whims. Timothy and Roger were terrible also. Boors, the lot of you. I daresay it runs in the family."

"Are you all right, Mother?" Beatrice asked, her eyes round with surprise.

"Of course I'm all right. I've been all right ever since your father died." Lady Weldon glared at Jason. "Like all men, he was a brute. The happiest day of my life was when he died."

Jason's eyes narrowed and he glanced angrily around the carriage—to no effect. The words continued to flow from Lady Weldon's mouth in an uncontrollable vituperative torrent.

"He expected to sleep in my bed once a week—even after Beatrice was born! I tried to guide his thoughts in a more proper direction by reading religious tracts aloud to him, but after I finished reading, he would want to engage in sexual congress! Once, I actually thought I was making some progress because he was gazing off into the distance with a very intent look on his face—but then I realized he was asleep! He had the most unusual ability to sleep with his eyes open. It could be quite disconcerting."

She shuddered. "It was a great relief when he finally acquired a mistress. But even then he managed to humiliate me—I discovered that he had given her a more expensive diamond necklace than the one he'd given me! I behaved like a lady, of course. I never let on that I was aware of the difference—even when I met the woman at a party and she had the vulgarity to finger her necklace!"

"Aunt Weldon," Jason said, "perhaps it would be better not to discuss such intimate matters in front of unmarried girls—"

"Why not?" Lady Weldon demanded. "Isn't it better they know the truth now? Isn't it better that they not be so naive as I was? I married my husband expecting to be treated with a modicum of respect. Instead, I received the most blatant insult! I solved the problem by purchasing an even *larger* diamond."

"Aunt Weldon," Jason warned, wishing he could strangle Vincent, "you do not seem to be yourself. I am sure you will shortly regret your words."

"The only regret I have was that I ever married at all. I had to tolerate his clumsy lovemaking, his interminably jovial nature—I wonder how other women put up with it. If I weren't so patient, I know I never would have. But I endured everything. I martyred myself on the Altar of Marital Duty—"

"Aunt Weldon, if you do not cease at once, I will be compelled to gag you with my cravat," Jason said. "And I am sure *all those present here* will not wish to see such an unpleasant spectacle."

Lady Weldon looked down her nose. The lines around her mouth quivered. "I refuse to be ordered about by a man. If you dare lay a hand on me, I will—" She stopped abruptly, a strange look passing over her face. "I . . . I beg your pardon, Jason. I . . . I don't know what came over me."

Breathing a sigh of relief, Jason said, "Never mind,

Aunt Weldon. I am sure it is the heat. It can have an odd effect."

"Yes, I . . . I suppose so." Looking uncharacteristically confused, she subsided into silence.

Jason glanced at Mary, but her gaze was still firmly fixed on her lap.

Damn you, Vincent, Jason swore silently. Had Lady Weldon's story of wedded life put Mary off of marriage? In truth, the tale was enough to put almost anyone off. He didn't know if he—let alone Mary—would ever recover from hearing about Lady Weldon's sacrifice on the Altar of Marital Duty. *You've gone too far this time, uncle. . . .*

The carriage pulled up to the house. Inside, Lady Weldon, leaning on Beatrice's arm, hurried up the stairs.

Jason waited for Mary to follow them, but she stopped in the middle of the hall, staring at him with wide, shadowed eyes.

He averted his gaze. He knew she was waiting for an explanation, for reassurance, but he couldn't give it to her right now. There was some business he had to take care of first. "Mary, you look tired. Go upstairs and rest before dinner. I'll talk to you later."

The shadows in her eyes deepened, making him feel a niggling guilt, but he suppressed it. He had no reason to feel guilty—but he knew someone who should.

He waited until Mary had disappeared up the stairs before he strode into the dining room.

A glowing form stood near the unlit fireplace.

Jason's hands tightened into fists. "I think you'd better start explaining, uncle."

16

Vincent took a pinch of snuff. "I have several abilities that you may not be familiar with. One of which is the fairly simple power of making people say what they're really thinking—much easier than actually entering someone's body. Although I must say, women are considerably more difficult. The female brain is completely irrational and illogical. The energy required to lower a woman's inhibitions is much greater than—"

"I don't want an explanation of your powers," Jason snapped. "I want to know why, after agreeing to let me deal with Mary in my own way, you persist in interfering."

Vincent arched his brows. "I persist because you fail to realize the mistake you are making."

"The only mistake I've made is allowing you to think you can rule my life. You've gone too far, uncle."

Vincent shut the snuffbox with a sharp click. "I haven't gone far enough. Can't you see what is happening? Don't you realize what you're setting yourself up for? I remember what it's like, believe me. It starts out innocently enough—you're attracted to a pretty face, a nicely turned ankle. You're drawn in slowly, thinking you're safe, that there's no danger. Then suddenly a simple attraction changes into desperate need, and you find yourself craving a kind look, a smile, a touch—"

Vincent paused, his hands shaking. Drawing in a deep

breath, he said more calmly, "She will ruin your life. Why can't you see that?"

"Why can't you see that you've lost? All your schemes have not driven her away. You've lost, uncle. Admit it, and leave Mary alone."

Vincent frowned. "Don't be a fool. Haven't you noticed how she runs from you at any hint of passion? Like all women, she's cold and selfish. Why would you want such a dreary little prude?"

"That's none of your business."

"She has bewitched you. I don't know how, but she has. Just as Elizabeth once bewitched me."

"Mary is nothing like Elizabeth."

Vincent's face hardened and he laughed sardonically. "All women are the same, you fool. Oh, I grant you, Mary hasn't shown the traits of her kind yet—but she will. Once she begins associating with the avaricious women of our society on a daily basis, that sweet nature of hers will fade away and she will become like all the others—manipulative, greedy, shrewish. And that's when she'll strike. She will destroy you, nephew."

His gaze met Jason's. They stared at one another, silently battling.

Jason was the first to break the silence. "For the last time—leave Mary alone," he said quietly, his gaze steady. "Or you'll regret it."

Vincent laughed at the ridiculous threat. "You can't be serious. You should listen to me and save yourself a lot of grief." He smiled, but Jason didn't smile back. Vincent stopped laughing. "You *are* serious," he said disbelievingly.

"I am deadly serious. Don't meddle with my life."

Vincent had never heard the boy speak in quite that tone. Keeping his face impassive, he took out his snuffbox and pretended to take another pinch. "And if I refuse?"

Jason's gaze didn't waver. "You've told me a lot about yourself these last six months, uncle. I know your weaknesses."

Vincent scoffed. "I have no weaknesses."

"No?" Jason smiled grimly. "I've noticed you have an aversion for the Pit."

Vincent gave a start of surprise. How the devil had the boy figured that out? Concealing a flicker of uneasiness, he shrugged. "Perhaps. But that is hardly a weakness."

"No? Did you never wonder why your aversion was so strong?"

"I know why. Because of a boyhood incident."

"Is that all? Are you certain that's the only reason?"

Vincent didn't like the slightly taunting note in Jason's voice. "Exactly what are you driving at, nephew?"

"Oh, nothing." Jason looked down, hiding his thoughts. "I've also noticed that after that first night you haven't bothered Mary when she's in the Blue Room."

Vincent's eyes widened. "Is that why you put her in there? You think I won't go in the Blue Room? You're wrong."

"Am I?" Jason's mouth curved mockingly. "I've warned you, uncle. Don't interfere." He strolled out of the room.

Stunned, Vincent couldn't move for a moment. Then, with a scowl, he strode after Jason.

Jason was in the hall talking to Kendall. ". . . in the Pit. Have it cleaned and brought up to the dining room before dinner."

Vincent stormed up to him. "You arrogant little puppy, do you really think you can threaten me?"

Ignoring him, Jason continued to talk to the servant in a low voice.

Vincent glared at him. "Did you hear me?"

Jason, his expression calm, waited until the servant left, then turned to Vincent. "Yes, I heard you."

"Then hear this," Vincent snarled. "You are wrong about the Pit and the Blue Room. In fact, I am going up to the Blue Room right now and frighten your prudish little fiancée all the way to London."

"You're bluffing."

Vincent smiled unpleasantly. "Am I?" He vanished.

For an instant, Jason froze. Then, with a violent oath, he ran up the stairs to Mary's room and threw open the door.

It crashed against the wall, and he was vaguely aware that Mary, seated at the dressing table brushing her hair, jumped. But he ignored her as he stared around the room. Heart pounding, he searched the corners and the ceiling and the floor. He crouched down and looked under the bed, then straightened and checked behind the door. He sniffed the air.

Nothing. There was no sign of the ghost.

His tension eased. Vincent *had* been bluffing.

"Jason? What on earth are you doing?"

He turned to Mary, an apology on his lips. The apology died, however, as he noticed for the first time that her shining, golden-brown hair was cascading down her back.

His throat grew dry.

He stared at her, unable to tear his gaze away from her hair. A memory flashed into his mind of the first night she'd come here, and how he had braided those long tresses. The silky smooth strands, amazingly soft and fine, had drifted through his fingers, making him yearn to bury his face in her hair. Fortunately, he had managed to resist the impulse. But he hadn't been able to resist touching her satiny skin. He could remember with tortuous clarity how her soft chin and full lips had felt . . . and the warm, enticing moistness of her mouth. . . .

His body responded with predictable lustiness to his thoughts. He groaned silently, then muttered an apology and turned to leave. But instead of doing so, he stopped, shut the door, and twisted the key in the lock.

He stared down at his hands in astonishment. What the hell? His hands had acted completely independently of his brain, as if they didn't belong to him. As if they belonged to . . .

Vincent.

Even as the realization hit him, he was jerked around and pushed forward. Jason struggled against the unseen force, fighting to regain control over his limbs, but his efforts were futile against the ghost's power. His legs were compelled to move across the carpet toward Mary.

As he approached, she lowered the brush to her lap and grew very still, her eyes wary.

He stopped in front of her. Without volition, his hands closed over her shoulders and pulled her up from her seat. He resisted fiercely. He could sense what Vincent was trying to do—the ghost was attempting to make him lose control, to shock and frighten Mary with his passion.

No, Jason swore silently, redoubling his efforts to fight the ghost. I won't let you do it.

The force increased.

Jason wrestled against it. He knew that the Blue Room must be draining Vincent rapidly. If he could hold out just a few more moments, he was certain the ghost would have to admit defeat—

"Jason?"

He glanced down at Mary. Her wide, blue eyes were staring up at him. Her hair framed her face and spilled down over her shoulders to rest provocatively against her breasts. . . .

Swallowing, Jason looked away, but he could still smell the faint blossom scent of her hair. Before he could stop himself, he drew in a deep breath, inhaling the sweet fragrance.

The force propelling him wavered.

Jason barely noticed. Memories were flooding his brain, of seeing Mary standing in Aunt Sally's room, clad only in her corset and drawers. He remembered kissing her in the sensual, intimate darkness of the dungeon, caressing her warm skin with wet, cool mud. . . .

The force flickered and faded.

Jason tightened his grip on her shoulders. "Mary," he whispered huskily. Her lips were slightly parted, her breath coming fast and sweet between them. Strands of her hair tangled about him, tying him to her like a silky web.

The force vanished.

But Jason was held in place by a much stronger force— a force that he had been fighting for what seemed like an eternity.

He bent his head and kissed her.

Her mouth tasted even sweeter than he remembered, like mint and honey. He explored every delectable nook, stroking and teasing and seducing her with his tongue.

With a gasp, Mary broke away. "No!" Her hands shaking, she pushed her hair back from her face. "I won't allow this. Not after what Mr. Quimby said."

She tried to step back, but Jason caught her hand and held it tightly. "Mary, please. Quimby was wrong. I didn't lead a wild life in London. I went to a few card parties, true, but that's all. I was never unfaithful to you, I swear it." He lifted her hand and pressed a passionate kiss to her palm. "Please believe me, Mary."

She turned her face away. "I don't know if I can."

"Why not?" Frustration and desire churned in his gut. "I've never lied to you. Surely you know that. Don't you? Don't you?"

"I . . ." She met his gaze, staring into his eyes for an agonizingly long, slow moment. He waited tensely for her answer.

"I . . . I know you wouldn't lie to me. But . . . "

"But what?"

"Jason . . ." Her fingers wiggled under his and he realized he was holding her hand in a near death grip.

"But what?" he asked more gently, easing his hold.

She wriggled her fingers a little more, but he refused to let go. "But what?" he repeated.

"Oh, Jason," she said helplessly. "Everything is so strange here. I always thought people married for love. But here, it seems as though everyone marries for convenience, or money, or status. I don't want a marriage like that. I don't want a marriage like Lady Weldon's—"

"Our marriage won't be like that." How could she even suggest such a thing? "You must know how much I care for you, Mary."

"Do you?" The shadows left her eyes and her expression softened. Her fingers curled around his. "Do you really?"

"Did you ever doubt it?"

"N-no, of course not."

"That's good." Holding her gaze with his, he undid the
buttons at her cuff. They were small—almost too small
for him to grasp. "You should never doubt me, Mary.
Don't you know I've wanted you ever since I first met you
at the Coopers'? I used to watch you sew. Your hands
almost drove me insane."

"My hands?" She sounded amazed, incredulous.

"Yes, your hands." He lifted her hand and kissed each
slender digit. "When I watched you, I imagined your fingers touching me, stroking me . . . "

She gasped, and tried to pull her hand away. He
released it, but only so he could lift the other one. The
Helsbury ring was on her finger. He'd never liked it
much—but he liked it on Mary. He unbuttoned her cuff
and kissed her wrist, his tongue caressing the delicate skin.
"The way I want to touch and stroke you . . . "

Her pulse fluttered under his lips. "Jason, I . . . I don't
think this is wise."

"Why not, Mary?" Releasing her hand, he kissed her
hair and her forehead and the curve of her cheek. "We'll
be married in a few days."

"I don't know . . . "

"Please, Mary." He kissed her ear and her chin and her
throat. "Let me kiss you. Let me kiss you and everything
will be all right."

Her hands clutched tightly at his lapels. "Jason . . . "

"Please, Mary." His mouth hovered over her tempting
lips. "Please. I want things to be the way they used to be. . . . "

"Oh, Jason." Her eyes grew bright and her lips curved
into a trembling smile. Her arms crept around his neck. "I
want that, too. I want that more than anything."

His mouth covered hers, heat surging through him at
her surrender. He deepened the kiss, wanting more, yearning for all of her sweetness, all of her. Hungrily, he
caressed her waist and side, and cupped her breasts
through the cloth of her dress.

She pressed more closely against him.

The feel of her soft curves ignited a blaze inside him. He pressed and teased her breasts until they swelled under his fingers. But it wasn't enough. He moved his hand away and a slight, incoherent murmur escaped her.

"Shh," he whispered huskily, moving his fingers to the buttons at her neckline. "I only want to get you out of this dress." He undid each button, kissing the deepening vee of her skin as the material parted. He tried to be patient. He wanted to go slowly and make this as pleasurable as possible for her. But when the dress was open to the waist, he could bear it no longer. He pushed the dress down over her shoulders and past her hips, popping off a few buttons in the process.

"My dress!" she cried.

"I'll buy you another. I'll buy you a hundred more."

She stiffened a little and looked up at him. "I don't want a hundred dresses."

"You don't have to wear them if you don't want to. In fact, I would prefer it if you didn't."

"That's not the point—"

"Mary . . ." He wished she would stop talking. He didn't care about the damn dress. He only wanted to kiss her. He pressed his mouth against the slight frown on her lips. "I'll do whatever you want, Mary."

Her frown remained. "I don't want dresses. I want you, Jason. That's all I've ever wanted."

"And I want you." He gathered her hair in his hands and kissed her. "Dear God, how I want you, Mary."

The slight tension in her shoulders eased. He continued to kiss her until her lips softened and parted, and then again until she was clinging to him as tightly as he was to her.

And still it wasn't enough. Their clothes remained an irritating barrier, preventing what he wanted with an almost feverish intensity—to feel her skin against his.

Not breaking physical contact any more than was necessary, he pulled off her petticoat. Tossing it aside, he glanced down. He grew still, staring at her. The air whooshed out of his lungs.

He had thought he'd noticed every detail of her appearance in the pale pink corset and white drawers. But looking at her now, in the soft afternoon light, he saw he had missed more than he would have thought possible—her small slippered feet and delicate, finely turned ankles; her shapely, silk-clad knees peeping out from her lace-edged drawers; the small padded bustle barely visible beyond the fullness of her hips; the tiny pink bow nestling on the corset between her breasts; and the points of her nipples standing out above the corset against the thin material of her chemise. . . .

"Mary," he said huskily. "Do you know how often I've thought of you like this? Ever since that day in Aunt Sally's room, I've dreamed of you, standing there in your drawers and corset. If Aunt Sally and all those silly seamstresses hadn't been there, I would have kissed you like this. And this. And this. . . ."

Pushing down the neckline of her chemise, he kissed the tops of her breasts and the hollow between, and circled around. He traced his tongue around the edges of the pink crests, tormenting himself, tormenting her, until he could endure it no longer. He closed his mouth over her nipple.

She cried out and arched her back. Her fingers tangled in his hair and pressed him closer against her breast. Still stroking the sweet peak with his tongue, he gripped her hips and pulled her up against the ache in his groin. The feel of the soft juncture of her thighs made him groan with pleasure—pleasure and anticipation.

Abruptly, he released her and stepped back, ripping off his cravat and coat. She watched wide-eyed as he unbuttoned his waistcoat, flung it on the floor, and pulled his shirt over his head.

Aching to feel her breasts against his chest, he drew her against him again. "Touch me, Mary," he whispered in her ear. "Touch me."

Her hands crept up to his chest, touching him timidly at first, then more eagerly, exploring the texture of the hair sprinkled there, traveling up over his shoulders and down his arms.

"You feel . . ." She paused, as if she didn't quite know how to explain.

"What, Mary? I feel what?"

"I don't know." Her fingers stroked his arm. "Hard. But smooth."

He groaned, thinking of another part of him that could match that description.

Her fingers, boldly curious now, moved to his chest again, seeking out the ridges of his ribs and the flatness of his stomach. He sucked in a breath when he felt her hands go lower, to trace along the waistband of his trousers.

"Mary . . ."

She blushed and pulled her hands away.

"Mary . . ." he groaned. He stopped and counted to ten, trying to slow the pulse of his blood. He wanted her to unbutton his trousers, but he didn't want to rush or frighten her.

He sat on a chair and tugged at his boots, the tension in his loins growing, his anticipation building to feverish heights. The boots came off, and he pulled her onto his lap so he could untie the strings of her bustle. He pulled the bustle out from between them and dropped it on the floor. Settling her more firmly on his lap, he groped for her corset strings, untying them and loosening them. The rigid garment fell away, and her chemise floated out.

"Mary," he groaned against the rapidly beating pulse at the side of her neck, "why must you wear so many clothes?"

She didn't respond. But then, he hadn't really expected her to.

Pushing her up, he stood and pulled the chemise over her head. It fluttered to the ground, leaving her wearing nothing but her drawers and slippers and stockings.

He lifted her in his arms, carried her over to the bed, and laid her there. He removed her slippers and untied the ribbons that gathered her drawers at the knees, before moving up to the ties at her waist.

"Lift your hips, Mary."

She complied, and he pulled them down slowly, his gaze drinking in the sight of the smooth planes of her belly and the rounded curves of her hips. He swallowed as the dark triangle between her thighs came into view, tight curls concealing the secrets there. He wanted to stop and explore the sweet nest, but he forced himself to tug the drawers lower, revealing the smooth white skin of her inner thighs and frivolous pink garters encircling her legs just above her knees.

He pulled the drawers the rest of the way off, then returned to her garters and stockings. Without bothering to untie the ribbons that attached them, he tugged them down and off, leaving her long, silky legs bare.

Stepping back, he surveyed the results of his handiwork. The full glory of her unadorned loveliness made his breath catch and his heart pound. From the crown of her golden brown hair, to the nails of her small pink toes, she was beautiful. "Mary," he whispered. "I want to kiss you all over."

A soft pink blush spread over her skin.

His gaze inspected every sweet inch. He bent and kissed the hollows of her throat and the undercurves of her breasts, reveling in the honeyed taste of her. With his tongue, he traced the red impression left by the corset on her side, down to the indentation of her navel, and back around to the curve of her hip. He frowned a little as he noticed the bluish bruise there on her backside, dark and unsightly against her pale white skin. He drew a finger gently around the edges. "Where did this come from, Mary?" he asked.

"What?" Her voice sounded dazed. "Oh, I . . . I think I fell on a stone in the brook yesterday."

His frown deepened. "That must have hurt." He kissed it softly, soothingly. "I'm sorry I knocked you into the brook. I'll make it up to you. I promise. . . ."

His mouth moved down to the top of her thigh, and then to the silky inner skin.

"Jason, I . . . oh, no, don't!" Her hands grabbed and pulled at him.

Reluctantly, he moved back up. "Mary," he said huskily, "I must . . . that is, will you help me with my trousers?"

Her eyes widened. She stared at him, then glanced furtively at his trousers. "I . . . yes."

Delighted by her answer, he stood up.

His delight soon faded, however, when she knelt on the bed and her hands fumbled with the flap of his trousers. The feel of her fingers brushing against him made his muscles grow taut and sent the temperature of his blood skyrocketing.

The blood pounded so fiercely through his veins, he wanted to groan with the pain of it. He wanted to forget the nicety of taking off his clothes, throw her on the bed, and take her in one hard, swift thrust. He wanted to drive into her again and again until the raging ache in him gave way to the sweet ecstasy of release.

He held his breath, fighting the urge to push her hands aside and rip off his trousers and drawers himself.

Finally, she managed to undo the flap. But then she paused, glancing up at him as if she were unsure what to do next.

Closing his eyes, he inhaled deeply, trying to maintain his control. The ache in him subsided infinitesimally. He opened his eyes and forced himself to give her a strained, but encouraging, smile.

She smiled back, then returned her gaze to his trousers. Tentatively, she tugged them down.

Barely restrained by the linen of his drawers, his arousal sprang forth. Her eyes widened. Hesitantly, she reached out and stroked him.

He groaned. He couldn't endure it any longer. He bent down and kissed her, pushing her back against the pillows. He pulled the strings of his drawers and shoved them down. They fell around his ankles, and he kicked them off. He stopped kissing her just long enough to dispose of his knee-high stockings, then lowered himself down onto the mattress beside her. He ran his hands over her breasts and waist and hips, pressing and kneading her soft flesh. He lifted his mouth from hers for a moment, his rapid breathing mingling with hers.

Her hands reached up and pulled him back to her, kissing him with innocent urgency.

He groaned silently, knowing he couldn't wait much longer.

He slipped his fingers between her thighs, stroking the sensitive flesh. A soft cry escaped her throat, and then she arched her hips up, moving instinctively, rhythmically against his hand.

He felt the slick moistness gathering there and he knew she was almost ready for him.

"Jason! I want . . . I want . . . "

"Yes, I know, Mary," he whispered in her ear. "I want it, too."

He moved over her, his knees spreading her legs. Positioning himself at her opening, he looked down, wanting to see her face.

Her eyes were half closed; her cheeks flushed. Her hair was spread out against the pillow. Sinking his fingers into the golden-brown strands, he held her still as he lowered his mouth to hers and slid smoothly and surely into her hot, tight, moistness.

She tensed, and he grew still. "Mary," he whispered, "am I hurting you?"

She shook her head and the tension in her muscles eased a bit. He pressed forward, up to the core of her. He stopped, knowing that there would be some pain for her, dreading having to cause it. Kissing her deeply, he caressed her breasts, bringing her passion to a fever pitch. When she was gasping and twisting against him, he pressed upward, breaking through the small obstruction.

Inhaling sharply, she grew suddenly still. He paused, not moving, worried that he had hurt her terribly. "Mary," he whispered, "are you all right?"

She nodded, and relief flowed through him. He pressed kisses against her lips and cheeks and eyes, still not moving, allowing her to become accustomed to his possession of her body.

He kissed her breasts, licking and stroking the nipples with his tongue. He felt her heart speed up again, and then race faster and faster as he continued to lavish attention upon her breasts. She began to writhe up against him again.

He pulled back, then pressed in.

"Oh!" she gasped.

He repeated the motion, and she gasped again.

He grasped her hips, adjusting her rhythm to his, moving faster and faster.

The beat of his pulse increased. Her arms encircled his neck. Sensation ebbed and flowed. He heard her soft, panting gasps multiply. Overloaded nerve endings strained. Her arms tightened. His groin ached with painful intensity as all sensation concentrated there, tightening, squeezing, condensing. She cried out. . . .

Ecstasy exploded through him in a fiery maelstrom of pleasure. He gave a hoarse shout. The pleasure went on and on as he strained against her, pouring his seed into her, kissing her with all the passion searing through his blood.

The pleasure dimmed and receded. All the tension that had been accumulating for the last year eased out of him and floated away, leaving him drifting on a cloud of fulfillment and contentment.

He looked down at her and saw a dreamy smile on her lips and in her eyes. Satisfaction filled him. He bent down and kissed her.

She was his. He had won.

Rolling onto his side, he pulled her against him, settling her head against his shoulder. She cuddled up to him, and he wrapped his arms around her.

He fell asleep with her tucked next to his heart, secure in the knowledge that Vincent would never be able to drive her away now.

The afternoon sun had sunk low in the sky, sending dark shadows across the room, when Jason woke. For a moment, he didn't know where he was. Then he heard a faint sigh, and felt warm female curves pressed against him.

Mary.

He turned his head and looked down at her sleeping face. His arms tightened around her. She couldn't leave him after this. They were irrevocably bound. Vincent could do nothing to frighten her away now—

A faint odor of autumn leaves entered the room.

Jason looked up sharply and saw a faint, wavering image standing by the door.

"Enjoy yourself, nephew?"

Jason stiffened. He tucked the sheet protectively around Mary and glared at Vincent.

Vincent smiled sardonically. "You've really put yourself in a bind. The idea was to scare her away, not to take her to bed. You'll have the devil of a time getting rid of her now."

Jason tightened his grip on the sheet. "You've lost, uncle. Mary will never leave now. You've caused enough trouble—why the hell don't you go away?"

Angry sparks glowed in Vincent's eyes as he opened his mouth, but before he could speak, a sleepy voice intervened.

"Jason," Mary murmured, her eyes still closed, "who are you talking to?"

17

Mary, *in a blissful state* of languorous lassitude, spoke hazily, barely awake. She was trying to hold onto the wonderful dream she was having . . . where she was wearing a plain gold band, and she and Jason were walking hand in hand along the seashore.

She was about to drift off again, when she became aware that Jason hadn't answered her. "Jason?" she murmured.

Still no reply. She opened her eyes a crack and a hard, masculine chest, lightly covered with hair, met her gaze. Blushing a little, she glanced up at his face.

His jaw was tight. His eyes, hard and gray and cold, were fixed on a spot by the fireplace.

"Jason?"

Hearing the uncertainty in her voice, Jason tore his gaze away from the mocking figure by the fireplace. He swore silently. Just when he'd settled everything with Mary, Vincent had to appear again. Knowing the ghost as he did, Jason had no doubt that his intent was to cause trouble.

Undoubtedly, the wisest course of action would be to try to get Vincent the hell out of there.

"Mary, I have to go," he said, keeping a wary eye on Vincent.

He felt her stiffen. "Don't you think we should discuss what happened?"

"What is there to discuss?" Glancing at the fireplace

again, he raised his voice to make certain Vincent heard. "We will be married on Wednesday as planned."

"But Jason . . . didn't making love mean anything to you?"

"Of course. I have taken your virginity. We *must* be married."

Vincent brushed his sleeve. "You are truly naive, nephew."

Jason, biting his tongue not to respond to the ghost's taunt, looked back at Mary. A flush had risen in her cheeks. "Is that all it meant to you?" she asked.

"Mary . . ." He clasped her fingers, which were suddenly clutching the sheet. From the corner of his eye, he saw the ghost wander over toward the dressing table and nudge the chemise lying on the floor. A wicked grin curled Vincent's lips. Glaring at him, Jason said distractedly to Mary, "What happened was going to happen sooner or later. I know you don't know a lot about men, but whenever a man is in close proximity with a woman, his passion will often overcome his common sense."

"Are you saying what happened last night could have happened between you and any woman?"

"No, that's not what I meant. I meant that I didn't mean for this to happen. It wouldn't have happened if it hadn't been for . . . "

"For what?"

"Yes, for what, nephew?"

Hearing the mocking challenge in the ghost's voice, Jason tightened his grip on Mary's hand. Taking a deep breath, he turned his full attention to Mary, knowing what he must do. "If it hadn't been for Vincent."

She stared at him. "Vincent?"

Jason nodded. "I should have told you before. He has done everything in his power to break our engagement." He met her gaze steadily. "I told him he has failed, but I doubt he will give up, even now."

"He won't?"

Jason shook his head. "He is capable of anything. Look what he has done already—he tricked me into coming into your room. It was him, this afternoon, not me."

She stared at him. "Vincent made love to me this afternoon?"

"No! That's not what I meant at all. He only forced me to kiss you."

"He had to force you to kiss me?"

"Yes. I mean, no. I wanted to kiss you. But I wouldn't have if he hadn't forced me. I couldn't stop him. Then he left and *I* couldn't stop. Damn it, Mary, stop looking at me like that. I want you to understand."

"Oh, I understand. You're insane!"

Jason ran his fingers through his hair in angry frustration. This was not going at all the way he'd intended. And the sight of Vincent standing by the fireplace, grinning, was not making the situation any easier.

"I am not insane," Jason said to Mary.

"That is a matter of opinion," Vincent drawled.

Jason cast a quick glare at him before turning back to Mary. "I'm trying to do what's best for both of us. Can't you see that?"

"The only thing I see is that you're lying to me." Angry tears rushed to her eyes and she blinked them back. "A ghost! Why don't you just admit that this afternoon meant nothing to you?"

"It did mean something to me."

"You expect me to believe that? I knew you had changed when I first came here—I just didn't want to believe it."

"I haven't changed."

"Yes, you have. All you need do to complete the picture of a selfish, arrogant aristocrat is cast me off now that you've seduced me."

"I have no intention of casting you off."

Vincent took a pinch of snuff. "Don't be a fool, nephew. This is your chance to do so."

Jason ignored him, watching in horror as a tear slipped down Mary's cheek. "Don't bother saying any more," she said. "I understand very well. You don't care about me at all. All you feel for me is lust." She wiped her cheek with the sheet.

"Excellent, nephew. You've made her cry. I am beginning to feel my presence is unnecessary. You are managing to bungle everything quite nicely. Shall I leave?"

"Yes," Jason snapped.

Mary's mouth fell open. "Yes, all you feel for me is lust?"

Vincent laughed.

"No!" Jason glared at Vincent. "I meant to say of course I care about you, Mary. I told you so earlier."

"I don't know if I can believe you, Jason. I feel as though you've taken advantage of me."

"You should leave now, nephew. Really, I'm a bit disappointed in you. Making love to her was taking an unfair advantage in our little game."

"I'll take whatever advantage I can," Jason snarled.

Mary gasped. "You admit it?"

Vincent laughed harder.

Mary gave Jason an icy stare worthy of Lady Weldon. "Please leave."

Jason gritted his teeth. "You are being unreasonable, Mary."

"*I* am being unreasonable? You almost make me laugh, my lord." She turned her back to him, revealing the long, delicate line of her spine.

Vincent whistled. "Nice view."

Jason rounded on him. "Will you get the hell out of here?"

Mary whirled. "This is *my* room, I'll thank you to remember! And I would very much appreciate it if *you* would leave!"

Vincent laughed so hard, tears were running down his face.

Controlling his temper with an effort, Jason said, "We must clear this up first, Mary."

"It's late, Jason. Lady Weldon will be upset if we're late for dinner. I must get dressed."

Vincent smiled, his gaze on Mary's bare shoulders. "This is starting to get interesting."

Jason glared at him. "You would not dare."

Mary's face flushed. "Do you intend to keep me naked in this bed forever, then?"

"My, my," Vincent drawled. "Perhaps I will give my blessing to your marriage after all—"

Jason climbed out of the bed and yanked on his drawers and trousers. Grabbing the rest of his clothes, he said coldly to Mary, "I will wait in the corridor for you. If you're not out in ten minutes, I'm coming back in." Ignoring the outraged look on her face, he strode to the door, unlocked it and held it open, staring challengingly at Vincent.

Vincent, with a sardonic smile, strolled through.

Jason followed him, shut the door, then turned around. "Well, uncle?"

Out of the Blue Room, Vincent's image grew brighter and more substantial. He still looked amused. "I must congratulate you, nephew. I think you have succeeded where I have failed."

Jason pulled his shirt on, glaring as his head emerged from the linen. "I warned you not to interfere. I'm sorry it's come to this, but you leave me no choice." He hopped on one foot, then the other, jerking on his stockings and boots. "Now I'm only sorry that I didn't take action sooner."

Vincent snorted. "Are we back to your empty threats again? What have you done? Summoned Cousin Horace to exorcise me?"

Before Jason could reply, a scullery maid rounded the corner, carrying a coal scuttle. She stopped short, staring at him with round eyes.

"She looks frightened, nephew. I don't believe she's used to seeing half-dressed men in the corridor."

Jason glowered. "Will you go away?"

The girl cowered. "I . . . I'm sorry, your lordship." She turned and ran, the coal scuttle bumping against her legs.

Ignoring Vincent's shout of laughter, Jason yanked on his waistcoat and coat and tied his cravat haphazardly around his neck, before pounding on Mary's door. "You have one minute left, Mary."

The door opened. Mary came out, her hair neatly coiled, immaculately dressed—except for the two pins fastening her gown where the buttons were missing. Jason offered his arm, but she ignored it. Looking cool and dignified, she strolled down the corridor.

Angrily, Jason followed her. "Mary, you must believe me. . . ."

Vincent floated along after them, laughing at Jason's futile attempts to explain. This was better than he possibly could have hoped for. And damned amusing, too. He'd never laughed so hard in his life.

Mary and Jason entered the dining room, Vincent close behind, where the rest of the family were already in their seats. Lady Weldon, apparently recovered from her ordeal in the carriage, sniffed at their tardiness, then stopped, her eyes bulging out of her head.

"Jason! What is the meaning of this?"

Jason, still trying to explain to Mary, stared at the older woman in confusion.

Quimby, also appearing recovered, cleared his throat. "It's, ah, not at all the thing to come to the dinner table looking so disheveled."

Jason glanced down at his wrinkled clothes. Belatedly, he buttoned his waistcoat and cuffs.

Cecil looked back and forth between Jason and Mary. His narrow face darkened.

Beatrice's rosebud mouth curved. "I'm sure Jason has an explanation."

"No, I don't." He turned back to Mary. "Mary, please listen—"

The door opened, interrupting him. Two servants came in with a large canvas-covered painting and set it against the wall, opposite the one where Vincent's portrait hung.

Jason hesitated, glancing at Mary, then at Vincent. The ghost was watching him with gleeful eyes. Jason tensed. Vincent had gotten out of hand. Over the last month, it had become increasingly obvious that he was going to have to do something about the ghost.

The time had come. His discussion with Mary would have to wait. He was certain he would be able to resolve everything with her—if his plan worked.

Turning his back on the ghost, Jason walked over to the painting and placed his hand on the canvas. "This is my wedding gift to Mary. It is a token of my high esteem for her." He bowed in her direction. "I know it's a trifle early, but I find I cannot wait the three days until our wedding to give it to you."

Mary stared at him, then at the canvas-covered painting, then back at him again. "Jason, I think we need to talk."

Jason sighed in frustration. *Now* she wanted to talk. But he couldn't, not right now. There was something he had to do first—something he should have done long ago. . . .

"We'll talk later," he told her, untying the rope that held the canvas in place.

"No, Jason." Her voice was insistent. "I really must talk to you now."

"It can wait." He pulled the rope off.

"No, it can't. I . . ." She took a deep breath. "I want to postpone our wedding."

Gasps filled the air.

The rope sliding to the floor, Jason turned to stare at her. Her chin trembled a little, but she met his gaze steadily.

"Postpone the wedding!" Lady Weldon cried. "At this late date? I will have to write letters to everyone—"

"No, you won't," Jason said, his gaze not leaving Mary's. "We are not postponing the wedding. Mary was only joking."

Mary frowned. "No, I wasn't. There are some things that bother me. . . . I don't always understand you—"

"You can understand me after the wedding," Jason said through clenched teeth. "We are not postponing the wedding, Mary, and that's final."

Mary looked at him, anger beginning to burn in her eyes again. "I'm afraid I must insist."

"And I'm afraid I must refuse." He turned back to the painting and took hold of the canvas.

"Then you leave me no choice." Her voice shook. "I am breaking our engagement."

Jason grew very, very still.

"Oh dear, oh dear, oh dear," Quimby cried.

Cecil's frown deepened.

Beatrice smiled.

The glow around Vincent flared for an instant. "Congratulations, nephew."

Jason stared at him, seeing the triumphant gleam in his eyes. His lips tightened. He pulled the canvas off the portrait.

Vincent's breath hissed through his teeth.

It was the portrait of Elizabeth.

The colors leached from Vincent's form, leaving him pale and weak. His aura flickered and dimmed.

Satisfied, Jason turned to Mary. "You are not breaking our engagement," he said coldly. Ignoring her outraged gasp, he instructed the two servants to hang the portrait on the wall.

"You go too far, nephew," Vincent said through pinched lips. His voice was muted, lacking its previous timbre and resonance.

Two spots of color burned high in Mary's cheeks. "I can't believe how arrogant you've become! You can't order me around." She tugged at the ring on her finger.

"I don't order you around," Jason said.

She tugged harder at the ring. "You do order me around. Without any consideration for what I think or feel at all."

"I always consider you—"

"The way you considered me when you decided we were going to Paris for our honeymoon without even asking me?"

"You said you wanted to go to Paris.

"I did. I do. But did you ever think that I might prefer the seashore?"

"I can give you Paris." He sounded impatient. "Why would you want the seashore?"

"For the same reason I want a simple engagement ring instead of this hideous heirloom."

Jason frowned. "I told you—"

"Yes, yes. I know. It's suitable for a countess. But is it suitable for *me*?" She yanked at the ring with all her strength.

"It is suitable for my *wife*," he said coldly. "I am the Earl of Helsbury, Mary. You will have to learn to accept that and to trust my judgment."

Mary laughed angrily. "The way I must trust your judgment with regards to Aunt Sally, Cecil, and Blevins?"

Jason's lips tightened. "Yes."

Mary stopped tugging at the ring. She stared at him for a long moment, his words echoing in her ears. Her anger faded away and she felt a pain in her chest, a pain that grew and grew until it enveloped her whole body. If he felt like that, then there was no point in continuing this conversation.

Blinking back tears, she opened her mouth to tell him so, when she noticed a sweet perfume in the air—a scent like roses in the springtime. She heard a noise.

Glancing over her shoulder, she saw the portrait that the servants had hung on the wall. It showed a smiling woman with laughing eyes. Mary started to look away, then noticed an odd light that seemed to be emanating from the portrait. The light grew brighter and brighter until it appeared to float down from the portrait.

Elizabeth Vale, her form radiant and slightly transparent, stood there, an almost imperceptible smile on her face.

Mary stared in astonishment. Another smell—like dried leaves—assaulted her senses. She heard a faint cursing. It grew louder and louder. She looked around and saw Vincent Parsell, the sixth earl of Helsbury, standing near his portrait, glaring across the room at Elizabeth.

Mary blinked, but the two ghosts were still there.

Shock exploded inside her brain. The room began to whirl. Faster and faster it spun.

Then the world became black and she sank into the merciful oblivion of a faint.

18

Vincent was vaguely aware that Jason had carried Mary to the sofa and that the other people in the room had gathered around them—but he could not tear his gaze away from the apparition at the other end of the dining room.

She was even more lovely than he'd remembered. Her face was partially turned from him as she watched the confusion by the sofa, but he could see that her white skin, framed by ebony curls, was as fine and silky-looking as ever. The seductive red of her lips was more enticing than he would have believed possible—as were the perfect curves revealed by the clinging gold gown.

She turned suddenly, looking at him with huge midnight blue eyes.

Her gaze had the effect of an electrical shock. A bittersweet pain swept through him.

Her delicate brows lifted. "Still causing trouble, I see."

Her insolent remark dispelled the witless sentimentality her appearance had evoked in him. He stared at her coldly. "What the devil are you doing here?"

She surveyed him from head to toe, her gaze cool and haughty. "You haven't changed a bit. Still arrogant, still ruining people's lives."

"Just answer my question."

She glanced around. "I'm not sure, but I suspect it's to fix the mess you've made of everything."

His eyes narrowed and his voice grew deadly soft. "Don't interfere, Elizabeth."

She tossed her head. "Don't use that tone with me. I'm not afraid of you."

Their gazes locked. Vincent felt the shock again, and then the draining force, even stronger than the Blue Room. In his already weakened state, he knew he could not prolong the confrontation. He concentrated on making his voice as menacing as possible. Summoning the last reserves of his energy, he warned, "I repeat—don't interfere with me," before he faded into his own portrait.

Elizabeth clenched her fists and glared at the man in the portrait, an almost-forgotten feeling of frustration welling up in her breast. How like him to try to frighten her. And how like him to refuse to talk to her. He hadn't changed a bit. He was an arrogant devil, and she wasn't sorry at all that she'd broken their engagement—

A slight moan distracted her from her thoughts, and she turned back to the sofa.

Several people clustered around it, blocking her view, so she floated up in the air to see better.

The pretty brown-haired girl she had seen when she first stepped out of her portrait was lying there, her eyes closed. A handsome, dark-haired man with blue-gray eyes was kneeling by her side, patting her hand and waving a bottle of smelling salts under her nose.

"Mary . . . Mary!"

A pang of guilt swept through Elizabeth. She had frightened the poor girl. She wished that she could have avoided that. She wished she could be an invisible ghost.

No sooner did she have the thought than the glow around her disappeared. Elizabeth looked down at her skirts and arms and hands in wonder. Was she invisible? There was only one way to find out. She moved closer to the sofa.

Mary's eyes fluttered open. Elizabeth held her breath. The girl seemed to be staring straight at her. But Mary showed no signs of seeing a ghost.

Elizabeth sighed in relief.

Mary turned her head and looked at the man kneeling next to her. "Jason?" she said, a bewildered expression on her face. Then her mouth tightened, and she turned away from him. Her glance flickered over toward the spot where Elizabeth had been. With a sigh, she closed her eyes again.

"Mary, are you all right?" Jason asked, his voice urgent.

Mary would not look at him. "I want to go to my room," she said, her voice muffled.

Jason swept her up in his arms, but even in that intimate position, Mary managed to look cold and haughty. Elizabeth followed them up to the Blue Room. She paused in the doorway, looking around at the familiar blue satin and ebony furnishings. Her throat tightened. Shaking her head, she floated inside.

Jason laid Mary gently on the bed. "Mary, I must talk to you—"

Again, she turned her face away. "Please go away." Her voice was full of an aching regret. "I'm not going to change my mind. Our engagement is over."

Jason hesitated, then said, "Rest for now. But I insist that we talk tomorrow." He strode out of the room.

As soon as the door closed behind him, Elizabeth wished herself to be visible again.

Mary, her eyes growing round, half rose from the bed. Then she perceptibly swallowed. "So I didn't imagine you."

"No, you didn't. But you must lie down. I fear my appearance has been something of a shock."

Mary lay back against the pillows, her eyes huge in her pale face. "You are Elizabeth. The woman who jilted Vincent."

"Is that the story he has told everyone? Ha!" Elizabeth flared brighter. Then, the glow around her softened. "Actually, it's true—I did. But that's really not important. What is important is that man, Jason. You have broken your engagement to him, have you not? I am here to help mend matters."

Mary twisted the edge of the sheet between her fingers. "It's too late. I don't ever want to see him again."

"Good heavens, child, what has he done to anger you so?"

Mary opened her mouth to repeat the ludicrous ghost story, then paused. He *hadn't* been lying about that, obviously. But what about everything else? What about his arrogance, his coldness, his lack of consideration for her? "I've had doubts ever since I came here," she said slowly, trying to explain her feelings. "I tried to ignore them, but I can't any longer. I should have heeded my instincts."

"But he loves you."

Mary stared off into the distance, then shook her head. "No, I don't think he does. Perhaps he did once, but he has changed. I don't think he knows the meaning of the word any more. He doesn't care about anything except his title and wealth. He's cold and hard. And I . . . I don't know if I love him anymore." Tears welled in Mary's eyes. "Please go away. I want to be alone."

Elizabeth stared at the forlorn figure on the bed. She wanted to help the girl. Indeed, she felt a deep compulsion to do so. She sensed, although she wasn't sure how, that that was why she was here—to help Mary and Jason.

She only hoped she could.

With a shake of her head, she floated toward the ebony door. She stopped, staring at it, an insistent memory forcing its way into her brain.

Ebony for your hair and blue satin for your eyes—I had it decorated especially for you, Beth.

Pushing the memory away, she floated through the door and down the corridor.

She'd been too concerned about Mary to pay attention before, but now she looked around, staring at the house she hadn't seen in almost twenty-five years.

It felt strange to be there. The house seemed not to have changed at all. The same wallpaper covered the walls, the same paintings hung there. She stopped midway down the corridor, staring at a portrait of a puritanical-looking lady. Twenty-five years ago, whenever she passed the painting, she'd tilted her chin up, refusing to be intimidated by the woman's cold stare.

She floated down the stairs, her fingers trailing along the shining mahogany railing. She wished she could feel the polished wood. She remembered how Vincent had trapped her against it once, kissing her in spite of her laughing protests. . . .

The hall was as dark and silent as ever. She remembered tiptoeing across the marble floor, trying not to let her heels click—she'd hated the way the sound had echoed in the cavernous room.

At least that wasn't a problem now, she thought, as she floated over the floor to the dining room.

Inside, she found servants clearing away the dishes that no one had eaten from. Elizabeth watched them warily, but none of them appeared to notice, or even sense, her presence. She floated over to the portrait of Vincent.

"I don't know how, but I'm sure you're somehow responsible for all of this," she said out loud.

The painted green eyes in the portrait seemed to grow colder, but there was no other response.

Elizabeth sighed and returned to her own portrait. She stepped up into it, feeling a surge of strength as she did so. Reveling in the sustaining force, she soaked it in.

She suspected she was going to need all the strength she possessed to fix this mess—and to fight the one man she'd never been able to beat.

19

By the next morning, Elizabeth was ready to take action. She stepped down from her portrait and stretched her arms over her head. The exercise felt almost as good as when she'd been alive—only instead of feeling the pull of her muscles, she felt pure energy streaming through every part of her. Lowering her arms, she glanced down at her gold gown and decided the first order of business was to change her clothes. As much as she liked the dress, she could not tolerate wearing the same thing every day.

Closing her eyes, she pictured a dress she'd always wanted but never dared to buy. Hearing a slight rustling noise, she opened her eyes and looked down. To her delight, she was now wearing a high-waisted bright turquoise gown with little puff sleeves.

Now all she had to do was find Jason. Judging from his behavior when Mary had fainted, he was her most likely ally.

Closing her eyes again, she imagined the master bedroom. She felt an odd dizzying sensation and quickly opened her eyes. She was still in the dining room.

Apparently, she would have to work on that one. Sighing, she floated out through the door, up the stairs, down several corridors, and into the master bedroom.

Unfortunately, Jason wasn't there. The chamber appeared to be no longer in use. She would have to search for him.

Sighing again, she floated out into the corridor and stuck her head through the next door.

She saw a young redheaded girl—Beatrice, someone had called her last night—talking to an older woman with gray hair and cold brown eyes. Elizabeth gasped with shock as she recognized her—Eugenia Farlow! Or Lady Weldon, she corrected herself. She remembered the woman pursuing the earl of Weldon with a single-minded purpose that had been almost frightening. She had never liked the woman. Elizabeth noticed the resemblance between her and the red-haired girl was striking—not so much because of their features, but because of the similarity of their expressions.

"How are you faring with the duke, Mother?" Beatrice asked.

"Very well," Lady Weldon responded. "As my favor for the glove game, I asked him to attend yesterday's evening meeting of the Society for Chastity Within Marriage. I believe he was impressed. I am certain it is only a matter of time before he pops the question. And you, daughter? Have you made any progress in ridding Helsbury House of that . . . that commoner?"

"Don't worry, Mother. I intend to have a little talk with her at the masquerade. I am certain she will run sniveling back to whatever provincial place she came from once I'm through with her. Then Jason will be mine. . . ."

Repulsed, Elizabeth pulled her head out of the room and continued down the corridor, making a mental note to advise Mary to keep her distance from those two harpies.

The rest of the bedchambers were empty. She went to the next corridor, where the Blue Room was, and peeked into the rooms. Only one other one was occupied.

The older blond woman in a frilly pink bed robe also looked familiar, but it took Elizabeth a bit longer to place her. She gasped when she did.

Sally Parsell! Dear Sally, who had stood by her during the most difficult time of her life.

Elizabeth watched the woman putter around amongst the various pots. "Sally? Sally!" The woman didn't pause. A shiver pulsed through Elizabeth. She and Sally had been the same age. If she were still alive, she would be old and gray too.

She shivered again.

She searched the rest of the rooms on the floor, but found no one else. She went up to the next floor, and looked inside the first chamber.

Inside, Vincent was pacing across the floor. She froze, staring at him, feeling for the first time the full shock of seeing him again. Her breath caught at the easy grace of his stride, the way his perfectly tailored coat and breeches molded to his muscled frame—he'd never needed to pad *his* calves, like some men she knew—and the way his hair glittered like spun gold. She'd always envied him his hair. She wished she'd been born with hair like that—

He reached the end of the room and swung around, green eyes beneath straight black brows looking straight at her. For a moment, she saw something in his gaze, something that transported her twenty-five years into the past, to the night when she'd gone to his chamber to receive a kiss. . . .

His expression turned cold and unwelcoming.

Something shriveled inside her, but she raised her head proudly and stepped inside. "Good morning, Vincent."

"What the devil are you doing here?"

Apparently even the common courtesy of a simple greeting was beyond him. "I want to talk to Jason. To see what I can do to help him and Mary."

"You truly intend to try to fight me?" There was a pulsing quality to the light surrounding Vincent. "You're wasting your time. I've been honing and refining my skills for the last twenty-five years. You can't hope to compete with my powers."

"Perhaps." Strangely, as the shock of seeing him again subsided, an unfamiliar exhilaration filled her. For the first time since she'd known him, she felt in control. For once, she didn't have to worry about the physical effect he'd always had on her. She could face him on her own terms. The thought gave her confidence. "Can't we at least talk about the situation like two civilized ghosts?"

Vincent stared at her suspiciously. "What is there to talk about? The girl has broken the engagement. He would be a fool to take her back. She would cause him even more trouble than you caused me."

Elizabeth arched her brows. "You make it sound as if I was some calculating hussy when I was alive instead of an innocent girl of nineteen."

"You, an innocent girl? You were born knowing how to twist a man's insides into knots."

Some of her satisfaction faded and she glared at him. "You weren't exactly a naive boy. I seem to recall a certain opera dancer that you escorted about quite blatantly. The stories of your dissipations were legendary."

"Not nearly so legendary as your flirtations," he drawled, pulling out his snuffbox.

"My flirtations! I was polite, nothing more. Speaking to a man hardly constitutes a flirtation."

"It does when a woman looks as you do."

"I should have known you would make it out to be all my fault. You haven't changed a bit." She watched him open the snuffbox with the lazy grace so innate to him and take a pinch.

"Nor have you. A man—or a ghost—would have to be insane to mix himself up with the likes of you."

She tossed her head. "Haversham wouldn't agree with you." She paused, then added, "He was ecstatically happy for the entire time of our marriage . . . and so was I."

Vincent grew very still. Then he snapped the box shut, and his mouth curled in a sneer. "I have no doubt you wound that fop about your little finger. The man was too stupid to see what you really are."

Elizabeth stiffened. "Perhaps you were the one who was too stupid to see what I really was," she said quietly.

"I doubt it." He slid the snuffbox into his pocket. "You haven't changed, Elizabeth. Your tongue is still as sharp as a knife, and you're still forcing your way into men's bedrooms."

She gasped. For a moment, hurt stabbed at her. Then anger pulsed through her with astonishing force. Her fists clenched. She wanted desperately to throw something at him.

A comb from the dressing table flew through the air, passing right through him to hit the wall behind.

Startled, she stared at the comb. Had she done that? She had never in her life done something so violent, so vicious.

Embarrassment trickled through her and she looked at him apologetically. "I'm sorry. I don't know what happened. I didn't mean—"

"Don't put on that pretty face of false regret," he said, his eyes glinting. "I always knew you weren't a lady."

Her embarrassment vanished, swallowed up by a flood of fury. She floated around the room, a furious hail of objects zinging toward Vincent as she passed. A brush followed the comb. He jumped to one side.

"You've always been an arrogant lout!"

A boot barreled toward him. He streaked up toward the ceiling.

"The most insensitive . . . "

An inkwell shot straight at his head. He dropped down to the floor.

" . . . rude, obnoxious . . . "

A handful of coal pelted through the air. He ducked.

" . . . insolent, sarcastic . . . "

A basin of water floated through the air and hovered over him. He glanced up and frowned. "Elizabeth—"

" . . . horribly conceited man I've ever met!" The bowl tilted, dumping its contents over his head.

Sparks shot out. Vincent flickered and disappeared.

Elizabeth stopped her rampage, shocked. "Vincent?"

There was no answer.

She bit her lip. Had she killed him? No, he was already dead, she couldn't have killed him. Had she deelectrified him, then? Oh, her terrible temper! She would have thought being dead would have cured her of that problem. But once again it had gotten her into a terrible fix.

"Vincent," she whispered, full of regret. She held out her hand to the spot where he'd stood. "I'm so sorry."

Soft laughter echoed behind her. Snatching her hand back to her side, she whirled.

Vincent's image, faint but discernible, stood by the fireplace, smiling mockingly. "You haven't defeated me yet, Elizabeth."

He vanished.

She was still glaring at the fireplace when the door opened behind her and a voice exclaimed, "What the devil—?"

Elizabeth turned. Jason, his coat over his arm, sweat beading his forehead as though he'd just indulged in some exercise, stood in the doorway, staring in disbelief at the chaos of his room.

She smiled at him. "I'm sorry about the mess, Jason. I wanted to talk to you."

Jason's gaze swung from the black ink dripping down the wall to the glowing form by the fireplace. "What do you want to talk to me about, Miss Vale?" he asked politely, shrugging into his coat.

Elizabeth studied him. He was a good-looking man, tall, with dark hair. He was perhaps not so handsome as Vincent, but there was something about his oddly familiar level gray-blue gaze that suggested a core of steadiness that Vincent lacked.

A memory flashed in her head of the night of the Helsbury musicale—and of going upstairs to the nursery with Jane Parsell, Gilbert's young wife. There had been a small boy, with bluish gray eyes, waiting in bed there. He had thrown his arms around Jane's neck and said, "Good night, Mama. I love you."

Elizabeth's throat tightened. She'd thought she would have a child of her own someday, one who would say those words to her—

"Miss Vale?"

Elizabeth looked up at those same gray-blue eyes—older now, and more cynical. "I remember you," she said slowly. "You are Gilbert and Jane's little boy. You are the earl now?"

Jason bowed.

Elizabeth frowned. "But how is it that you have inherited the title? Gilbert was Vincent's youngest brother. Did none of the other three have children?"

"My uncles all died unwed. Vincent saw to that."

Enlightenment dawned on Elizabeth. "And now he's trying to make sure you don't marry, either. But why?"

"Vincent doesn't want any Helsbury earl to endure the pain he suffered—the pain he claims you caused him."

"I see." Elizabeth fingered her locket. "Am I correct that you do not appreciate his interference?"

Jason laughed without amusement. "You are. His 'interference' caused Mary to think that she needed to break our engagement."

Elizabeth looked up in alarm. "You can't allow her to do that!"

"I didn't. I refused to accept her termination."

Elizabeth smiled. "I'm glad to see one of the Helsbury earls has some sense."

Jason arched his brows, but said nothing. He crossed over to the nightstand and picked up the clean towel lying there. He started to wipe the sweat from his brow, then paused and glanced warily about the room.

Elizabeth, floating over to a chair, did not notice his actions. "We must formulate a plan, Jason."

He stopped looking around the room and stared at her. "We?"

"Of course." Experimentally, she sat down. She went a little too far and found her head where her derriere was supposed to be. She floated up until she was in a more conventional position. "I'm here to help you."

He gave a slightly bitter laugh. "Frankly, Miss Vale, I'm not eager to have another ghost interfering in Mary's and my business."

Elizabeth frowned. "Then why did you summon me?"

"I did not summon you. At least, I didn't intend to do so. I only hoped the portrait would make Vincent leave."

"I see." She mulled this over in her mind. Judging from Vincent's appearance a short while ago, she did not think Jason's plan had succeeded. "I think it would be wise of you to accept my help."

Jason wiped his face with the towel. "What do you propose?"

"You must talk to her alone."

He crumpled the towel into a ball and tossed it onto the wash stand. "I don't think she will agree to that."

"I will persuade Mary. You must make certain to make the best use of the opportunity."

Jason hesitated, then nodded. "If you can convince her to agree to see me, I will do my best."

Elizabeth smiled. "Go to the garden in one hour. She will be there, I promise you." She tried to vanish the way Vincent had, but failed. Sighing, she walked through the door.

She was definitely going to have to work on her powers.

Vincent frowned at the sway of Elizabeth's hips as she left. He had forgotten how she could tease a man just by the sensuous movements of her body—the way she had this morning, when she stepped down from her portrait and stretched with catlike pleasure.

He had no doubt she'd done it on purpose. He was equally certain she had changed her dress—right in front of him!—on purpose as well. Not that he had been able to see anything—but that had almost made it worse.

She hadn't changed at all. She was still a teasing, forward wench, and she still could make him more furious more quickly than anyone he'd ever known.

Haversham wouldn't agree with you. He was ecstatically happy for the entire time of our marriage . . . and so was I.

He closed his eyes and clenched his fists. A familiar hollow feeling filled his chest.

She was lying. Just as she had been twenty-five years ago when she'd written him that she'd fallen in love with Haversham. He'd been going to make her confess her lie that night twenty-five years ago, but he'd died before he could reach her.

Now he had another chance. He only had to think of a way.

A way to make her admit that she didn't love Haversham—and never had.

20

Jason, his hands clasped behind his back and his feet slightly spread, gazed at Mary as she sat on the stone bench, staring straight ahead. In her blue dress, her hair coiled high on her head, she looked the picture of prim virtue—the complete opposite of how she'd looked yesterday in the Blue Room.

He knew how that hair looked uncoiled, spread out on a pillow, how soft it felt in his hands and how heavenly it smelled when he buried his face in it. He knew what she looked like under that prim blue dress, her skin soft and rosy with blushes, how luscious her breasts looked and tasted. He knew that if held her in his arms and touched her in certain spots—the sensitive curve at the juncture of her neck and shoulder, the delicate skin just below the indentation of her navel, or the place covered by sweet curls between her thighs—she would squirm and sigh with pleasure. He knew how incomparable she had felt against him, how glorious she'd smelled and tasted and sounded as he'd made mad, passionate love to her.

Yesterday afternoon had been perfect. So how the devil had everything gone so wrong? Making love with her should have solved all their problems. Instead, it seemed to have made them worse.

Jason took a deep breath. "Thank you for seeing me, Mary. I want to explain about Vincent. He has been trying to frighten you away since you arrived. He was responsible for pushing me into Beatrice's arms and for making Quimby and Aunt Weldon say those insane things. He has the power to make people say what they're thinking."

He picked a pink rose from a bush by the bench. "But even though he tricked me into going to your room, I was fully responsible for what happened there. I apologize for my behavior yesterday, Mary. I want to work this out between us." He handed her the rose.

She took it, and some of the rigidity seemed to go out of her spine. "I would like that also," she said. She looked at him earnestly. "I am so confused, Jason."

He sat down next to her and took her hand in both of his. "I've been confused too, Mary."

She looked up at him, her eyes blue and sincere. "I feel as though I don't know you any more. I don't know what you want from me."

He smiled tenderly. "I want to fondle your breasts."

She stiffened.

"I mean, I want you to be part of my life." He glanced about furiously. There was no sign of Vincent, but the redolent smell of autumn leaves lay heavy in the air. He turned back to Mary. "You are important to me. More important than you can imagine." His hands tightened on her fingers. "I want to marry you and cherish you. Most of all, I want you in my bed."

She gasped and pulled her hand from his grasp. "If that's all you care about—" She rose to her feet, the picture of outraged indignation.

"No, Mary, wait!" Leaping to his feet, he seized her arm. "That's not what I meant to say. I meant to say that I want you *naked* in my bed and I want to kiss your lips and your breasts and your belly and your—"

"Jason!"

Sweat popped out on his forehead. "Mary," he said through gritted teeth, "it's Vincent. Can you smell that scent like autumn leaves? He's making me say these things. Remember I told you that he has the power to make people say things? The way he did with Quimby and Aunt Weldon."

"All I smell is roses." Mary eyed him coldly. "And you told me he had the power to make people say what they're thinking."

Jason raked his fingers through his hair. "That's not the point. The point is it is my duty to wed you. I took your virginity, Mary. We must be married whether you like it or not."

"The point is," she said, her face pale and set, "nothing has changed. Please excuse me, Jason. I find I am a trifle weary of your company." Tossing aside the flower he'd given her, she stalked out of the garden.

No sooner was she gone than Elizabeth, now wearing a red dress, floated out from behind a bush and hovered over the stone bench. "You certainly botched that."

He bent over and picked up the rose Mary had thrown away, his lips tight with annoyance. "It was Vincent."

Elizabeth looked at him quizzically. "Can he really make you say things you don't mean?"

A flush rose in Jason's cheeks. "Not exactly . . . never mind. Mary is furious. I never realized how stubborn she can be. She refuses to see that we must marry."

"And no wonder," Elizabeth said. "You weren't very flattering. You should have been more conciliatory. You should have asked her, not ordered her to marry you. Any woman would rebel at such an insult."

His fingers closed around the bloom. "I know I did not handle her well. I lost my temper." He looked up at Elizabeth again. "You must convince her, Miss Vale. She has to marry me."

Elizabeth nodded. "I will see what I can do." She glanced down the path Mary had taken. "But perhaps I should allow her an hour or two to calm down. She seemed very angry indeed."

Elizabeth floated down and sat on the bench. "In the meantime," she said, a trifle dryly, "I think we should rehearse what you will say to her next time."

*   *   *

Vincent, lounging on a tree branch above Jason and Elizabeth, smiled with satisfaction at the success of his most recent endeavor. He'd definitely scored a victory. He laughed silently, remembering the expression on Mary's face when Jason had said he wanted to fondle her breasts. Really, the boy needed to control his lustful thoughts.

As for Elizabeth . . . if this was her best effort to "help," then he needn't worry at all.

Smiling, he bent his ear to hear what she was saying to Jason.

". . . Ask her to dance, tonight. Afterward, take her out on the balcony. And remember, you must treat her gently. With respect. . . ."

Vincent's smile vanished. Elizabeth had always wanted to be treated like a queen on a throne. When he'd first met her, she'd been surrounded by men—morons who'd worshipped at her tiny feet and begged for the opportunity to serve her. It had been something of a game for him to bait her, to make her hiss with indignation and turn a cold shoulder to him. But her coldness had been belied by her furtive glances and rosy blushes whenever he caught her at it.

He'd enjoyed the game—until that first time he'd made the terrible mistake of kissing her.

He'd intended only to tease her when he'd caught her alone in the corridor at the opera. He'd pushed her into a shadowed corner, taken her sputtering into his arms, and kissed her. She'd been stiff with indignation at first. Then slowly, subtly, her body had relaxed. Her arms had crept up around his neck, and she had responded.

Oh, sweet lord, how she had responded. The earth had stood still, stars had shot crazily through the skies, and a rainbow of colors had burst throughout the universe. When he'd finally released her, he'd been able to do nothing but stare at her.

Vincent sat up on the tree branch. The sun was shining brightly in the sky, but he couldn't feel it. He felt cold— cold in every particle of his being.

"Very clever."

Startled, Vincent glanced up to find Elizabeth, arms folded across her chest, hovering before him.

From long habit, he instantly concealed his thoughts and regarded her with the mocking smile that had become his protection against emotions he didn't want to feel. Inclining his head, he drawled, "Thank you. Making people say what they're really thinking is a useful talent of mine."

"Useful . . . but a trifle childish."

Vincent's brows drew together. "Childish?"

"Don't you agree that all this maneuvering is rather silly?" She floated over to a branch opposite him and sat down. "Why not let Jason make his own decisions?"

"Because I care about the boy, that's why," Vincent said coldly. Her ebony curls and white skin were stunningly beautiful against her red dress and the backdrop of dark green leaves. It almost hurt to look at her, she was so lovely.

Swinging a tiny slippered foot, Elizabeth gave a tinkling laugh. "You sound like an overbearing father. Really, you must allow Jason to live his own life."

Vincent watched her shapely ankles peeking out from under the hem of her dress. "Until he can show some wisdom, that is impossible."

"You can't win, you know. They love each other." Her smile was seductive, beguiling.

He steeled himself against it. "Love is a highly overrated emotion."

Her foot stopped swinging. "There's no reasoning with you, then?"

"No. Unless . . ." He paused, inspiration flashing through his brain. "Unless you would care to make a small wager."

"A wager?" She frowned. "What kind of wager?"

"You seem so convinced that Mary and Jason love each other. If you can persuade Mary to wed Jason on Wednesday, I will pay the forfeit of your choice."

Elizabeth thought about it for a moment. "I would like to learn that trick of making people speak their minds."

"I will teach you—if you win. But if you fail . . . "

"If I fail, what?"

He smiled provocatively. "It's too bad I can't ask for a kiss."

She didn't take the bait. "If I fail?" she repeated.

"If you fail, you will answer a question I shall put to you—and you must swear by your eternal soul that your answer is true."

She stared at him uneasily. "What question?"

"Ah, you will only find that out if you fail. Do you agree to the wager?"

"I don't know." She fingered her locket. "You won't interfere?"

"Oh, no, I didn't say that. There are no restrictions for this wager."

She stared at him a moment longer. "Very well. I accept your wager."

Triumph blazed within him, but he tamped down the revealing glow. "Excellent. Perhaps you should go rest. Conserve your energy for tonight. As a ghost, you must be careful about these things, you know. You could be sucked away in an instant and not be able to come back."

"Oh? Thank you for the warning. But I think I would rather go talk to Jason—and tell him to be on guard for your tricks."

Smiling, Vincent watched her float away. It didn't matter what she said to Jason. It was doubtful Jason could do anything—not when Mary was so angry at him.

But perhaps it would be wise to make sure Mary's anger didn't cool. Perhaps he should have a little talk with her. . . .

Bracing himself to withstand the draining force, he transported himself to the Blue Room.

Mary was there, pacing about. Feeling the pull of the room, Vincent remained invisible, watching her. She looked angry, but he could also see a trace of tears on her cheeks.

Feeling the pull of the room again, he appeared and said, "Good afternoon, Miss Goodwin."

Mary swung about, her expression startled. "You!"

He bowed. "I think it's high time we met, don't you?"

She faced him, arms folded across her chest. "No, I don't. I have no desire to meet you."

Anger simmered inside him at her rudeness, but he managed to smile. "I understand your feelings. I only wanted to apologize."

"Don't pretend that you're sorry," she snapped. "This is what you've wanted all along. You should be very happy now. You and Jason can wallow in your arrogance and conceit together, free from the pernicious influence of women. I don't know how I've put up with him as long as I have."

Vincent gritted his teeth. Miss Mary Goodwin was not so sweet as he had thought—her temper was downright shrewish. But he forced himself to say soothingly, "I, too, am amazed at your tolerance."

"I refuse to be treated so shabbily any longer," Mary said angrily, dashing a tear from her cheek. "I don't know how I've held my tongue at his insults."

"You have been extremely patient," Vincent agreed, "and much too accommodating. I know I wouldn't like to marry someone who had proposed only from a sense of duty."

Mary stared at him. "A sense of duty?"

"Yes. To marry and produce an heir." He feigned a look of surprise. "Surely you knew? Or you must have at least suspected. Didn't you think it was strange that he proposed to you so quickly after he discovered he was the new earl?"

Mary bit her lip. No, she hadn't thought it strange—she'd been surprised, delighted, ecstatic. But now that she thought about it, it did seem rather odd. A faint nausea rose in her. Duty!

"I'm sure he thought you would be an excellent wife—in bed at least. After rescuing you from a life of drudgery, it would be only fair for him to expect you to demonstrate your gratitude."

"Demonstrate my gratitude!" Her face paled. "How dare he? I do not think I can endure his insults any longer!"

Vincent nodded with false sympathy. "You intend to leave in the morning, then?"

"Oh . . . I hadn't thought about that. I suppose I should, since I have broken off our engagement. I don't want to spend a minute longer here than I have to." She looked at him. "I would appreciate it if you would leave now. I don't want to spend a minute more than I have to in *your* company, either."

In spite of his satisfaction at his success, Vincent stiffened at her insult. With a curt bow, he went out into the corridor. He glared at the ebony door a moment, incensed at her rudeness. But then his anger faded, and a slow smile curled his lips.

She was leaving tomorrow. There would be no chance of a reconciliation.

And at last—at *long* last—he would have the answer to the question that had been eating at him for twenty-five years.

21

Jason, dressed as a cavalier complete with a sword and wig, greeted a fat Greek god and an elderly Marie Antoinette. The couple moved forward to join the other gaily dressed guests milling about the hall. Jason tugged at his blue, gold-embroidered frock coat, pushed a long, irritating curl out of his face, and scowled.

He hated the ridiculous outfit that the earls of Helsbury traditionally wore on this occasion. The high-heeled buckled shoes and the lace frothing at his wrists and throat made him feel like some ridiculous fop, which was bad enough. But the wig, with its profusion of long, sausage-shaped curls, made him feel like a damned fool.

He loathed the wig.

And to add to his foul mood, Mary still had not come down yet, even though guests had been arriving for the last hour.

Beatrice, dressed as a Turkish princess, with a little veil revealing just her eyes, pressed against his side. "I do hope Mary is not ill. I wonder if she understands that she should be here to greet the guests. It is fortunate that I am here to take her place."

Elizabeth, hovering behind Jason, glared at Beatrice. "I detest that girl," she hissed in his ear. "Can't you get rid of her?"

Ignoring her and Beatrice, Jason greeted several more guests.

Elizabeth sighed. "I suppose not. Oh, well." She fluffed up the red skirt of her Gypsy outfit. "Just remember to ask Mary to dance, then take her out on the balcony. Be kind and patient. And *apologize*. Don't forget that."

"I won't," Jason murmured. He greeted several more guests, then said out of the corner of his mouth, "If she comes."

Lady Weldon, dressed as a rather aging Aphrodite, turned to him. "If who comes? Are you referring to Mary? I must agree with Beatrice, Jason—I find her behavior shocking, absolutely shocking. She should have been down an hour ago."

"Now, Mother," Beatrice said. "You know that Mary is not familiar with all that is expected of her. We must be patient with her vulgar, ill-bred manners." She smiled sweetly at Jason. "You know how much I like Mary. I have even forgiven her for hitting me in the nose with the shuttlecock."

"It appears that all of the guests have arrived," Jason muttered. "I believe it is time for us to join the party. Please excuse me." He turned to walk away, when a movement caught his eye. Glancing up, he saw Mary at the head of the stairs.

A hush fell over the hall.

She descended slowly, wearing a gossamer gold dress that glowed and sparkled in the candlelight, similar to the one Elizabeth wore in the portrait. But Elizabeth had never looked so sensuous, so lovely that it stole one's breath.

Jason could not tear his gaze away. The way she walked, shoulders back, hips swaying, was no longer concealed by the full skirts she usually wore. The outline of her legs and the curves of her breasts and hips were tantalizingly displayed. As if she knew the effect it would have, her lips curved upward into an amazingly seductive smile.

With an effort, he lifted his gaze to the gold and diamond tiara glittering in her hair, which was caught up in a profusion of curls at the back of her head. The style revealed the long expanse of her throat and shoulders and chest, which was not covered by so much as a string of pearls. The barely existent bodice cleaved to her breasts, the fabric so thin that the thrust of her nipples was plainly visible—

Jason glanced around the hall and saw the other men in the room staring at her, their polite smiles not quite masking the lustful gleams in their eyes.

A tight white line appeared at the corner of Jason's mouth. He stalked over to the stairs. When she reached the bottom, he took hold of her arm and snapped, "What the *devil* do you mean by wearing that dress?"

Mary stiffened at his tone. "Why shouldn't I?"

"Because you look like a doxy, that's why. It's indecent."

His sharp comment hit her like a blow. Secretly, foolishly, she had hoped that he would like the gown. Hurt, combined with the guilt and misery she'd been feeling all day, grew and metamorphosed into hot, simmering anger. She closed her fingers into a fist, fighting the urge to slap him. "Elizabeth wears a dress like this. My own mother wore dresses like this," she said coldly. "There's nothing indecent about it."

She started to walk away, but Jason caught her arm and pulled her aside. "Elizabeth's dress never clung to her like that. Probably because she had the good sense to wear something underneath." He glared down at her. "You're behaving disgracefully."

"I? *I* am behaving disgracefully?" She drew herself up to her full height. "You almost make me laugh. I refuse to put up with your rude, insensitive behavior any longer. I am leaving tomorrow."

"What!"

Mary tilted her chin up. "I am taking the morning train to Liverpool. The Helsbury ring is on my dressing table. Perhaps you will be able to find another bride to wear it." She turned, and walked toward the ballroom where she could hear the strains of a waltz being played.

"You have a ticket?" his hateful voice drawled from behind her.

She paused. He had only sent her a one-way ticket to come to Helsbury House. Slowly, she turned. "No, but I assure you I will reimburse you for the price of one."

"No."

"No, you don't want me to reimburse you?"

"No, I won't buy you a ticket."

Mary gasped in outrage. "What do you plan to do? Shackle me in the dungeon and keep me a prisoner here?"

His cold gaze flickered over her. "Not a bad idea."

Before Mary could reply to this astounding piece of arrogance, Beatrice and Lady Weldon strolled up.

Lady Weldon cast a disapproving look at Mary's dress. "Jason, you should be thankful that Mary has broken your engagement. I doubt she will ever learn what is tasteful and what is vulgar. It's very plain that she will never be a suitable countess—which is no surprise. Girls like my Beatrice spend their entire lives preparing for the responsibility."

The words hit Mary like sharp hailstones. For a moment, she couldn't breathe. But then, straightening her spine, she managed a glittering smile. "Yes, I can see one needs to spend one's whole life learning how to deal with rude, petty, small-minded people." She turned away, her eyes burning. She had to get away. "Please excuse me. I see Cecil, and I wish to speak to him."

Ignoring Lady Weldon's angry glare, Mary walked over to the group of men standing by the ballroom door.

Cecil, dressed in chain mail and the red cross of Saint George, eyed her admiringly. "You look beautiful, Mary."

"Absolutely charming," the duke of Stafford concurred. He tugged at the tight-fitting red coat of his Admiral Nelson costume. "Dresses like that were very common in my youth. Much more appealing, in my opinion, than squeezing the female form into the horrendous fashions of today."

"Thank you, your grace," she said, fluttering her lashes. "I am glad you approve." She glanced angrily over her shoulder. "Jason doesn't."

"Eh, Helsbury, you've always been a touch too conservative," the arch-Tory duke called to Jason who stood frozen a few feet away. "Lovely ladies deserve lovely gowns. Miss Goodwin, the dancing has begun. May I have the honor? I want to talk to you about the Reform Bill. I've been thinking about what you said. . . ."

Vincent, frowning deeply, followed Jason, who was following Mary and the duke, into the ballroom. Jason leaned against a pillar by the door and folded his arms across his chest, glaring at Mary as she and the duke took their places on the dance floor.

Slowly, Vincent's gaze traveled to Mary, who was nodding and smiling as she danced. He was almost as shocked as Jason was by her appearance. She wasn't beautiful—not the way Elizabeth was—but she looked surprisingly . . . sensual.

"Very pretty, isn't she?" a familiar provocative voice whispered in his ear.

He turned to see Elizabeth, a smile on her tempting lips. Forgetting Mary, he stared at the woman he had once intended to marry, noticing the long black lashes and sparkling dark blue eyes. In the tattered red Gypsy costume, with her black curls tumbling about her shoulders, she looked impossibly young and innocent. Something in the region of where his heart used to be tightened.

Before he was quite aware of what he was doing, he bowed and held out his hand.

She looked at him with surprise. "You wish to dance with me?" Her surprise changed to suspicion. "Are you planning something, Vincent?"

"Certainly not. I just don't have too many opportunities to dance any more—and especially not with such a graceful partner." Smoothly, he pulled her into the dance.

He wasn't touching her—not really—but he could feel the pulsing of her aura and the warmth of the glow around her. "You are as light as—if you will forgive me—as air."

"A compliment, Vincent? I hardly recognize you when you are being so pleasant."

He whirled her in a circle, floating upward over the heads of the mortals below. "Why not enjoy ourselves while we discuss terms of surrender?"

"Oh, are you ready to concede, then?"

He shook his head, smiling. "Come, come. Be realistic. She's been downstairs less than ten minutes, and already they're fighting. Give it up, Elizabeth."

Her laughter rang out over the music. "Oh, Vincent, don't you see her?" She looked at him with pitying eyes. "Jason will never be able to resist her."

Vincent stared down at the woman in his arms as he guided her around the brightly lit chandelier. "You may be right. Certainly I couldn't resist you. Do you remember, Elizabeth?" He moved closer. Their auras mingled and sparked. "Do you remember how I came to your room after the masquerade and made love to you? Long, slow, sweet love, and still you wanted more. I was happy to comply. We made love for hours, and still you begged—"

Her cheeks bloomed fiery red, but she met his eyes directly. "As I said, Jason will never be able to resist her." The music stopped, and she stepped back. "Now if you will excuse me, I wish to speak to Jason and give him some hints."

Frowning, Vincent watched her float down toward Jason, then turned his gaze to Mary. She was standing in the middle of a group of men, laughing and flirting with amazing adroitness. The men hung on her every word, smiles on their lips and admiration in their eyes.

His frown deepened. Elizabeth was right, damn her. He had underestimated Mary all along—and that was never more apparent than tonight. The thin gold gown bore silent testimony to the full extent of the danger she represented. Jason would no doubt do whatever was necessary to keep her. He would never let her go. Unless he, Vincent, could think of a way to put her forever beyond Jason's reach.

Vincent took out his snuffbox and flicked open the lid. He grasped a pinch of snuff between his fingers, his gaze still fixed on the group of people below.

As he watched, a man dressed as Saint George leaned over and whispered something to Mary. She smiled and nodded, but didn't speak. Vincent glanced at the man.

It was Cecil. He had been in the hall too, Vincent recalled. Now he was looking at Mary, an expression of concern in his eyes.

Vincent, lifting the pinch of snuff to his nose, paused. He glanced at Mary, then back at Cecil, studying the man's worried face.

Thoughtfully, he brought the snuff to his nose and inhaled.

Cecil and Mary.

It just might work. . . .

As the duke droned on and on and on, Mary smiled and nodded and understood absolutely nothing of what he said. All she could hear was the echo of Lady Weldon's words.

It's very plain that she will never be a suitable countess.

She didn't know why the words hurt so much. She had never aspired to be a countess. But still, she felt as though she were on the verge of tears, that what Lady Weldon had said had some significance that Mary couldn't quite articulate—at least not yet.

She brushed a hand across her eyes. She had to stop these melancholy thoughts. She needed to plan what she was going to do after she left Helsbury House.

She could go to her brother's. But she hated to be a burden on him. Perhaps Mrs. Cooper would hire her again. Mary was sure her former employer would be glad to have her back. Of course, Mary would never be able to tell her everything that had happened. She would have to keep the fact that she was now a ruined woman a secret. Which should be easy enough. Unless . . .

"Mary," a voice whispered in her ear. She turned to Cecil, who was eyeing her worriedly. "Are you *certain* you're all right? You look a trifle peaked."

Suddenly, Mary couldn't keep up the charade any longer. "I . . . I'm not feeling very well," she said, the burning sensation in her eyes increasing. "I think I need some fresh air."

His chain mail clinking, Cecil drew her away from the group, through the crowded ballroom and out onto the balcony. She sank onto the wrought iron seat beyond the circle of light coming from inside the house. She breathed in the cool air, rich with the scent of jasmine, and fought for control.

Cecil sat down next to her and grasped her hand. "Mary, please tell me what's wrong."

She looked down at his hand covering hers. In the background, she could hear the music from the ballroom and the chirp of cicadas from the garden. The need to confide in someone was overwhelming. She gazed at his narrow, shadowed face. The chain mail covered his hair, but she could see his hazel eyes, dark with concern. "I don't know what to do," she admitted, her throat tight with unshed tears. "I did something very foolish. I . . . I allowed myself to be compromised."

Cecil's hands tightened on hers. "Jason?"

She nodded. "It was stupid of me, I know. I was so uncertain about him, yet I allowed him to make love to me. Now I'm ruined."

Cecil had an angry glint in his eye. "Jason ought to be shot."

"It wasn't his fault. Not really. I should have said no."

"He never should have asked. You are much too generous, Mary. He is no gentleman."

"Don't say that, Cecil. I don't want to be the cause of

ill will between you and your cousin. I will be all right, honestly. I don't mind for myself so much, but . . . oh, what if there's a baby?" She blurted out her greatest fear, the fear that had belatedly occurred to her less than an hour ago. "I cannot bear the thought of a child being brought up under such a heavy burden."

Cecil picked up her other hand. "I wish there was something I could do," he said helplessly.

Mary smiled at him through the tears in her eyes. He was so sweet. And he was looking at her with such warm concern, such sympathetic worry—

His expression suddenly changed. His eyelids drooped, the planes of his face seemed to tighten, and his shoulders drew back. His warm, slightly damp grasp grew icy cold.

"Maybe there *is* something I could do."

Even his voice sounded different. Lower, more assured. But his words diverted her attention from the changes in his demeanor. "What could you possibly do?" she asked, perilously close to tears again.

"I could marry you."

Her tears disappeared as she stared at him in astonishment. "You would do that for me?"

A shaft of light caught a glint of green in his hazel eyes. "For you . . . and Jason. I have sensed all along that you were not right for each other, and I know he feels the same. But his sense of honor would never allow him to break the engagement—especially after taking you to his bed."

Mary's heart sank. "His sense of honor?" she whispered.

Cecil nodded. "He can't break the engagement—or allow you to—unless there is someone else to take care of you."

She grew pale. "I see. It's kind of you, but I can't. I will just have to hold firm to my refusal."

"But what if there's a baby?" Cecil said, his voice strangely intense. "You must marry someone. You don't want to hurt an innocent child, do you?"

"No," she said slowly. "But perhaps we could wait and find out whether or not there's a child?"

A cool breeze blew as Cecil shook his head. "You know how people are. They delight in counting on their fingers. And although I'm willing to accept responsibility if there is a child, I would at least like it not to be public knowledge that it isn't mine." She glanced at him, and he shrugged apologetically. "I hope you don't think me too selfish, Mary."

"No, of course not," she said. She forced herself to smile. "You're being exceedingly kind and generous." Her head was beginning to ache. The diamond tiara in her hair felt unbearably heavy. She wanted to do the right thing, but she had never been so confused about what that was. It seemed wrong to take advantage of a man and marry him for her own convenience. Usually, she would never consider it. But if there was a baby . . .

"Very well," she said wretchedly. "I will marry you."

His eyes glittered in the dim light. "You won't regret this, Mary." He smiled and his arm slid around her waist. "And I'm sure you won't mind sealing our bargain with a kiss."

She did mind. Everything within her protested, but how could she object? She nodded.

His mouth closed over hers. She expected a light, friendly kiss. But instead, his mouth was bold, demanding. She loathed the kiss—it was too practiced, too knowledgeable, too emotionless.

She tried to pull away, but his arm, surprisingly strong, tightened around her waist, the chain mail pressing into her skin.

She struggled, but to no avail.

She was beginning to panic, when suddenly he was torn away from her. She breathed in great gulps of air and glanced up, only to have the air whoosh out of her again.

Standing before her, his hand gripping Cecil's collar, was Jason.

And there was murder in his eyes.

22

"Jason!"

He barely spared her a glance. He was too intent on strangling Cecil. Pushing the smaller man back against the stone railing, he applied greater pressure to his throat.

Mary jumped up and grabbed his arm. "Jason, stop! Are you insane?"

"No," he snarled through clenched teeth. "Cecil is the one who is insane to try to take advantage of what is mine."

Mary stiffened, relaxing her hold on his sleeve. "Have you forgotten I broke our engagement? You have no right to interfere. Let him go."

"You are the one who has forgotten. I refused to accept your termination of our engagement." Turning to glare at her, Jason loosened his grip on Cecil's throat. Cecil managed to punch him in the stomach, catching him by surprise. Grunting in pain, Jason released the other man.

Cecil stepped back, gasping, and Mary rushed to his side. "Are you all right?" she asked. He nodded, and she turned furiously back to Jason, who was adjusting the fall of the lace over his wrists. "I refuse to accept your refusal. I am going to marry Cecil."

Jason's hands froze on the lace.

Cecil laughed. Mary looked at him in surprise. The laugh sounded very odd for Cecil. "Seems like you're out of luck, old boy."

Jason's eyes widened, then narrowed. "I think you are mistaken . . . *old boy.* I am going to marry her, and nothing you can do will prevent me." More quietly, he said, "You've lost. Why don't you admit it and go away?"

A muscle quivered in Cecil's cheek. "I never lose. Something you would be wise to remember."

Jason ignored the implied threat. "I won't allow you to marry her."

"How will you stop me?"

Jason fingered the hilt of the sword hanging from his belt. "I will fight you if necessary."

Cecil laughed again. "You think you can kill me?"

"I think I can drive you away."

"What's it to be, then?" A smile lingered on Cecil's lips. "Swords?"

"If you like. Shall we adjourn to the fencing room?"

"Why go so far?" Cecil made a gesture as if reaching for his pocket. "There are swords in the dining room."

Grimly, Jason strode to a door hidden in the shadows at the far end of the balcony. He entered the house, Cecil a few steps behind.

Mary stood frozen in place, her mind racing with images from the fencing contest—of Jason pressing Cecil mercilessly, and the flashing, lethal-looking swords. . . .

Her hand flew to her mouth. Oh, dear God, *no.*

Her heart pounding with fear, she rushed after them. She went through the door and found herself in a pitch-black room. She stepped forward and bumped into a piece of furniture. Reaching for the object so she could use it to guide her, her hand encountered piano keys. A crash of chords resulted. Snatching her hand back, she stared through the inky blackness, trying to see.

It was impossible. But realizing that she was in the music room, she groped her way through in the general direction of where she knew the door to be. She bumped into a few chairs, but managed to reach the door. Breathing a sigh of relief, she opened it and entered the blessedly well-lit hall.

She hastened across to the dining room, where she found Jason and Cecil lighting the wall sconces and the candelabra on the table. She ran to Jason's side and clutched his arm.

"Are you insane?" she cried. "Cecil is no match for you. Stop, or I'll go to the guests for help."

He shook off her grasp. "If you do, we will only meet another time. Stay out of this, Mary."

Disbelievingly, she watched as he pulled the long curled wig from his head and threw it across the room. He unfastened the ornamental sword at his waist, then shrugged out of his heavy frock coat and waistcoat. In breeches, knee-high stockings, and shirt frothing with lace at the collar and cuffs, he grabbed a sword from the wall under Vincent's portrait and turned to Cecil. "Are you ready?"

"Almost."

Mary glanced at Cecil. His chain mail in a pile at his feet, he stood in nothing but a plain thigh-length linen shirt and hose. He crossed the room and took the other sword from the wall. He put the point to the wall and, without regard for the wallpaper, pressed the blade until it curved into a perfect half-circle. "Ah, excellent." He slashed the sword through the air. "Are we agreed that Mary goes to the winner?"

Ignoring Mary's outraged gasp, Jason nodded curtly. "*En garde.*"

"*En garde.*"

They crossed swords in a brief salute, then pulled back. Mary clasped her hands. "Jason . . . Cecil . . . "

Cecil lunged.

With amazing speed, Jason parried. Cecil lunged again, but Jason sidestepped, and the blade smashed through the glass door of the china cabinet.

Cecil withdrew the blade and turned to face his opponent. He attacked again, driving Jason back toward the end of the room.

Mary watched in equal parts fear and astonishment. She had thought Jason would butcher Cecil. But Cecil was proving very adept with a naked sword. Mary closed her eyes. If either of them were hurt, how could she bear it?

Her eyes flew open when she heard a loud crash.

Cecil had swung his blade across the buffet table, knocking a priceless tea set to the floor. It smashed onto the floor, breaking into a thousand pieces.

Mary cried out, but the men didn't stop. She was beginning to be very afraid for Jason. Cecil was like a man possessed, the fury of his thrusts continuing unabated. The clanging of steel against steel grew louder and louder until Mary covered her ears with her hands. Jason seemed to be able to do little else except defend himself.

But even as the thought passed through Mary's mind, Jason made a sudden jab at Cecil.

Vincent jumped back, barely evading the deadly blade. He cursed silently. He had expected this to be easier. He had forgotten how heavy a physical body could be—he'd grown accustomed to his weightlessness. His movements felt cumbersome, awkward, sluggish—and the effort of maintaining his control over Cecil's body was draining his energy.

But he needed to hold on. All he had to do was win this fight and Mary would no longer be a threat. He glanced at her, standing in the corner, her hands clasped over her ears. Once she was gone, things would revert to the way they'd been before she arrived—the way things had been for the last twenty-five years.

Vincent shook the sweat from his eyes and stepped back, needing to catch his breath. To cover his weakness, he laughed. "Give it up, Jason. You can't win. You'll be happier without her. Don't be a fool."

"The only foolish thing I've ever done was listen to you. Ever since I arrived here, you've told me what to do, what to say, what to think. Like an imbecile, I allowed you to control me. I won't tolerate it any longer, uncle."

Vincent stared at him. "Why, you ungrateful puppy. You would have been lost without me."

"I would have managed somehow. From now on, I will make my own decisions about what I want and whom I will marry, and you will have to accept that."

"And if I refuse to do so?"

"Then you will have to leave."

Vincent laughed again. "Surely you don't think you can beat me, nephew? I am the best swordsman in all of England. I am the earl of Helsbury, after all."

"No," Jason said, his gaze unwavering. "*I* am the earl of Helsbury."

Vincent felt the color drain from his face. He made a thrust, but Jason blocked it easily.

"Do you think I don't know what this is all about?" Jason asked, defending himself from another thrust. "Do you think I don't know why you persist in lurking about? It's because you know you made a mistake. Because if you hadn't been so stupid, you might still be alive. Because you had to have complete and total control, you gave up everything—even the woman you loved—"

Vincent grew still. *You gave up everything—even the woman you loved. . . .*

The words echoed and reechoed through his head. A sudden pain pierced him, making it difficult for him to breathe.

You gave up everything—even the woman you loved.

A white-hot fury exploded inside of him. Rage poured through his veins, driving away all weariness, all awkwardness.

He attacked with a sudden ferocity, swinging his blade around in a wide arc.

Jason parried in the nick of time, and they moved back, around the table.

"I really think," Vincent said between gritted teeth, "that perhaps you deserve to die after all. . . ."

The fight took a lethal turn.

*   *   *

Jason blocked thrust after thrust, his strength dwindling, his concentration wavering. An odd regret was filling him, regret for what he knew he must do.

In spite of his words, Jason knew he'd have had a difficult time without Vincent. The ghost had been almost like a father to him. He hated for everything to end this way, but he knew he had no choice. Vincent had ruled the roost for far too long. Someone had to stop him. And if the task fell to Jason, so be it.

He bided his time, watching for an opening. When Vincent stumbled over the curled wig on the floor, Jason took immediate advantage and thrust.

But the other man ducked and Jason's blade plowed into the portrait of Vincent, piercing his right arm.

Vincent clapped a hand to his arm, gasping. Sweat dripped down his forehead, and he looked unnaturally pale. His breath came in harsh gasps from between his lips, but still he smiled. "Even if you kill me, nothing will change. Mary cares nothing for you."

"You know nothing about what Mary feels," Jason said, doing his best to hide the weariness rising in him.

"Don't I?" Vincent grinned wolfishly. "Did I tell you how sweetly she kissed me when she thought I was Cecil? Did I tell you how her lips clung to mine? How she pressed her body against mine? As if she were begging for me to—"

Jason's weariness vanished. Blood pumped through his veins like a raging river. His lips parting in a feral snarl, he leapt at the other man.

Vincent stepped neatly to one side. Jason, unable to stop his forward motion, ran into a chair, knocking it over. Stumbling, he lost his balance and fell to the floor with a heavy thud. The sword flew out of his hand.

Vincent did not pause. He thrust again, his blade heading straight for Jason's heart.

Mary screamed.

At the last possible moment, Jason seized the chair and pulled it in front of himself, blocking Vincent's arrowing blade. He scrambled back, seized his sword, and swung it around, slicing into Vincent's arm.

Gasping, Vincent dropped his sword and clutched the wound. He stared at Jason, two red spots burning in his white cheeks, blood seeping through his fingers and dripping to the floor.

Jason, breathing heavily, leaned on his sword.

As if in slow motion, Vincent collapsed.

"I hope this settles everything," Jason said coldly. He straightened and held out his hand to Mary. "Come, Mary."

She stared at his hand and then at his face. "You beast! How could you? I will never marry you!"

She rushed over and knelt beside Vincent. "Cecil, my poor dear friend, speak to me, please."

He opened his eyes and gazed up at her. "Will you"— he coughed weakly—"will you marry me?"

She hesitated barely a moment. "Of course I will." She hugged him gently. "If it's truly what you want."

Over her shoulder, Vincent looked at Jason.

He smiled and mouthed silently, *You lose, nephew.*

23

An odd noise, like someone in pain, made Mary turn around. Jason stood there, his face pale, his eyes bleaker and grayer than she'd ever seen. "I'll find the doctor," he said quietly and walked out of the room.

A lump rose in her throat. It was over. Her engagement to Jason was really over. Her eyes burned again.

A moan brought her attention back to Cecil. He suddenly went limp. Alarmed, she tightened her arms around him as a cold draft brushed by her. "Cecil! Are you all right?"

His eyelids lifted and he blinked up at her, a confused expression on his face. "W-what happened?"

Mary's brow creased with worry. "Hush, you've lost a lot of blood." She looked around the room until she spied a folded napkin on the table. Hastily, she retrieved it and returned to kneel at Cecil's side. "You fought a duel with Jason," she said as she gently pressed the linen cloth against his blood-soaked shirt.

He closed his eyes. "Am I dead?"

"No, of course not." She tore a strip from his tunic with the red cross and helped him into a sitting position so she could tie the pad in place. "You're very much alive, and we're to be married."

Cecil's eyes shot open. "I asked you to marry me?"

"Don't you remember?" Frowning, she pulled the strip of cloth tight.

"Yes," he said hesitantly, looking more confused than ever. "But . . . but it's all very strange. It was like a dream. As if it was someone else."

"You must be in shock from your wound. Or . . ." Her fingers grew still on the bandage. "Cecil, have you changed your mind? Do you not wish to marry me after all?"

His brow knit. "I remember . . . you may be with child. Yes, we must get married. It's the perfect solution. I should have thought of it before."

"You did think of it before." She knotted the strip of cloth.

"Oh, yes. So I did."

She sat back on her heels and looked at him searchingly. "You are certain you haven't changed your mind? I know you are making a great sacrifice for me."

"It's not a sacrifice. You will be doing me a favor, protecting me from all the matchmaking mamas. I like you, Mary. You're not like the London ladies I've met."

"No, I'm not," she said somberly.

The door opened, and Dr. Scott, dressed as a Roman gladiator, entered. "Helsbury said someone was hurt—"

He stopped, glancing around at the wreckage of the dining room. "Good heavens," he exclaimed, before catching sight of Cecil, barely visible in the shadows behind the table. "Ho, ho, what have we here? Miss Goodwin, could you please bring some light?"

Mary grabbed the heavy candelabra from the table and held it aloft as the doctor tore Cecil's sleeve open and laid bare the wound. She swallowed. Blood still oozed from the nasty gash. Dr. Scott examined it briskly, not wasting any breath on awkward questions. "You're a lucky fellow, Parsell. The wound is fairly superficial." He cleaned and wrapped Cecil's arm. "You should rest for a day or two, but it's nothing serious. I'll call a servant to help you upstairs."

"No, that won't be necessary." Stiffly, Cecil rose to his feet. "I feel fine."

"You young idiots always do," the doctor muttered. Shaking his head, he left.

When the door had closed behind him, Mary turned to Cecil. "Oh, Cecil, I'm so sorry. This was all my fault!"

"Nonsense," he responded. He smiled weakly. "I'm glad this all happened. It means I will have a bride of whom I am very fond." He swayed.

"Cecil, be careful!"

He grabbed the back of a chair. "Don't worry. You heard the doctor. The wound is superficial. Which is fortunate, because I must leave at once."

"Leave?" she said blankly.

"Yes. I must go purchase a special license." His gaze met hers. "Will you come with me?"

Unconsciously, Mary recoiled. "I . . . I don't think that would be proper."

He smiled, a little wryly. "You're right—it wouldn't be proper at all. But if I leave now, I will be back by tomorrow night."

With a bow, he left the room, holding his arm against his side.

Mary watched him go, shame heating her cheeks. He was such a gentleman.

I will be a good wife to him, she promised herself fiercely. He deserved nothing less.

Slowly, she walked back into the hall. From the open ballroom doors, she could hear the laughter and music. Suddenly, she knew she could not return to the party. Grabbing the train of her dress in her hand, she hurried up the stairs.

She entered the Blue Room a few moments later to find Elizabeth pacing about, her bright aura lighting the room.

"There you are, girl!" Elizabeth cried. "Jason told me what happened—I can't believe what a bumblebroth you've made of things!"

Mary stiffened. "It wasn't my fault—"

"You goosecap," Elizabeth interrupted rudely, "don't

you realize that it was Vincent who proposed to you, not Cecil?"

Mary sank onto her bed. "Vincent?"

"Yes, Vincent! I'm surprised you didn't guess at once!"

Mary remembered Cecil's strange behavior. She remembered his confusion about the duel and his proposal—and no wonder! It had been Vincent! "Dear heaven," she murmured, staring down at the carpet.

"So you see," Elizabeth said, her hands upon her hips, "you can't marry him."

Mary looked up, her lips tightening to a straight line. "Oh, yes, I can."

Elizabeth stared at her. "Don't be a fool. You can't marry a man who didn't really ask you."

"Perhaps he didn't ask me at first, but he did afterward. He wants to marry me, and I want to marry him. He has gone to purchase a special license and will return tomorrow. We will be married the next day."

"You can't be serious—you're in love with Jason!"

Mary lifted her chin. "I most certainly am not in love with that arrogant, thoughtless brute. He could have killed Cecil."

Elizabeth rolled her eyes. "I told you, it was Vincent Jason fought."

"But Cecil was the one who was hurt," Mary pointed out. "My mind is made up. I am going to marry Cecil."

Elizabeth, recognizing the stubbornness in Mary's face, nearly threw her hands up in defeat. Only the memory of her own unhappiness prevented her. "Marrying a man you don't love is the worst mistake you could make. You might think it won't be so bad, but once the ring is on your finger, you will realize that he now has the right to touch you, and you cannot refuse him. . . ." A deep shudder coursed through her. "Think about that, Mary. I hope by tomorrow you will have come to your senses."

Leaving Mary to contemplate her warning, Elizabeth went in search of Jason.

She looked in the ballroom. The guests danced and

laughed, completely unaware of the drama that had taken place a few feet away. Jason was nowhere to be seen.

She peeked in his bedroom, but it was empty. The fencing room was similarly unoccupied.

She finally found him sitting in the library, removing chess pieces from an ebony and ivory board. There was an almost frightening air of control about him.

He rose automatically to his feet, a chess piece in his hand. "It's over, Miss Vale. Mary has made her feelings plain. There's no use in fighting any more."

Elizabeth eyed him coldly. "I will pretend you didn't say that. You must stop her."

He shook his head. "She's made her choice."

"You must stop her," Elizabeth repeated, "or she will marry Cecil instead of you."

She glided through the wall, casting the room into darkness again with only a single candle to fight off the shadows.

Sinking back into his chair, Jason looked at the white queen between his fingers.

She will marry Cecil instead of you.

With a sudden sweep of his arm, Jason sent the chess pieces crashing to the floor and leapt to his feet. He strode out of the library, up the stairs and down the corridor to the Blue Room.

Without hesitation, he threw open the door, sending it crashing against the wall.

24

Mary, sitting at her dressing table, examining the Helsbury ring in the light of a single taper, looked up. A sense of déjà vu washed over her as she saw Jason silhouetted in the doorway. He still wore his satin breeches and frothing-lace shirt, the material taut across his muscled thighs and shoulders; his face was sharply angled, his eyes blackly shadowed.

He looked dark and wild. And dangerous.

The ring slipped through her fingers onto the table. Her heart began to pound. Trying to hide her apprehension, she looked down her nose, doing her best to emulate Lady Weldon's most intimidating stare. "I suppose earls are not required to knock."

He slammed the door closed and strode across the room. Seizing her shoulders, he dragged her up from the chair and kissed her.

Desire blazed through her. She struggled against him, trying to resist the passionate demand of his mouth. His hands slipped from her shoulders to her wrists, pushing them behind her and arching her back. His lips trailed down her throat to a place just above her wildly beating heart. He lingered there a moment before returning to her mouth and kissing her deeply, ardently, unendingly.

For a moment, the room faded away, and all she could feel was his mouth on hers. His kiss, his touch, felt so wonderful. So good. So right. . . .

But it wasn't right. It was wrong. Terribly wrong.

"No!" With a sob, she broke away, trying to escape the lethargy that was stealing over her. She bumped against the dressing table, knocking over the candle. It went out, casting the room into blackness.

Mary stumbled back against the satin drapes, her head spinning in a dizzying swirl of yearning and self-denial.

"Mary . . . "

She froze. His voice floated through the darkness, low and deep and seductive, reminding her of another time when they had been together, alone, in the dark. A time she didn't want to remember. . . .

"Mary, do you remember that time we were locked in the Pit?"

A tiny, almost imperceptible moan escaped her.

His voice turned immediately in her direction. "You told me why you liked the dark—that everything seemed richer, fuller, more intense. . . ."

His voice sounded the way it had in the Pit—soft and persuasive, urgent and compelling. Her throat tight, she stepped back again, her fingers sliding across the satin drapes. The material rustled slightly.

"Mary?" His voice came closer. "Remember yesterday afternoon? I want to make love to you like that again, only in the dark this time. I want to know what it's like to kiss you in the dark—your mouth and throat and hands. . . ."

She remembered his tongue on the palm of her hand, his mouth on her fingers and wrist, the sensuous pleasure of discovering nerve endings she hadn't even known existed. And the huskiness of his voice saying *I used to imagine your fingers touching me, stroking me. . . .*

"You were so lovely. I thought I would expire before I was able to remove all those clothes. Those damnable, teasing, tormenting clothes."

She remembered how he had unbuttoned her dress, kissing her throat and neck, until suddenly, impatiently, he had shoved it down, ripping off two buttons.

"You looked so delectable in your corset and drawers and stockings. . . ."

She remembered how he had pushed down the neckline of her chemise and kissed her breasts. How he had pulled her up against him and she had felt the hardness between his thighs.

"I remember how you touched me. . . ."

She remembered, too. His chest and arms had felt hard and smooth, the hair on his chest coarse. He'd felt so strong—and she'd reveled in that strength, so different from her own yielding softness.

"I took off your corset and chemise and drawers and you looked . . . dear God, you looked so incredibly beautiful without them. I could have spent hours just looking at you."

Her fingers curled around a fistful of satin. A tingling warmth spread over her skin as if he were looking at her naked body right now. He had made her feel so beautiful. So desirable. She closed her eyes, trying to banish the warmth.

"But I had to kiss you. To taste you. You tasted so sweet . . . your throat and your breasts and your belly and your thighs. Remember how I kissed your thighs, Mary?"

A memory of his mouth caressing her popped into her brain before she could prevent it. She remembered how his mouth had ventured too near that place where their bodies had later joined. She'd been shocked at the time. But now, the memory sent a flaring heat to that very spot. She choked back a sob.

"And then you unbuttoned my trousers and pulled them down. Do you know what sweet torture that was, Mary, to have your fingers brushing and pressing against me? To have your hand stroke me so softly, so gently, so provocatively? I could barely restrain myself."

He had felt so . . . big. She had been embarrassed. But curious. She had felt him shudder when she touched him, making her aware of the pleasure she was giving him. And she had been glad of it.

"But that didn't compare to the feel of the tight, hot, moistness of you around me. . . . Our bodies fitted so perfectly together. You felt so wonderful, Mary. When I entered the sweet depths of you, I thought surely I must be in heaven. I thought surely you must have been created especially for me."

It had hurt a little at first. But he had been so gentle, so patient. She had felt so cherished, so loved. And then she had been caught up in the sensation. The rhythm. The pleasure. . . .

"I have never known such pleasure, Mary. Remember the pleasure? Remember, Mary?"

The drapes rippled under her fingers as if another hand touched the satin, but she barely noticed. She was caught up in a maelstrom of memories—memories of pure, intense, indescribable pleasure. . . .

"Mary, don't run away. Come here. I only want to make love to you. . . ."

His arm encircled her waist. The sob escaped her throat, but then his mouth was on hers, hot and hungry. He tasted of smoke and brandy and a slight saltiness. He smelled of soap and tobacco, slightly musty linen and masculine sweat, and the increasingly familiar musk of desire.

He hiked up the skirt of her gold gown, up past her stockinged calves to the bare skin of her thighs. There was nothing, no petticoat, no corset, no drawers to impede his progress.

His fingers stroked between her thighs, and she cried out. He inserted a finger into her and she writhed against him.

"You are so hot and wet and tight," he murmured.

He fumbled with his trousers, and then she felt the potent maleness of him spring forth against her. His hands cupped her buttocks, lifting her against him. Before she quite realized what was happening, he entered her.

She gasped. He pressed her back against the satin drapes, sliding all the way into her, then pulling back out.

"Wrap your legs around my waist," he muttered hoarsely.

Mindlessly, she complied. At first, she could only hear the primitive music of their lovemaking—the gasping of breaths, the rasping of skin, and the thrusting of their bodies.

But then, for a few moments, the sounds became submerged in a soft, tactile world of touch. Everything felt of lace and satin. The lace at his collar brushing against her breasts. The satin of the drapes sliding along her back. The lace at his cuffs brushing against her bottom. The satin of his breeches sliding along the length of her legs. The lace of his breath brushing against her lips. The satin of his manhood sliding between her thighs. . . .

The sensations became more and more intense. He delved into her again and again, until she began to sob and gasp. Fiery sensation began to concentrate deep within her, building and building until suddenly, she exploded.

Wave after wave of pleasure shot through her body. She cried out, and with a hoarse shout, he poured into her, holding her tightly against him. Mary, her eyes closed, felt a moment of pure, intense completion.

And then it was over. The pleasure faded slowly, leaving her shaky and breathless, unable to move or speak. She could feel his heart pounding against her breasts, the heat of his body slick with sweat. He still held her thighs splayed around his hips, showing no inclination to put her down.

She heard him inhale, a deep satisfaction in the sound. "You're mine, Mary," he whispered in her ear, sounding possessive and triumphant. "Mine. I'll tell Cecil tomorrow that you can't marry him."

She stiffened, the passion draining from her.

Cecil.

Dear heaven. Dear heaven above, what had she done?

She pushed at Jason's shoulders. "Let me down."

Her voice sounded shaky even to her own ears. She

could sense him staring down at her through the darkness. "Is something wrong, Mary?"

"Is something wrong? Is something wrong?" Her voice rose in pitch as she repeated his question. "How can you ask that!" She pushed at him harder.

Slowly, he released her legs and lowered her to her feet, his body still holding her against the drapes. "Mary . . . "

"How could I have betrayed Cecil like this?" she burst out, trying to push him away. "He's been so good, so kind to me. Oh, I am so ashamed!"

He held her tightly. "There's nothing to be ashamed about," he said, his voice hard. "You're mine. You know it, I know it. Your body knows it."

He pressed up against her, his leg pushing against the still-exposed vee of her thighs. She couldn't restrain an involuntary moan.

"You see, Mary?" His tone softened. "We were made for each other."

"Perhaps once we were." Tears burned at the back of her eyes. "You've changed, Jason."

He kissed her softly, gently. "No, I haven't. It's only because of Vincent that you're having these doubts."

"No, it's not. It's not Vincent at all. It's you. And me. Can't you understand that?"

He frowned. "The only thing I understand is that I want you. I've always wanted you."

"You used to care about what *I* want. You used to be concerned for other people. Now all you care about is what you want. Is this what our lives will be like? Caring only for what we want, never giving a thought to who we might be hurting? I'm becoming a person I don't even like."

His mouth grew still on hers. Silence pulsed through the room.

Then he stepped away from her. Her skirt slithered down her thighs. Her legs felt weak and wobbly. She stared through the darkness, trying to find a shape, a silhouette, to tell her where he was. But she could see nothing.

A moment later, she heard the faint sounds of flint striking tinder. A tiny flame flared by the fireplace. He lit a candle and a soft glow spread throughout the room.

He set the tinderbox down on the mantle, turned, and began to walk toward her, his face dark and unreadable.

Her hand flying to her throat, she backed away.

He stopped, his forehead creasing. He looked away from her, his gaze passing over the dressing table, glancing by the Helsbury ring. She saw him pause, then look back at it. He picked up the heirloom and stared at it, some nameless emotion crossing his face. His fist closed tightly around the ring.

"I'm sorry," he said quietly.

Then he turned and left the room.

Mary did not come out of her room at all the next day until after dinner, when she received a message from Cecil that he had returned and would like to talk to her in the library.

Her feet dragging, she went downstairs.

She could not look at him as she entered. He came to her side and kissed her cheek. "I have the special license."

She glanced at him, then quickly averted her gaze. "There is something I must tell you first. Something happened last night—"

"You don't have to tell me anything," he interrupted swiftly.

"Yes, I do." Willing back the tears, she lifted her gaze to his face. "You will not wish to marry me after I tell you what happened."

He gripped her hands. "Please don't say another word. I do want to marry you. I don't care what happened. I only care that we put the past behind us and concentrate on the future."

Mary pressed a handkerchief to her eyes. "You are so good. So kind. I am the most fortunate woman in the world."

"No, it is I who am fortunate. Please don't cry. Tomorrow we will be married and we will leave this place."

"Tomorrow!" Mary felt a wrench of dismay at how quickly everything was moving forward—especially after the long, slow days of her engagement to Jason. "But . . . but tomorrow is the day I was supposed to have married Jason!" She frowned. "In fact, I don't think Jason canceled the wedding. Everyone will come to the church expecting to see Jason marry me."

"If they're coming expecting to see a wedding, then let's not disappoint them," Cecil said. "There's no reason you and I shouldn't go ahead with our marriage."

"But everyone would be shocked, outraged—"

"Then let them. I am not embarrassed to be marrying you. I want the whole world to know. It's better that we face the busybodies from the outset."

Mary looked at him doubtfully. "I don't know, Cecil . . . "

"It would please me greatly."

"Very well," she said unhappily. "If that's what you wish."

"Thank you." He pressed a kiss to the back of her hand. "Now I will let you go to bed. Tomorrow will be a big day."

Mary returned to her room. She pulled her blue dress out of the wardrobe and hung it on a peg. Reaching out, she touched the delicate embroidery.

Something inside of her crumbled and died.

Covering her face with her hands, she burst into tears.

In another room, not too far away, Jason lay on his bed, staring up at the ceiling and remembering how excited he'd been when he'd first heard the news of his inheritance.

It had seemed like a dream come true, gaining a fortune, a title, and an estate all at once. But he hadn't thought of that so much, not at first. At first, his windfall had meant only one thing. He could support a wife.

He could propose to Mary.

He remembered that day he'd proposed to her—he'd been looking for her to tell her the news about his inheritance, and he'd found her in the garden, her arms full of flowers. She'd been the most beautiful sight he'd ever seen, the sun glinting off her hair, her arms full of yellow and orange roses. Her gentle blue eyes had smiled up at him with a sweetness that he'd never seen before, a sweetness that stole into his heart and promised him a joy greater than any he'd ever known.

He'd never known anyone like her—not when he was a law clerk, and certainly not since he'd become earl. There was a goodness about her that permeated her every thought and action. Like the virtuous woman in the Bible, Mary was more valuable than rubies—why had he not seen it sooner? Why hadn't he valued her as she deserved?

Because he was a fool. A selfish, arrogant fool. He had failed her. If only he could have another chance—

A knock sounded.

He sat up on the bed, staring at the door. Who would come to his room at this time of night? His heart pounded. Could it be . . . ? Could she have changed her mind?

The knock sounded again.

Hope unfurling inside him, he strode to the door and yanked it open.

Cecil, his jaw tight and his face grim, stood on the threshold.

"May I come in?" he asked coldly.

Jason's hope turned to ashes. Equally cold, he stepped back and allowed his cousin to enter.

"I won't take much of your time." Cecil's voice was curt. "I only want to tell you that if you ever go near Mary again, I will kill you."

"You are certainly welcome to try."

A flush darkened Cecil's cheeks. "How can you be so

flippant? Don't you see what you've done to her? You're tearing her apart. If you care for her at all, for God's sake, leave her alone."

Cecil's low, intense words were like a hundred blades thrusting into Jason's heart. In his mind, he heard once again Mary's voice, trembling with pain and confusion.

I'm becoming a person I don't even like.

What had he done to her? Dear heaven, what had he done?

He turned away, staggering under a weight of guilt and regret. He had to make it up to her. He had to do something.

And he knew, in his heart, what that something was.

"Very well," he said quietly. "I wish both of you well."

"You do?" Cecil sounded half surprised, half disbelieving.

"Yes." Jason stuck his hand in his pocket and closed his fingers into a tight fist around the object there. He could feel it cutting into his palm, but the pain was barely noticeable next to the pain in his heart. "I'm glad you're marrying her. She will be much happier with you."

Cecil hesitated a moment, then nodded. "Good-bye, Jason." He left.

Jason drew his hand from his pocket and slowly unfolded his fist to reveal the Helsbury ring.

The ruby in the center glinted evilly.

He strode to the window, threw open the sash, and flung the ring out as far as he could, sending it disappearing into the cold, dark night.

Staring after it, his chest tightened. For a moment, he couldn't breathe. The pain in his lungs was excruciating, but the ache in his heart was greater as he rested his forehead against the cold glass.

Mary . . .

25

The day of the wedding dawned bright and clear.

Elizabeth, having mastered the knack of appearing and disappearing, materialized in Mary's room with only a few stray sparks floating about.

Mary, stroking the conch seashell, was seated at the dressing table in her petticoats.

"Well," Elizabeth said, arms folded across the bodice of her white silk dress, "have you come to your senses yet?"

Mary looked around. Elizabeth's forehead creased. The light that had seemed to glow from within the girl was gone. Her mouth curved up in an approximation of a smile, but it didn't reach the depths of her sad, dark eyes.

"Yes, I have," Mary said. "I'm going to marry Cecil." In a low voice, she added, "I wish I'd never met Jason."

Elizabeth clutched her locket, a wave of pain washing over her as she remembered saying very similar words herself twenty-five years ago. "Don't say that."

Mary looked at her, sad comprehension in her eyes. "I didn't quite understand before . . . but I think I do now. You were in love with Vincent, weren't you?"

Elizabeth turned away, not answering.

"What happened?" Mary asked. "Why did you break off your engagement?"

"It's a long story," Elizabeth said, staring at the intricately carved ebony bedpost.

"I would like to hear it," Mary said. "After everything that's happened, I would like to know."

Elizabeth sighed. "I wouldn't know where to begin."

"Begin at the beginning." Mary set the shell on the table. "Did you fall in love with him at first sight?"

"Good heavens, no. But there was something about him. . . ." Elizabeth stared off into the distance. "He was—oh, I don't know. Exciting, different. There was a vitality, an air about him that made every other man seem dull. Oh, he was arrogant—I knew his attentions were nothing but a game to him. He infuriated me because instead of composing poetry to my beauty and begging me to marry him, he advised me to accept some poor fool so that the rest of my court could be put out of their misery. I loathed him—but somehow, whenever we were in the same room, I couldn't stop watching him. I suppose we would never have progressed much beyond insults, but one day he took it into his head to kiss me. And I was lost."

Elizabeth fingered her locket. "I had no hope that he would ever marry me. He'd made his opinion of marriage very plain. So no one was more surprised than I when he called one day, dressed in his finest clothes. He carried a single rose in his hand, and he asked me to marry him."

"Oh," Mary said involuntarily. "How romantic!"

Elizabeth smiled wryly. "Yes, wasn't it? I was deliriously happy—until I made the mistake of allowing him to take me to his bed."

Mary looked down at her lap.

"He changed after that. He became a little more arrogant. A little more careless of my feelings. It was as though he suddenly had all the power. He wanted to marry immediately, but I didn't want to. I wanted to have a church wedding with all my friends and family there. It was foolish of me, I admit, but at the time, I just wanted everything back the way it was."

She shook her head. "I was very naive. We couldn't go back. But instead of admitting it, I fought him—fought him until he gave me an ultimatum—marry him or return his ring. I returned his ring."

Mary gasped.

Elizabeth smiled sadly. "I regretted it for the rest of my life." She looked at Mary. "Don't make the same mistake I did."

Mary stared down at her petticoat. "Thank you for telling me your story. But the situations are completely different."

"No, they're not. It's not too late. Think about what I've told you, Mary."

Mary, a tragic look on her face, opened her mouth to reply, but the door opened and a pretty, buxom blond entered the room.

"Kathryn!" Mary rose from her seat to embrace the woman. "I'm so glad to see you. I wasn't sure you'd be able to come. Is John here, too?"

"Of course!" Kathryn said. "He would never miss his baby sister's wedding. We just arrived and I came directly up, hoping to have a chance to speak to you privately."

"Oh?" Mary glanced at Elizabeth.

Elizabeth made a face at Mary, but took the hint that Mary would like to be alone with her sister-in-law. Obediently, she dematerialized. Once invisible, however, she floated up to the corner by the ceiling so she could hear what Kathryn had to say.

"What do you want to talk to me about?" Mary asked.

"What do I want to talk to you about!" Kathryn gave her an exasperated look. "Didn't you think that we'd find it a trifle odd to arrive for your wedding with the earl of Helsbury only to find that the bridegroom has changed?"

"Oh, that." Mary toyed with a lace flounce on her petticoat. "Things didn't work out between Jason and me, and I . . . well, I decided to marry Cecil instead."

"Just like that?" Kathryn asked in disbelief.

"Well . . . yes."

"Don't you think this is a trifle sudden?"

"Not really."

Kathryn gave her a penetrating stare. "Are you sure, Mary? You know you are welcome in our house any time, your ridiculous independence notwithstanding."

"I know, Kathryn." Mary smiled a bit shakily. "But I promise you, this is what I want."

"Very well," she replied. "Your brother and I were worried, but if this is truly what you want, then of course we will respect your decision. We met Cecil downstairs. He seems like a nice man."

"He is," Mary murmured. "One of the nicest men I've ever met—"

Up in her corner, Elizabeth snorted. Nice! Cecil might be the nicest man in the world, but it still didn't change the fact that Mary loved Jason—

Without warning, a presence appeared at her side. Startled, she looked over and saw Vincent. His image was very dim, as though he had very little strength. "Is something wrong?" she asked, a trifle anxiously. "You are very faint."

"Concerned about me, Elizabeth?" He grinned mockingly. "I'm touched."

Her concern vanished. "You—! Why are you here? Have you come to gloat? Or to play Peeping Tom?"

"She does improve without her clothes," he drawled.

"Oh! You lewd wretch, you always were a disgusting lout."

"And you're as charming as ever, Elizabeth. You must have made Haversham's life hell."

She glared at him. "Would you please be quiet? I'm trying to listen to Mary's sister-in-law."

Vincent arched his brows, but complied.

"I hope you and he will come visit us," Kathryn was saying. "We would love to have you."

"Thank you," Mary murmured. "I am sure Cecil and I would enjoy that—"

The door opened again, and Beatrice, dressed in a festive yellow dress, came in. "Oh! I'm sorry. I didn't mean to interrupt."

"You're not interrupting," Mary said, forcing a smile. "Lady Beatrice, this is my sister-in-law, Kathryn Goodwin."

"It's a pleasure to meet you, Lady Beatrice," Kathryn said.

Beatrice inclined her head, then looked at Mary. "I can come back later if you like."

"No, that's not necessary," Mary said.

Kathryn looked at Mary, a question in her eyes. "Would you like me to help you dress?"

"No, thank you, Kathryn. I can manage."

Kathryn hesitated a moment more, then nodded. "Very well." She hugged Mary, and whispered in her ear, "I'll talk to you after the wedding."

Beatrice waited until the door closed behind Kathryn before she spoke. "Good morning, Mary. I see you're not ready for the ceremony yet." She looked at the dress laid out on the bed. "How . . . quaint. I think you were right to insist on making your own gown. It suits you."

"Thank you," Mary said tonelessly.

Beatrice moved across the room and put her hand on Mary's arm. Mary stiffened but didn't pull away. Beatrice smiled sympathetically. "I wanted to tell you how sorry I am things didn't work out between you and Jason."

"That's very kind of you, Lady Beatrice."

"I must say, though, that I think you're making a wise decision. I hesitated to say this before, but I don't think you and Jason ever could have been happy together. He needs a more . . . sophisticated wife. Cecil is much more your sort. He will be satisfied with what you can give him. I wish the both of you every happiness."

"Thank you," Mary said again. She turned away a little, moving away from the touch of Beatrice's hand on her arm. "Lady Beatrice, I hate to be rude, but I would like to be alone for a few moments. Perhaps we could continue this conversation at a later date?"

"Of course, Mary. Don't apologize, I understand. I must go anyway. I want to ask Jason if he will drive me into the village after the ceremony. I need some more perfume and a few other items from the haberdasher's."

Beatrice sailed out.

Elizabeth frowned after her. "I detest that girl," she muttered to Vincent. "She's a troublemaker if I ever saw one. I saw her clinging to Jason at the masquerade. As soon as Mary's gone, she'll be after him like a duck after a bug, the brazen jade."

"Rather like you after Haversham," Vincent said.

"I did *not* pursue—oh, never mind. Believe what you want. It was never any use talking to you. Why are you here, anyway?"

"To make certain you don't talk Mary into changing her mind, of course."

"It would appear there's little chance of that," she said bitterly. "You must be very proud of yourself."

A slight crease appeared between his brows, but he didn't respond.

She glared at him. "Why don't you go away? You've accomplished what you set out to do. You've condemned two people to misery for the rest of their lives, but your selfish needs have been met."

Vincent's mouth tightened. "My selfish needs? You forget—I did this for Jason, not for myself."

"You don't seriously believe that, do you? You've never cared about anyone but yourself. You always wanted everything your own way. You didn't want anyone to take your place, did you?"

"You sound like Jason." His mouth tight, he opened his snuffbox and took a pinch. "Perhaps you're right. Perhaps you're both right. But perhaps there was another reason. Perhaps I couldn't bear to see another woman in *your* place."

Her face turned white. "I don't believe you—"

The door opened and a woman in a frilly pink dress entered the room.

Elizabeth tore her gaze away from Vincent's, fighting a ridiculous urge to cry. "Good heavens," she said, trying to regain her composure. "That's—"

"Aunt Sally!" Mary said, looking startled. "You left your room!"

Aunt Sally glanced around nervously as if expecting to see Vincent lurking in the corner. "Jason asked me to give you a message."

Mary grew still. "He did?"

"Yes, he wanted me to tell you he was sorry and he wouldn't bother you anymore."

"Oh. I see." She forced a smile to her trembling lips. "Thank you for leaving your room to come tell me. I greatly appreciate that."

"You're welcome." Aunt Sally hesitated. "I thought you might need some help dressing."

Mary's smile this time was a little more genuine. "Thank you," she said gently. "I would like that."

Her face brightening, Aunt Sally hurried over to the bed and picked up the dress. She helped Mary lift the gown over her head and settle the skirt into position. "I had a long talk with Jason," the older woman said.

"Oh?"

Aunt Sally began fastening the long row of buttons at the back. "Yes. He told me he'd talked to Vincent and Vincent wasn't angry at me any more."

"He did?" Mary didn't know whether to laugh or cry. "And that made you decide you could leave your room?"

"Not at first. I was still nervous because I was afraid that Vincent might find out somehow that I was the one who told the servants to put Elizabeth's portrait in the Pit. But then Jason told me something that decided me."

"What was that?" Mary asked.

"He told me that he's finished repairs to the dower house. Eugenia and Beatrice are moving there, so he needs someone to manage this house. He asked me if I would do it." A soft pink flush rose in her cheeks. "I did manage the house before Eugenia came. And I think I was quite good at it, if I do say so myself."

Mary stared at her. It almost sounded as if Aunt Sally

had been more afraid of Lady Weldon than the ghost. Had Jason realized that, too?

Mary blinked rapidly. Perhaps he had been right. Perhaps she should have trusted his judgment.

"I thought I would come to your wedding too, if you don't mind," Aunt Sally said.

"Of course I don't mind," Mary said. "I would love to have you there."

Aunt Sally beamed. "If you're going to be married, I want to see it. It will be good to see a wedding again." She stepped back. "There you are, my dear. You look beautiful. The blue is very becoming."

Mary stared in the mirror. The dress was a bit old-fashioned—the sleeves were too small and the skirt not wide enough—but Aunt Sally was right—the blue was becoming. The dress was modest and sweet, like the girl she'd once been. She looked at the delicate stitchery on the dress, remembering the hours she had spent bent over the material. She remembered the love that had been in her heart and her hopes and dreams for the future.

Tears pricked at the back of her eyes.

"What's the matter, dear?" Aunt Sally asked anxiously.

"Nothing, Aunt Sally." Mary turned her face away, trying to hold back the tears. Jason . . . dear Jason. She loved him so much. If only . . . if only . . .

"Mary, you're not crying, are you?"

"No, Aunt Sally." Mary's throat was so tight she could barely speak. The burning at the back of her eyes was growing stronger.

"Mary . . ." Aunt Sally's voice was full of despair. "Don't cry. I can't bear it if you cry. It reminds me too much of Elizabeth."

Elizabeth stiffened. Vincent glanced at her curiously.

Mary blinked back her tears. "Elizabeth?"

"We *were* best friends, in spite of everything. I was her maid of honor. I helped her dress for her wedding to Haversham. She was very distracted the whole time. She kept looking out the window as if she was waiting for someone." Aunt Sally put her hand in her pocket and clutched something. "All through the ceremony, she behaved strangely, her gaze drifting toward the door. She had to be prompted in her responses. She hesitated so long before she said 'I will' that everyone thought she wasn't going to answer. When the ceremony was over, I went upstairs to help her change. Once we were alone, she began to cry. She didn't sob, just big tears rolling down her cheeks. I started to cry too, although I didn't know why."

Elizabeth could feel Vincent's gaze on her, but she kept her face averted.

"Elizabeth . . ." he said.

Without a word, she floated through the door out into the corridor.

26

Frowning, Vincent followed, catching up to her at the head of the stairs. He stared at her, this woman who had caused him such misery—but who had also once brought him indescribable joy. He felt as though he was on the edge of a precipice, that he was about to discover the answer he had been seeking for twenty-five years.

"Why were you crying?" he asked slowly.

She still kept her gaze averted. "All brides cry on their wedding days."

"Oh?" He stepped closer so that he could feel the warmth of her aura. "Was that truly why you were crying, Elizabeth?"

"What other reason could there be?"

"That's what I would like to know. Tell me, Elizabeth. Why were you crying?"

"I . . . oh, if you must know, I thought you would stop me. I sent you that horrible letter, and I was certain you would come." She raised tear-filled eyes to his. "Why didn't you? Why didn't you?"

"I tried." Shaken by the anguish he saw in her eyes, he stepped back. "I tried. There was a storm. I was thrown from my horse and fell into the river. I was dead within minutes."

She inhaled sharply. "Oh, Vincent. I didn't know."

He glanced away. "Perhaps it was for the best. I am sure you were very happy with Haversham."

She laughed shakily. "Our marriage was decidedly ill-fated. We planned to go to Italy for our honeymoon, but two days after we set sail, our ship sank in a storm off the coast. Everyone drowned."

"Dear God, Elizabeth." Vincent stepped closer, an expression of intense pain on his face. "No one ever told me. I'm sorry. I wish you could have been spared such a death."

"Somehow it seems fitting. In a way, it was almost a relief. Haversham was not too pleased with me."

Vincent frowned. "I thought you said he was ecstatically happy." His gaze wandered over her face. "He should have been—even if it was for only two days."

"I think the glow wore off a little when I showed no signs of recovering from the seasickness that plagued me from the moment I stepped on board."

Vincent stared at her. "Are you saying he never touched you?"

Elizabeth gave a watery sniff. "In truth, I believe it was more the thought of him touching me than the motion of the ship that made me ill."

The fierce gladness that had enveloped Vincent dimmed. "You never did like to be touched."

"That's not true."

He laughed bitterly. "Don't pretend now that you wanted me. Every time I touched you, you tried to freeze me out."

"I was frightened, you big looby. Is that so hard to understand?" She smiled without humor. "Every time you touched me, I melted into your arms. And you took advantage of that, Vincent. You can't deny it."

"If I did, I didn't mean to." Restlessly, he paced the length of the room. "I wanted to marry you and make love to you, Elizabeth. Was that so wrong?" He paced back and stopped at her side, "Was it?" he demanded fiercely.

"No, Vincent," she whispered, her eyes bright with unshed tears. "But I wanted more than that. It seemed that all we had between us was that intense physical attraction. You didn't seem to care about anything else."

He looked at her face—so beautiful it made his heart ache. "I . . ." His throat tightened, the words hovering on his lips. He'd never been good with words. He'd tried to show her instead. He wished he could show her now. He wished he could take her in his arms and hold her and kiss her and make love to her.

But he couldn't. All that was left to him now were words. The words he'd never been able to say when he was alive.

He might never have another chance. He had to tell her. He had to.

He had to.

He took a deep breath. . . .

27

But he couldn't do it.

He couldn't say the words. Not when he couldn't be certain how she would respond. Not when her response had the power to condemn him to an eternity of pain and suffering.

"What, Vincent?"

He turned away. "Never mind. It's really not important. It's too late for us now, Beth."

The soft glow in her face dimmed as if a light had gone out inside her. "Much too late," she agreed, fingering the locket at her throat. She raised her gaze to his. "But we can at least do something about Jason and Mary. They love each other, I know it. We can't let them end up like us."

Vincent watched her fingers playing with the locket. He felt sad and drained. But he no longer felt the compelling need to save the Helsbury earls from marriage. The years he'd spent preventing his brothers from marrying suddenly seemed empty and wasted.

"I suppose it would behoove me to try to correct the damage I have done," he said slowly. "In spite of your low opinion of my motives, I do care about my nephew's happiness. But what can we do? Mary is to wed Cecil in less than an hour."

She turned to gaze at him hopelessly. Silently, he returned her stare.

They needed a miracle. And they both knew it.

Unfortunately, there were no miracles forthcoming.

After a long silence, Elizabeth said, "We must talk to them."

Vincent raised a doubtful brow. "They both seem uncommonly stubborn."

"We must try, at least," Elizabeth insisted. "Please, Vincent. You go to Jason. I'll speak to Mary once more."

Vincent hesitated, then shrugged and vanished.

Elizabeth returned to the Blue Room. Aunt Sally was still there, chattering as she pinned flowers in Mary's hair.

"I grew these bluebells myself, Mary, and I thought they would be perfect with your dress. Do you like them?"

"Yes, of course," Mary murmured.

"I do envy your marrying," Aunt Sally continued with barely a pause. "I always hoped . . . but alas, it was not to be. I've never told anyone this, but at one time I was quite partial to the duke of Stafford. But I was plump and plain, and he was in love with Lady Helen. He was quite devastated when she died—or so I've heard. . . ."

Finally, after what seemed like an eternity, Sally went to check on the carriage. Elizabeth materialized instantly.

"Mary, you can't go through with this wedding."

Mary looked up in surprise. "We've been through this already. I'm not going to change my mind."

"Jason loves you. And you love him. Can you deny it? Can you?"

Mary stared at her, then bowed her head.

Elizabeth breathed a sigh of relief. "Then you won't marry Cecil? You'll break the engagement?"

Mary's lips tightened. "No. I'm still going to marry Cecil."

"What?" Elizabeth stared at her in astonishment. "I don't understand! Why?"

Mary stroked the blue silk of her gown. "When Jason proposed, I hadn't thought too much about what being a countess would mean. It isn't just Jason and me. There are tenants, Parliament, responsibilities. I think Jason tried to warn me, but I didn't really understand. It's not fair to him, Elizabeth. He needs someone to be a countess. Someone who can handle the duke of Stafford with poise and grace. Someone who will support and uphold the position. Someone who will prefer Paris to the seashore. He shouldn't be saddled with plain Mary Goodwin."

"So he must give up the woman he loves?"

Mary shook her head sadly. "He will find someone else to love."

"And what of you? Will you also find someone else so easily? Don't be a fool! You love him."

"It's because I love him that I can't marry him. I could never do anything that would harm him."

Sally returned. "The carriage is ready, Mary."

Helplessly, Elizabeth watched Mary leave. How in heaven's name could she argue against such unselfishness?

"You're making a mistake," Vincent said, watching Jason stab at an invisible target. "Don't let her slip through your fingers."

Jason slashed the sword through the air. "Why are you suddenly so eager for me to wed Mary?"

Vincent averted his gaze. "I realized I was wrong."

"You, wrong?" Jason lowered the sword. "Did I hear correctly? Are you ill, uncle?"

Vincent gritted his teeth. "Listen to me."

"I'm all ears."

"You love Mary and she loves you. Marry the girl and end all this grief."

Jason shook his head. "No. I can't." He stared down at his sword. In a quiet voice he said, "I hurt her last night. In a way that she can never forgive me for. You were right when you said living here would change her. How can I allow the woman I love to be destroyed?"

"Don't be so damned noble."

Jason smiled bleakly. "I don't feel noble at all. Go away, Vincent. I don't want to discuss this any further."

Vincent glared at him. The boy was impossibly bull-headed.

He went down to the dining room, where he found Elizabeth waiting.

She looked up eagerly. "Well?"

He shook his head. "He admits he loves Mary, but he believes she would be miserable as his wife. He is impossible to reason with."

Her face fell. "Oh, dear. Mary confessed she loved Jason, but insists she is the wrong kind of wife for him." Tears welled up in her eyes. "They love each other desperately. They're so unselfish. So noble. So—"

"So stupid." Vincent paced around the table. "How the devil are we going to resolve this mess?"

"I don't know. They're both so stubborn. They were made for each other. But she is going to marry Cecil anyway."

"We must find a way to stop this wedding."

Elizabeth twisted her hands. "But how?"

How indeed?

Vincent considered the matter. He'd frightened off innumerable Helsbury fiancées.

Stopping one small wedding couldn't be more difficult than that.

"Come with me, Elizabeth," he said grimly. "I'll think of something. . . ."

28

The church was filled to the rafters. Mary stood at the end of the aisle, looking at the crowded pews.

There was no sign of Jason.

She did see Lady Weldon in the front pew, however. Even sitting down, the older woman somehow managed to look down her nose at Mary. Next to her was the duke of Stafford. On his other side sat Beatrice, smiling as though it were Christmas.

"Good gracious," Aunt Sally said, gazing around. "I've never seen the church so full." She tapped her chin. "Of course, it would be, though. This would have been the first wedding of a Helsbury earl since Vincent's father married over fifty years ago."

Aunt Sally slipped her hand in her pocket. She hesitated a moment, then pulled out a gold locket.

Mary gasped, recognizing Elizabeth's necklace. "Aunt Sally, where did you find that?"

"Elizabeth gave it to me right after she married Haversham. She asked me to return it to Vincent, but he was already dead when I returned to Helsbury House."

"What's in it?"

"I don't know. The catch is stuck. I tried to pry it open once, but it didn't work." She handed the locket to Mary. "I know it meant something special to Elizabeth. I want you to have it now."

Mary gasped again. "Are you sure?"

Aunt Sally nodded. "Let me put it on for you." She slipped the chain over Mary's head.

Tears in her eyes, Mary thanked her. Aunt Sally gave her a fierce hug, then hurried down the aisle to take a seat behind Lady Weldon, next to Mary's brother and sister-in-law.

Trying not to sniffle, Mary saw a movement near the front of the church. She looked up to see Cecil, running a finger around his collar, come in through a side door and take his place. Catching sight of her, he met her gaze and smiled.

Mary forced herself to smile back. Cecil was such a good man. He was so kind and gentle. She would be happy with him, she knew.

Taking a deep breath, she walked down the aisle to his side.

He took her hand in his. "Have you talked to Jason?" he whispered.

"No. Why?"

"I spoke to him last night. He said he wanted to wish us well. He said he was glad you were marrying me—that I was the better man and you would be happier with me."

Mary stared at him in stunned amazement. Jason had said all that? She felt the prick of tears again.

Cecil gazed at her keenly. "Will you be happier with me, Mary?"

"I . . . I . . . of course." She stared down at their entwined fingers. She *would* be happy with Cecil. And she would make him happy, too. In a few years, she would forget all about Jason. . . .

Quimby signaled to someone standing in the shadows. The man stepped forward and lit the candles. As the flame flared, Mary saw his face. She gasped.

It was Blevins, the man who had importuned Jason for a job at the mill.

"Cecil," she whispered, "why is Mr. Blevins here?"

Cecil glanced at the man. "I believe he is working as curate for Quimby. Jason discovered that Blevins had taken holy orders years ago before falling on hard times. He convinced Quimby to take him on as an assistant."

An assistant! Numbly, Mary absorbed this information. It was perfect—Blevins had a job, and Quimby could make sure he didn't imbibe too much.

The vicar cleared his throat. "Dearly beloved friends, we are gathered together here in the sight of God, and in the face of his congregation, to join together this man and this woman in holy matrimony."

Mary's throat felt tight. So Jason had listened to her after all. He had always tried to be fair. To do what was right. That was one of the first things that had struck her about him—his kindness. Perhaps becoming an earl hadn't completely taken that away from him.

"Marriage is to be undertaken for the procreation of children, as a remedy against sin . . . "

Mary pressed her free hand against her stomach. *This is for the best,* she told herself, tears brimming in her eyes.

". . . and for the mutual society, help and comfort that one ought to have of the other. Thus these two persons present come now to be joined in this holy estate. Therefore, if any man can show any just cause why they may not lawfully be joined together, let him now speak, or else hereafter forever hold his peace."

The church was silent. Mary's tears overflowed and trickled down her cheeks. It was too late—

A loud clap of thunder resounded throughout the church.

Startled, Mary glanced at the stained glass window high above the altar. It seemed to darken before her eyes.

There was another thunderclap and then a gale-force wind struck the church. It whistled through the cracks in the door and up under the eaves. The congregation shifted in their seats. The interior of the church grew darker.

Quimby glanced fearfully about, then bent his head over his prayer book. "Then I require—"

The door crashed open. Rain and sleet and snow blew through the church with all the fury of a hurricane. People gasped. The wreath of flowers blew from Mary's head and her hair swirled around her. Cecil put his arm around her, trying to shield her from the storm's fury. Quimby staggered back a few steps. The women in the congregation clutched their hats and shawls. Several men tried to make their way to the door, but the wind was so strong they could only step forward an inch at a time.

Up on the church rooftop, Elizabeth, dressed in a silver-spangled black gown, looked at Vincent with new respect as the wind and rain howled about them.

"How do you do that?" she asked, watching him in awe.

"It's all a matter of concentration." He clapped his hands together and thunder boomed again. He blew, and wind whipped out of the north.

"I'm impressed."

Pausing to take a breath, he grinned at her. "Why don't you see what's going on in the church? I can't keep this up much longer."

Elizabeth nodded and stuck her head through the church roof.

The parishioners were shouting at each other to be heard over the wind. Two men were still trying to reach the door. In one pew, Elizabeth could hear a quiet sobbing.

It was Aunt Sally.

"I knew I should have stayed in my room! This is all my fault!"

"Hush, it's no such thing," the duke of Stafford said over his shoulder. He rose to his feet, braving the wind and rain to move to the seat next to her. Patting her hand, he said, "Please calm yourself, Sally. I'm sure it's not your fault."

Lady Weldon glared at the two of them. Beatrice, pushing her pelisse out of her face, wore an identical expression.

At the front of the church, Mary was pale, but calm.

"Pray proceed, Vicar," she shouted over the howling wind.

The vicar looked at her as though she was crazed. He glanced at Cecil, who hesitated, then nodded.

Quimby, his robes flapping out behind him, leaned forward and peered down at his prayer book. "Let's see, where was I?"

Frowning, Elizabeth pulled her head out of the church. "It doesn't seem to be working," she said to Vincent. "Mary is quite calm, but Sally is almost hysterical. She thinks the storm is your way of punishing her for leaving her room. Whatever did you do to that poor woman?"

Vincent stopped blowing. The rain stopped and the wind died down as he turned to glare at her. "Absolutely nothing, I assure you. Lady Weldon put that idea into her head."

Elizabeth's lips tightened. "That horrible woman! I never did like her."

Vincent shrugged. "She will receive her just deserts. Look in the church again. I'll try something else."

Elizabeth put her head through the roof again.

The church had calmed down considerably. The men, their hair flattened against their skulls, wiped off the pews with their handkerchiefs. The ladies, their hats drooping, tried to restore some order to their clothing.

The vicar cleared his throat. "Ah, here we are—"

Before he could continue, the ground began rolling beneath his feet. He grabbed the pulpit.

Mary clutched Cecil's arm to retain her balance. One of the glass windows broke, scattering shards. Several people tried to crawl under the hard wooden pews to protect themselves. Screams echoed throughout the church.

"It's an earthquake!"

"It's the end of the world!"

"Heaven help us!"

Cecil, looking shaken, said, "Mary, perhaps we should postpone the wedding. . . ."

"Nonsense," Mary said, her lips tightening. "They can't keep this up forever."

"Who can't?" Cecil asked, looking half confused, half frightened.

Elizabeth pulled her face out of the roof and shook her head at Vincent.

He frowned a moment, then beckoned to her. "Follow me, Elizabeth. I have another idea."

Together, they floated down through the roof into the church.

The shaking stopped.

Mary smiled a little unsteadily at Cecil. "You see? Shall we proceed?"

Still looking shaken, Cecil whispered something to Quimby, and the vicar, a trifle pale about the gills, nodded. He opened his mouth.

"Oooooohhhhhhhhhhhhhhhhhhhhhhhhhhhhh."

Quimby's mouth snapped shut. He looked around in confusion. The parishioners—some of them whispering, some of them sobbing from the shocks they had already suffered—all grew silent.

The eerie moaning came again.

"Ooooooooooooooooooooohhhhhhhhhhhhhhhhhhh."

The parishioners, their eyes wide, their faces pale, looked at each other.

"OOOOOOOOOOOoooooooooooohhhhhhhhhhhhh."

"It's the Helsbury ghost!" someone cried from the back of the church. "We're all doomed!"

Screams broke out again. En masse, people rose to their feet and rushed for the door.

"The Helsbury ghost! The Helsbury ghost!" they all cried in panic.

Chains rattled ominously. A mischievous wind blew down the aisle, knocking hats askew and lifting skirts.

The stampede for the door grew chaotic. A man reached the door and fumbled with the latch. A solid mass of bodies pushed up behind him and other hands fought to lift the latch, hindering and impeding each others' efforts.

Maniacal laughter rang out over their heads.

The latch lifted. The door opened. Screaming and yelling, the crowd poured out into the churchyard. Some jumped in their carriages. Others didn't wait. They ran down the road until they were out of sight.

In the church doorway, Elizabeth and Vincent watched the retreating crowd. Elizabeth smiled at Vincent admiringly. "You're very good at that."

"I've had a considerable amount of practice," he said modestly. With a puff of air, he blew the door shut and turned back toward the front of the church. He stopped, staring.

Elizabeth followed his stare and saw the vicar standing frozen in the front of the church, his face pale. Mary and Cecil were still standing before him.

Disbelievingly, Elizabeth looked around and saw a few pews still full. Mary's brother and sister-in-law, pale and shaken, sat in one. In another, Aunt Sally was on her knees, her hands clasped, praying out loud.

In yet another pew, a young couple who were clasping each other's hands sat next to an elderly woman. "Cynthia, Peregrine, why did those people leave?" the old woman asked querulously, in the overly loud tone of some deaf people. "Frightfully rude, if you ask me."

A few pews behind them, a woman pulled at her husband's arm. "Please, please, Mr. Trumball. Let's leave. I'm frightened."

"Now, now, Mrs. Trumball," the man replied. "We came to see a nob's wedding, and see it we will. Even if it *is* only the cousin of the nob. I must say it doesn't seem quite right to lure us here with the promise of seeing an earl get married and then to palm us off with his cousin. But still, we're here, so we might as well see it. Ghost or no ghost."

In the front pew, Lady Weldon and Beatrice stared down their noses as if daring any ghost to take *them* on. Behind them, the duke leaned toward Sally and said in a perfectly audible whisper, "We have a few ghosts at Stafford Castle, too."

Her face composed, Mary said, "Pray continue, Mr. Quimby."

The vicar seemed to come out of his trance.

"Ahem," he said, his voice shaking a bit. "Where was I?"

Despairingly, Elizabeth turned back to Vincent. "It didn't work. Nothing did. It's over, Vincent. We can't stop them."

He frowned. "Don't say that. We can't give up, Elizabeth."

"What else can we do? Even if we do manage to prevent them now, what's to stop them from leaving here and marrying elsewhere? We've lost, Vincent."

Vincent's frown deepened. He hated to admit it, but Elizabeth was right—

"Ah, yes," the vicar mumbled. "Here we are. If any man can show any just cause why they may not lawfully be joined together, let him now speak, or else hereafter forever hold his peace."

Quimby peered nervously around the silent and nearly empty chapel. "Then I require—"

The door burst open.

Jason stood in the doorway.

29

Everyone stared at the new arrival, jaws dropping and eyes widening.

Mr. Trumball hitched up his pants. "Well, what do you think of that?" he exclaimed to his wife. "I would have thought Helsbury would have stayed away after being jilted by Miss Goodwin. Very civil of him, if you ask me."

"Uh-oh," the duke whispered to Sally. "I don't like the look on his face."

Elizabeth couldn't agree. She *loved* the look on Jason's face. "Stop them," she urged. "*Stop* them."

"My pardons, Vicar," Jason said, striding forward. "I did not mean to interrupt." He walked to the pew where the duke and Aunt Sally were seated and sat down. Beatrice smiled over her shoulder at him.

The chapel was silent for a moment more. Elizabeth waited, hoping against hope that Jason would speak.

But he didn't. He only nodded to the vicar to continue.

Despair settled over her like a shroud.

"Elizabeth," Vincent said.

She looked at him. His voice held a tinge of excitement. "Perhaps you were right," he said. "Perhaps we've made a mistake trying to stop the wedding—"

"A mistake?" she said. "What do you mean?"

He smiled at her, his eyes glinting. "I mean perhaps we should be trying to make sure a wedding takes place. . . ."

* * *

Mary stared at Jason, a foolish hope fading from her heart. For a moment, when he'd walked in, she had thought—

Her eyes burned. She loved him. She had realized that the night of the masquerade when she'd allowed him to make love to her, but she hadn't realized how much until right this moment. His kindness to Aunt Sally and Cecil and Blevins made her ashamed for ever doubting him. She loved him so much, she thought her heart would burst with it—but she knew she could never tell him so. Not when she would be the wrong kind of wife for him. He needed a countess. A real countess.

The vicar cleared his throat. "Ah, let's see, where was I? Ah, here we are. I require and charge you both that if either of you do know any impediment why you may not be lawfully joined together in matrimony, that you now confess it."

Mary bit her lip. She wanted to cry out, but she knew she couldn't. She had to be strong. . . .

A strange sensation came over her. Without volition on her part, her mouth opened. "There is an impediment."

As soon as the words were out of her mouth, she gasped. Where had those words come from? She was aware of a murmur from the few people still remaining in their seats. She opened her mouth to take back what she'd said, but again, strange words came out of her mouth. "I can't marry Cecil."

The murmur grew louder.

The vicar blinked at her. "You can't? Why not?"

"Because I love Jason."

Mary gasped again. The sound was drowned out, however, by the gasps from the audience. Helplessly, she turned to stare at the shocked congregation. Her pleading gaze fell upon Jason.

He rose to his feet, looking very pale. "She doesn't know what she's saying." But then, suddenly, his body jerked and new words came out of his mouth. "I mean, I love Mary also, and I want to marry her right now."

The murmurs in the chapel became an uproar. Aunt Sally smiled. Lady Weldon looked disapproving, Beatrice furious, and the duke confused.

The vicar looked astonished. "This is highly irregular." He squinted at Cecil, who appeared bewildered. "You agree to this?"

"I suppose," Cecil said slowly. "If it's what Mary truly wants."

Mary felt an unbidden affirmative working its way up her throat. She pressed her lips together, but her head jerked up and down.

Cecil studied her a moment, then smiled. He kissed her cheek gently, then went and sat down in the place Jason had vacated.

"No!" Jason shouted. "This isn't—" He broke off, his mouth snapping shut. He moved with odd, spasmodic steps to the front of the church, almost as if someone was forcing him.

Mary looked at him worriedly when he reached her side. "What is happening?" she managed to whisper.

"Vincent and Elizabeth have apparently decided to take matters into their own hands," he hissed through clenched teeth. "We must fight—" His head whipped around to the vicar and he said loudly, "You may proceed, Vicar."

Quimby looked at him uncertainly. "This is most peculiar. I will have to start over."

"Then do so," Jason said.

Quimby cleared his throat again. "Very well. Dearly beloved friends . . . "

He spoke more quickly this time, flashing nervous glances at Mary and Jason. Mary struggled to protest, but her mouth refused to obey. She peeked at Jason. His face twitched as if he too was trying to speak.

The vicar turned to Jason. "Wilt thou have this woman to thy wedded wife? Wilt thou love her, comfort her, honor and keep her in sickness and in health? And forsaking all others, keep thee only to her, so long as you both shall live?"

Jason did not respond. The muscles in his face twisted into incredible contortions. "I . . . I . . . I *will!*" The last word, sounding as though it was torn from him, was almost a shout.

The vicar, looking startled, turned to Mary. "Wilt thou have this man to thy wedded husband? Wilt thou obey him and serve him, love, honor and keep him, in sickness and in health? And forsaking all others, keep thee only unto him, so long as you both shall live?"

"I . . . I . . . I . . . "

The vicar stared at her wide-eyed.

"I . . . I . . . I . . . "

Jason's hand tightened on hers.

"I . . . I . . . I . . . " She clamped her lips together.

Everyone leaned forward in their seats.

Invisible hands pried her lips apart. "I . . . I . . . I *will!*"

Everyone sat back in their seats and sighed. The vicar mopped his brow. To Jason, he said, "Do you have the ring?"

Jason hesitated, then removed a plain gold band that had been his mother's wedding ring from his little finger. In slow motion, beads of sweat rolling down his forehead, he put it on Mary's finger.

Hastily, the vicar said, "Forasmuch as Jason and Mary have consented together in holy wedlock, and have witnessed the same before God and this company, and have given and pledged their troth and have declared the same by giving and receiving of a ring—I pronounce that they be man and wife together. In the name of the Father, and of the Son, and of the Holy Spirit. Amen."

Dazed, Mary bowed her head, the fight draining from her. She and Jason were married—

A bright, brilliant joy flooded her heart. Her thoughts faded and blurred. . . .

Elizabeth looked up at the man at her side. The glow inside him expanded, superimposing Vincent's features over Jason's. He smiled down at her, a gleam in his eye. "It looks as though I will get that kiss after all."

She laughed.

He laughed too, but then his laughter died away, and he clasped her hands. "Elizabeth," he said huskily. "I don't think I ever told you . . . "

"Yes?" she said, a bit breathlessly.

"I . . . I . . . oh, the hell with it. I love you, Beth. I always have and I always will."

Tears brimmed in her eyes. "Oh, Vincent."

"Damn it, Beth, is that all you can say? I've waited twenty-five years to ask you this, so tell me now—do you love me?"

"Of course I do. Forever and always, Vincent."

"Then kiss me, Beth."

She did. With all the love she could muster.

And he kissed her back, with all the love he had denied for so long.

And as they kissed, the locket she wore around her neck opened, and the petals of a single rose drifted out, filling the entire church with a sweet perfume.

Horace Quimby ran a finger around his collar, trying not to stare at the couple before him. It was extraordinarily warm in here, he thought. The heat must be affecting him again. He could have sworn he heard them calling each other Elizabeth and Vincent. And they seemed to be *glowing*. "Ahem. We have yet to sing the psalms, my children. There will be plenty of time for . . . other activities later on—"

The glow around them intensified, growing brighter and brighter. Sparks shot outward. And still the light grew brighter and brighter until the people watching had to shield their eyes. The lights floated upward from the couple, then merged. With a bright flash, they vanished, leaving behind only a soft glow.

Jason broke off the kiss and stared down into Mary's eyes. Slowly, in unison, they turned to look at the congregation. Everyone was gaping at them.

"Oh, dear heaven," Mary whispered.

Jason's arm tightened around her waist.

Then, without further ado, he swept her up in his arms, carried her down the aisle and out of the church, leaving the astonished congregation behind.

30

He bundled her into the carriage and climbed in after her. He sat next to her and the coach took off with a jolt, almost throwing Mary from her seat.

His arm went around her waist to steady her. "Dear God, what have I done?"

Mary looked away. She felt breathless, her hair was falling around her face, her dress was in disarray. "I think you married me. We should be able to get an annulment, though." She bowed her head. "We could say we were married against our will."

"Oh, yes," he said, his voice a trifle sardonic. "We could say that we weren't in possession of our faculties. That ghosts were forcing us to marry."

His hand was still on her waist, his fingers stroking the material of her gown, she noticed. "We must do something," she said feebly.

"Yes." His stroking fingers grew still and his voice husky. "Unless we want to stay married."

She kept her head down, not wanting him to see the tears in her eyes. "No. It's impossible."

"Impossible?" His fingers tightened on her waist. "Even if I told you I love you?"

She looked up at his face. He looked different. His features were alight with tenderness and love. The tears spilled down her cheeks. "Please, don't. I can't bear it."

"Why not? It's the truth. I love you. I know I'm asking

a lot of you. I know I'm asking you to live a life full of onerous responsibilities. I know you may end up hating me because of it. But I love you, Mary."

"Oh, Jason. Don't you see? I wouldn't mind the responsibilities. But I'm not right for you. You should marry a lady who is haughty and beautiful . . . a countess."

"You are the perfect countess."

She choked back a laugh. "No, I'm not. I don't have much fashion sense and I don't like going to parties where I have to watch what I say. You can't love me."

"I do love you. I always have. Your joy and laughter lighten the dreariness of my life."

She fingered the lapels of his coat. "I prefer the seashore to Paris."

"Then that's where we'll go. We can be unfashionably happy." He tilted up her chin. "I love you, Mary."

She smiled mistily. "I love you, too. And I will try to be a good countess."

"Mary . . . "

"Yes?"

"The first rule of being a good countess is to be quiet when the earl is trying to kiss you."

Her heart swelling with joy, Mary put her arms around her husband's neck and proved that she could be a very good countess indeed.

Epilogue

Quimby, convinced that the events at the church were a sign from God, became a proselytizer, wandering about the country predicting that the end of the world was nigh. Blevins took his place as Helsbury vicar and was much loved due to his deep understanding of human frailty.

Cecil, after brooding for a month or two, realized that he would much rather have Mary as a cousin-in-law than a wife, and proceeded to enjoy himself . . . until he met a pretty little brunette who quite stole his heart away.

Meanwhile, Lady Beatrice, deprived of her prey, set her sights on a new victim—the duke of Stafford. Her mother, Lady Weldon, did not appreciate the competition from her own daughter and the two argued bitterly. When they stopped their bickering long enough to come up for air, they were amazed to discover that Sally Parsell had stolen him right from under their noses. Lady Weldon was so upset, she had a fit of apoplexy and died. On her deathbed, she blamed Beatrice for everything and swore never to forgive her.

A few months later, Mrs. Trumball unfortunately passed away, and Beatrice, who had no other prospects, married Mr. Trumball. The marriage was not a success, however, for whenever Mr. Trumball tried to make love to his bride, his mother-in-law's disapproving face appeared. They remained childless.

Mary and Jason, however, were blessed with twins— whom they named Vincent and Elizabeth. As the children grew up, they accompanied their parents on holidays to France and Italy and Austria. But their favorite holidays of all were the ones at a little cottage at the seashore, the very place where their parents had spent their honeymoon. . . .

And in the dining hall of Helsbury House, the portraits of Vincent and Elizabeth were moved next to each other and a vase of flowers placed on the table below them.

Legend has it that those flowers still bloom, unfaded— as bright and eternal as the love of all the Helsbury earls and their wives.

Let HarperMonogram Sweep You Away

◆◆◆

SIREN'S SONG by Constance O'Banyon
Over Seven Million Copies of Her Books Are in Print!
Beautiful Dominique Charbonneau is determined to free her brother, even if it means becoming a stowaway aboard Judah Gallant's pirate ship. But Gallant is not the rogue he appears, and Dominique is torn between duty and a love she might never know again.

THE AUTUMN LORD by Susan Sizemore
A Time Travel Romance
Truth is stranger than fiction when '90s woman Diane Teal is transported back to medieval France and must rely on the protection of Baron Simon de Argent. She finds herself unable to communicate except when telling stories. Fortunately she and Simone both speak the language of love.

GHOST OF MY DREAMS by Angie Ray
RITA and Golden Heart Award-winning Author
Miss Mary Goodwin refuses to believe her fiancé's warnings that Helsbury House is haunted—until the deceased Earl appears. Will the passion of two young lovers overcome the ghost, or is he actually a bit of a romantic himself?

A ROYAL VISIT by Rebecca Baldwin
An affair of state becomes an affair of the heart when Prince Theodoric of Batavia travels to England to find a bride. He is looking for a titled lady, but a resourceful and charming merchant's daughter shows him that love can be found where one least expects it.

And in case you missed last month's selections...
KISS ME, KATIE by Robin Lee Hatcher
Bestselling Author
When high-spirited suffragette Katie Jones takes a job at a local Idaho newspaper with her childhood friend, Benjamin Rafferty, she never expects love to be the top story. A warm and touching romance from one of the most beloved Americana writers.

TEMPTING MISS PRISSY by Sharon Ihle
Award-winning Author
For Priscilla Stillbottom, working as a saloon singer in a Colorado mining town is hardly a fairy-tale existence—until handsome saloon owner Payton Cobb becomes her very own Prince Charming.

BLACKSTONE'S BRIDE by Teresa Southwick
Jarrod Blackstone is stunned when Abby Miller appears on his doorstep with his sister's orphaned children. But even more surprising—and thrilling—are the sparks that ignite between the rugged bachelor and the independent woman.

STEALING MIDNIGHT by Sonia Simone
Disguised as a highwayman, Darius Lovejoy happens upon Zoe Sommerville, a beautiful woman he believes can lead him to his prey. He steals her jewels, but she threatens to capture his heart.

Special Holiday Treat
CHRISTMAS ANGELS: THREE HEAVENLY ROMANCES by Debbie Macomber
Over Twelve Million Copies of Her Books Are in Print!
The angelic antics of Shirley, Goodness, and Mercy are featured in this collection that promises plenty of romance and dreams that come true.